Praise for Melani

The Roswell Quest, the prequel

Her discovery could change the world forever…

Readers' Favorite wrote: If you're a fan of TV shows like Stranger Things, you're going to love *The Roswell Quest*. DJ Schneider masterfully incorporates real-life events to craft an engaging narrative that keeps you hooked from start to finish.

The Tale of the Tarot, Book One

Her destiny lies in the cards…

Reviewer, Sally Altass wrote: An exciting teenage thriller set in the 1960s. Spies, UFOs, cover-ups, and much more. There's a rising tension throughout the book, and the ending had me gasping for breath.

The Map of Orbis Terrarum, Book Two

Her fate rests with the map…

Kim Anisi for Readers' Favorite: 5 Stars. A fantastic story!

Reviewer Sally Altass wrote: Nothing is simple and straightforward. The story twists and turns and throws curveballs that even the most ardent mystery reader wouldn't expect.

Melanie Simpson Mystery Book Three

THE STONES OF CARNAC

Her Future is Chiseled in Stone

DJ SCHNEIDER

Published deBoys Press, LLC
Copyright © 2024 David Schneider
All Rights Reserved

The only real events in this book are the historical facts depicted around UFOs and government coverups—and, of course, the crash that occurred outside Roswell, New Mexico in 1947 and the alien material from that crash.

ISBN 979-8-9908324-0-4

*This novel is dedicated
to all those who strive to
fulfill their destiny*

Contents

Call to Action!

Acknowledgements

About the Author

THE STONES OF CARNAC

To this day, whoever erected the Carnac Stones,
remains a mystery

MK-Ultra

Seattle, Washington, 1967

Agent Miller slapped Tom across the cheek. "Wake up."

Tom stirred and moaned. His eyes fluttered and tried to focus. "Where am I?"

Miller leaned down so he was only inches from Tom's face. "*Where* doesn't matter. You're broken, Tom, in case you haven't figured that out yet. It's possible you may never walk again. You need medical attention soon if there is any chance of recovery." Miller smiled and leaned back. "So, you help me, and I'll help you."

Tom tried to look around, but a bright lamp on a long arm hung over his bed and made it hard to see. It was the kind of light used in operating rooms to direct intense light onto a small area—in this case, his face.

He knew he was in some sort of hospital bed. He could just make out the railing sides. The bed had been raised so his head was higher than his feet. He tried to get up, but something stopped him. His wrists were tied down and he felt a tightness around his torso. Some sort of full-body restraint. He couldn't feel anything below his waist.

"No sense trying to move, Tom. We have you in traction. It's for your own safety. Otherwise, you could make your injuries worse. Once you have shared what you know, we'll arrange medical attention. For now, you are stable enough for our needs."

Miller walked to the foot of the bed, picked up a chart, and flipped it open. "Just so you know, you are in a secured room in a nameless government hospital. After the accident in Seattle, you were taken to the emergency room at Swedish Medical. We transported you here as soon as you were stable."

Tom tried to focus on Miller. "Melanie?"

"You mean the cat with nine lives? She's fine, as far as we know. She managed to escape our grasp once again and is apparently safely back in Lake Oswego. Safe for now, anyway. Much of that has to do with what you tell us."

Tom shook his head and shut his eyes.

"Since you brought her up," Miller said, "why don't you tell us what you were doing in that van? Where were you going, Tom? Where was *she* going?"

Tom tried to remember what happened. They were trying to lose the car chasing them. Danny ran an intersection and a large truck of some sort t-boned his van, tossing it up into the air and onto its side. Tom remembered slamming against the passenger door as it landed on the road, lying there until it skidded to a stop. Then looking up to see Melanie holding herself against the seats above him, tears streaming from her eyes, talking to him. Checking on him. And the vision of Danny above her, crushed between the steering wheel and the driver's seat, obviously dead; blood flowing from his face.

They were on their way to see a professor who had been working with Melanie's father. She had the alien material from the UFO crash site with her. She wanted him to have it for study. But more importantly, she wanted to see films the professor had taken of her father and the Orb—a device given to her father by a dying alien at the crash site.

Twenty years ago, he had helped her father smuggle the Orb and material out of the site before the military arrived. He knew that whoever this guy was, he wanted the debris, but there was no way he could know the Orb existed. Tom planned to keep it that way. He had no intention of sharing any of this with the man standing at the foot of his bed.

Tom heard him walk closer. He opened his eyes to see the lower half of the man appear by the railing of his bed. The top half cut off at mid-chest by the sharp edge of the lamplight. The bottom half showed a dark suit, white shirt, and black tie. His black belt had a silver buckle that reflected the lamplight into his eyes.

Miller leaned down and patted Tom on the arm again. "Perhaps it would be good for you to know we recovered the crash material from the Simpson girl. So really, all I am doing here is tying up loose ends. Like where you were going before the accident. Or, better stated, whom you were going to see. The thing is, we need to know about anyone who has seen or knows of the alien material. It's important we slam such doors shut, and lock them tight."

Tom squinted against the bright light. "Melanie never told me. We were on our way to see a man. That's all I know. She kept the address to herself, just in case something like this happened."

Miller studied Tom's face, looking for the small tells of lying—the fluttering of the eyelids and licking of the lips. "I have no doubt that is the case. Miss Simpson is a very smart girl. But, let's make sure, just in case, shall we?"

Miller went to a table, picked up an object, and carried it back to Tom. He shoved the tip of a small spray bottle into Tom's nostril and squeezed.

Tom gasped and then coughed. His eyes went wide in reaction.

"That was an aerosol of lysergic acid diethylamide. Also known as LSD. A small dosage, really. Only 50 micrograms. Just enough to set the stage for the sodium pentothal."

He patted Tom's arm again. "Alrighty then, let's give it time to do its magic." He went over, dropped the aerosol bottle on the table, and picked up something else. "While it does, I'll fill you in. CIA has done quite a bit of experimentation with LSD and other drugs. We wanted to develop interrogation and mind control techniques through brainwashing and psychological torture. We called it Project MK-ULTRA. The program has been in play for over a decade, but I got involved a few years ago.

"I was in charge of administering the drugs and assessing the results. I became quite good at understanding certain combinations to achieve specific effects. I found a particular combination that is rather persuasive as a truth serum. When I came to work for Bull and his black ops group, it soon came in handy. And that is what we are doing here. So, why am I telling you this? Because you won't remember, and it thrills me to share such secrets, just on the off-chance you might."

He pulled a chair from across the room and scooted it up next to the bed. "Just a little bit longer. We need the LSD to take effect."

A few minutes later, Miller pulled Tom's eyelid back and studied his pupil for the telltale signs. Satisfied, he held up a syringe, tapped the side to release any bubbles, and pressed the plunger until a drop of liquid appeared at the top of the needle. He tied some rubber tubing around Tom's upper arm, pulled it tight, and tapped at a vein. "There we are." He pushed the needle into the vein and pressed the liquid out of the syringe.

"A little sodium pentothal. The right amount, in tandem with the LSD, to gain the perfect effect." He released the tubing and gave Tom a big smile. "You *will* soon tell me everything."

The Decision

Lake Oswego, July 29, 1967

Mel

I heard a knock on my door. Emilee called, "Melanie, can I come in?"

I'm in my PJs and putting my hair up, about ready to go to bed. "Sure."

She came in wearing her night clothes and a terry bathrobe. She sat on the edge of my bed, patting the spot next to her. I went over and sat down. Emilee is my grandmother and came all the way from England to take care of me after my mother died a month ago.

"Melanie, things are a bit muddled right now. I understand that. So, I want you to think about what I say next. No need to answer right away."

I could see a touch of doubt turn to resolve as she pushed forward. "I would like you to consider going to England with me. There is still enough time before your education starts up again for us to make the trip."

I jumped in. "England? But I thought we were staying here."

"Just to visit. I want you to see what life is like over there, and see our family home—which will be yours one day." She patted my hand. "And, I think things might become clearer if you did."

What could she mean by that? I studied her, and something in how she looked told me she was right. But still, I had to wonder. "If you are trying to get me to think about moving to England, I won't. I don't want to lose my friends."

She smiled. "I understand. Let's just take little steps for now. What about if you bring your chums with you on the trip? I'll cover their expenses. Will that suffice?"

I brightened. "Really? You'd do that?"

"Certainly."

I thought for a moment. Even if I liked England I still wouldn't want to live there, so what was the sense of going? "Emilee, that's really nice of you to offer. But I don't want to go. There really isn't a reason to. I hope that's okay with you?"

She gave me a hug. "All I ask is for you to think about it. Will you?"

I hugged her back. "Sure."

Emilee sat back and stroked my arm. "Good. Now, I have something for you."

"For me?"

"Yes. I found it when going through Gloria's things while you were gone."

She took something from her pocket and set it in my hand. Whatever it was, it felt heavy. Then she pressed her hand over mine and looked at me. "I know your mum would want you to have it." She gave me a kiss on my cheek and left the room, closing the door behind her.

I looked down to see a silver locket on a chain in my hand. I took the chain and raised the locket so it dangled in front of my eyes. It felt kind of heavy; more than I would imagine lockets to weigh. And it seemed bigger than the few lockets I'd seen. My eyes went wide when I noticed the shape. Most lockets are round. This one was oval but tapered toward the top, just like the shape of the Orb my dad held in the films I had seen at Professor Lofton's.

The locket slowly spun on the chain to reveal both sides. It looked like one side had some sort of space scene on it, little stars all over, with three bigger stars angled in a diagonal line across that side. The other side had what looked like tall stones lined up in rows.

I jumped up from the bed in shock. These were the Stones of Carnac! They had to be. They looked just like the ones in the film which showed my dad at the Stones, studying them.

I took the locket to my desk and turned on a small lamp so I could see it better. I looked at the side with the stars again. The three stars looked familiar. I tried to remember from where, and suddenly my body radiated with excitement. They had been pointed out in the night sky to me by Katch's grandmother outside their home. They were the three stars making the belt in the constellation Orion. The stars she pointed out while telling me they were *my* sky people.

I turned the locket over again, to the Stones. They were definitely the Stones of Carnac. Had I not seen the film of my dad, I never would have known what these stones were. It really did seem a path had been laid out for me and I was on it, even right now, sitting here. Destiny. Dharma.

I studied the rest of the locket and found a small latch pin on the side. It took a moment to figure out how to open it, but I finally did. I cried at what it revealed—a picture of my mother on one side and my father on the other. The pictures were of them when they were younger, not much older than me now, maybe just after getting married.

I took a handkerchief out of my drawer and wiped at the tears on my cheeks. Then I held it against my eyes for a while to capture the free-flowing tears until I could pull myself together. I didn't hurry, though. The crying was a release I really needed.

I finally settled myself enough to continue. I looked over at my music box on the dresser. My dad had given it to me on my fifth birthday. I got it and sat in the chair again as I placed it on my desk.

I still remember that day, when he got down on his knees, his eyes bright with excitement as he put it in my tiny hands and said, "You will always be my Mel Belle. My little ballerina."

He told me he gave me that nickname because it came from the French fairy tale, *La Belle et la Bête*. Beauty and the Beast.

He nodded to the lid and said, "Open it." I did. A little ballerina jumped up and danced a beautiful dance of pirouettes. *Swan Lake* played across the room. "Now look at this," he told me. He reached into the small compartment in the music box and pressed a tiny latch along the side wall. A hidden drawer popped out of the back. I remembered my eyes going wide with surprise. I looked up at my dad. He said, "This is where I will always keep my love for you. A secret place no one can find, so no one can ever take it." He made the motion of kissing the air, grabbing it, and placing it in the drawer before closing it. "Love for my Mel Belle, anytime you need it. Our little secret forever."

I opened the music box to watch the ballerina dance to *Swan Lake*. I had done this so many times since Dad died, I was surprised it hadn't broken from wear and tear. I watched and listened until it wound down, the song finally clicking its last notes and ending. The little ballerina stopped mid-pirouette, which seemed very sad to me every time it happened.

I reached into the box and clicked the little latch. The hidden compartment popped open and I took out a piece of memory metal from the spaceship crash. I balled it up in my fist and then dropped it on the desk. It remained crumpled up for a moment before flowing back into its original, seamless shape. I smiled. Not all of the evidence from the Roswell crash had been lost up in Seattle.

I decided to put it in the locket. I planned to wear that locket every day for the rest of my life and wanted to keep the metal with it, with my dad. I took a nail file from my dresser and studied the picture of my father in the locket. It was held in place by little metal stays in four corners. I slipped the tip behind one edge of the picture and popped it out. The memory metal was thinner than the foil from a cigarette pack, so it easily folded small enough to fit in the space. I took my dad's picture and fitted it back into the locket to cover the metal.

I looked at the picture of my mother, then picked up a small hand mirror and studied myself. It was amazing how much I looked like her. I touched the picture, just to feel close to her again. As I ran my finger across it, I accidentally knocked it out of the locket. The picture fluttered to the floor. I picked it up to replace it when I noticed something where the picture had been.

It looked like an odd-shaped coin or token of some sort. I took the nail file and popped it out of the locket. It fell on the desk. I picked it up. It was about the size and thickness of a quarter, but only half of one, looking like the other half was missing. The edge where it would connect was jagged, like a piece of a jigsaw puzzle, where only its counterpart could fit. I turned it around in the lamplight for a better look. It was made of shimmering silverish metal, brighter even than platinum. The metal was very smooth, as if a film of some sort covered the surface, giving it a slick feel. I had never seen anything like it before.

I studied the first side; a pattern of circles and lines. I ran my finger across them and could feel the pattern stand out in relief. The circles were of various sizes. The lines ran between them, connecting some of the bigger circles with thicker lines. Other lines, smaller, ran to smaller dots. Many of them ran off the edge of the token to where the connecting piece would fit.

I rolled the token over in my hand to see the other side. It had what looked like a pyramid on it—a stepped pyramid, just like the one we saw my dad standing next to on the film at Professor Lofton's. It was also in relief, so it stood out against the flatness of the token. I sat back in my chair. Could it be the same pyramid? What did the professor call it? Oh, yeah. The Temple of Inscriptions. I studied the token again. It had the same stairs going up the front to a small temple on top, only on the coin this was all cut in half. I could see tropical trees around it, like in the film. But I suddenly stopped because I saw something that wasn't in the film. An oval shape next to the top of the pyramid, floating in the sky. That's funny, it sure looks a lot like a UFO. A chill hit me. It was a UFO!

I turned the coin back over to look at the other side again. Those lines and circles—something about them felt familiar. But from where? I thought for a moment. And then I knew. I jumped up from my chair and ran to my closet where I kept some books. I took one down and went back to my desk. It was *The Interrupted Journey*, about Betty and Barney Hill's abduction. I turned to the page of the map Betty Hill drew. I compared it to the circles and lines on the token. They matched! The circles were the planets on Betty's map, and the lines were the travel routes.

I sat there, stunned. How could this be? What could it all mean? I had to think. How did my mother get it? Maybe of more importance was, *who* made it and why? I only now began to absorb the significance of what it meant. Somehow all of this fits together. Spooky. But then I thought of the most important question of all—where was the other half of the token, *and who has it?*

A thought hit me and I went over to my closet again, got on my knees, and dug through all the school stuff I had dumped out of my bookbag in my haste to run away. I found a thick geography book and carried it to the desk.

I flipped through it until I found the map I was looking for; a map of Europe. The professor said the Carnac Stones were in Brittany, France. It took a moment to locate the area, and even longer to find the town of Carnac. But there it was. I looked at the spot on the map as if I was standing right there in the middle of the Stones. I drew a line from there to the Isle of Wight where my grandmother said she lived, just across the channel from France. Not close, but not that far, either.

I thought for a moment, looking at the small amount of water separating England from France. I tried to remember. It was only about twenty miles across at one point in the channel, and here I am in Lake Oswego, Oregon, more like 5,000 miles away, with an entire continent and the whole of the Atlantic Ocean between us. The Stones may as well have been on Mars.

I closed the book and thought for a moment. Maybe what Emilee offered earlier wasn't such a bad idea after all. I walked out to the living room. Emilee sat comfortably propped in a chair reading a book. She glanced up when she heard me coming. I stood there for a moment, to make sure what I was going to say made sense.

Emilee closed her book. I must have had some sort of look on my face while standing there. She sat up and said, "Melanie, what is it?"

I knew this was what I needed to do. "I want to go to England."

The Key

Mel

Frankie dropped into the chair by his desk and looked at me like I was crazy. "You're doing what?"

"Going to England with Emilee. I have to go. My dad was at Carnac. You saw the film. I need to find out what he was doing there."

I had gone to bed after talking to Emilee, but laid there for hours thinking about going to England and wondering how I could get to the Carnac Stones in France. Then, I worried about telling Frankie. It was so sudden. I couldn't just call him. I needed to tell him in person, and as soon as possible. That thought kept at me until I finally got up, put on my clothes, and snuck out of the house. It was well after midnight, but I needed to do this now.

When I got to his house, I tapped lightly on the sliding glass door until he finally came out to see what was making the noise. At first, he probably thought I was there for another reason. At least until I opened my mouth about going to England.

He wore boxer shorts, an old Motown tee shirt, and a perplexed look on his face. He turned on the gooseneck lamp sitting on his desk and it threw a spot of light across the surface. The rest of the room stayed in total darkness. I kneeled next to him, took his hand, and looked at him. One side of his face stood out against the reflection from his desk. The light danced across it as he slowly shook his head in frustration.

"This is just crazy, Mel."

"I know. But I have to." I let go of his hand and pulled the locket out from under my shirt and unhooked it from around my neck. "Emilee gave this to me tonight. She found it in my mother's jewelry box." I scooted over to the desk and held the locket under the light. "See how it's shaped like the Orb we saw in the films the professor showed us? And look here." I held the locket so he could see one side better. "These have got to be the Stones of Carnac." I looked over at him. "You saw the film. They look just like those stones."

"But why would they be on this locket?"

"That's the point. I don't know, but it must mean something." I turned it over. "See these three stars? They're just like the stars Katch's grandmother pointed out to me that night at her house." I looked at him. I'm sure the excitement showed on my face. "I wouldn't have any idea what these scenes meant if I hadn't gone to see Professor Lofton. Somehow this is all falling into place, and in screwball ways."

He took the locket and studied it under the light, switching it from one side to the other. "Then it really must be some sort of destiny." His face suddenly changed and took on a look of despair as he turned to me. "You know I won't be able to go with you. Not after what I pulled by taking the Mustang up to Seattle. The ruling party in this family, namely my parents, have taken away my keys and pretty much grounded me for life. And, I don't even have a passport." He handed the locket to me. "Do you?"

"Yeah. From when we took a trip to South America a few years back." I attached the chain around my neck and tucked the locket into my shirt. "I need you to stay here anyway."

He looked surprised. "What? Why?"

"Emilee is going to call tomorrow to book a flight. I think we'll be leaving really soon. Maybe in just a couple of days. We only have a little over three weeks before school starts again, and I'll need to be back by then."

"That still doesn't answer my question."

I reached into the pocket of my cut-off jeans, took something out, and put it in his hand. He looked down to see the key Professor Lofton had given me. "Because I need you to find the safe deposit box this key fits. I won't be able to look for it since I'll be over in Europe."

Frankie shifted in his chair and leaned closer to me. "Oh. I see. Have me do *your* dirty work while you're off traipsing around Europe drinking tea and eating crumpets with the Queen of England." He smiled at his little joke. Maybe trying to reset his mood.

"Funny." I took his hand. "But I'm serious, Frankie. I need you to figure out where the key goes, so we can find out why my dad left it for me."

"Do you think it holds the Orb?"

"I don't know. It could. But one thing we do know is it has to hold something important. Why would he leave it for me otherwise?"

"And the way he did it, almost like a reward for making it to the professor's house."

I gave him my most hopeful look. "So, will you look for it while I'm gone?"

"I'm not sure how. I'm grounded, remember?"

I turned the chair so he faced me. "I'm sure you'll figure out a way." Then I thought of something. "Maybe George could help you somehow."

He gave me a funny look. "What? Captain Thornton? How could he help?"

"I don't know." My eyes brightened. "What if you're still grounded and you need a ride to wherever this place is, once you figure it out? He could take you. And I don't think your parents would say no to the captain of the Lake Oswego Police Department."

Frankie shook his head. "Look, I understand you've gotten to know him pretty well, but I'm still not so sure about him."

"Frankie, believe me." I scooted in between his legs, reached around his neck, and pulled his head toward me to give him a soft kiss. "You can trust him."

He liked my move and wrapped his arms around me, pulling me closer. "Well, if we do figure it out, we'll need a way to get there. I doubt my parents would turn down the Chief of Police."

"Good." I kissed him again.

"But first," he said. "I have to find out what the key fits. Maybe, with Beanie and Katch's help, I can."

"Not Katch. She's going with me." I gave him a bit of a guilty look. I knew he wouldn't like what I just told him.

He scooted back and pulled my arms from his neck. "Well, thanks for thinking of me first. You know, so I at least had the opportunity to say I couldn't go." He dropped the key on his desk and pushed his chair back some more. The lamplight from his desk distorted the deep look of hurt on his face as it penetrated into me. He stood, sidestepped me, and took a few steps away.

I jumped up, wrapped my arms around him from behind, and placed my cheek against his back. "Look. I already figured you wouldn't be able to go. It's not like your parents would ground you, take the Mustang away, and then let you go jaunting off to Europe."

He pulled my arms from him and turned around to face me. "And what makes you think Katch will be able to go?"

I gave him another guilty look. "I've already talked to her. Emilee said I could bring someone. You know, moral support. I knew Katch had a passport because she told me about a trip her family took to Italy a while ago. To visit the Gallo side of the family. And remember, she told her mom she was going to Seattle, so didn't get into trouble. It was no problem once her parents found out Emilee would pay for everything."

"So, you called her right away and waited until, what … now to tell me?"

"I had to call her to make sure she could go, and to let her parents know as soon as possible since we need to leave so soon. Once Emilee got off the phone with Katch's dad, it was all worked out."

I put my arms around him again. "I was going to tell you in the morning, but I couldn't wait. I lay in my bed thinking about you, and how I wouldn't see you for weeks. I couldn't sleep. I had to come over now." I gave him a long kiss to let him know how much I cared about him. "I'm really grateful for what you did for me in Seattle, Frankie. It was a big risk coming up there to help me, knowing what you would face from your parents when you got back. Thank you."

"Nice try in changing the subject. But what I want to know is exactly how you plan to get to this Carnac place in France, when your grandmother's place is in England. Have you thought about *that?*"

I let go of him and sat on the bed. "I haven't got a clue. Not yet, anyway. But I have to figure it out. I just have to."

Taking Flight

Mel

We had a whole big group at the airport: Katch's mom, who brought us, plus Emilee, Katch, and me. Then the boys came along to say goodbye. Somehow they had worked it out with their parents. It probably went something like this, "But Mom, what if Mel dies in a plane crash? You would deny me my last chance to see her!" No doubt the same for Beanie. Whatever they did, it worked, because they were here.

Luckily, Mrs. Gallo had a big Rambler station wagon that could hold all six of us, along with our luggage.

We were sitting in the waiting area for our flight to be called. It seemed like the first pause in what had been a long string of whirlwind days.

I bumped Frankie in the side. "So, you promise, right?"

He turned to me. "I already did, but I will again if it makes you feel better." He crossed his heart and said, "I promise that Beanie and I will try to figure out the key thing." He smiled at me. "Better?"

I set my new backpack at my feet. I had Emilee take me to Andy and Bax in Portland where they have all sorts of

Army surplus stuff. I found an old Army backpack just like my dad's that I had lost up in Seattle. I knew it wasn't his, but it still made me feel connected to him.

I wrapped my arm around Frankie's and gave him my most serious look. "I'm counting on you. It's important to me. If I wasn't going on this trip, that's exactly what I'd be doing. So, thanks."

"At least it'll give me something to do and make me feel useful while you're gone. I'm definitely going to miss you." He leaned over and I turned to him so we could kiss.

"You two just can't help yourselves, can you?" Beanie said. He and Katch were sitting next to us.

I looked over to see Katch giving Beanie a 'what about us' look. She said, "Maybe that's because they will miss each other. I don't see that from you at all."

Beanie feigned surprise. "How can you say such a thing? All I do is ogle you."

I had to cut in. "Beanie, you do know ogle means to stare at someone in a lecherous way?"

He looked off into space for a moment. "No, I thought it meant something else. But actually, that fits pretty well." He raised his eyebrows and leered at Katch.

"Yep. I see that look a lot," Katch said. "I suppose ogle does fit." She was about to say more, but Beanie dove in and gave her what looked like a very messy kiss.

Right then, the announcement came over the speakers to board our flight to Seattle. We had to go there first, and then catch a flight to somewhere on the east coast, and finally another flight to England. It would be a long trip.

Emilee said it was the best the travel agent could do on such short notice.

We all stood and walked toward the gate.

"Okay girls, make sure you have your tickets ready," Mrs. Gallo said.

Katch and I held them up for her to see.

"Good." She pulled Katch into her and gave her a big hug. "Tune to the earth, and hear the song of the universe."

"Huh? Hear what?" Katch said.

Mrs. Gallo chuckled. "The song of the universe. That mysterious little message is from your grandmother. You know how she is a Hopi medicine woman twenty-four seven. She caught me just as I was heading out the door. You were already getting into the station wagon. She said it was important to tell you, as her protégé. Apparently, a last-minute vision of some sort."

Katch and I exchanged looks. "How do I interpret that?" she asked.

"I guess it'll give us something to talk about on the plane."

I felt Frankie reach over to hold my hand as we got in line. I looked at him. He was checking out the plane we would be boarding. "You aren't going to be on a prop plane all the way to England, are you?"

"No. This is just to Seattle. I think we catch a jet plane from there."

He turned to me. "Okay. Good. It would take forever otherwise."

I studied his eyes because I knew the memory of them would have to last me for a while. "I really do love you."

He smiled. "I love you, too. I wish I could come, but it was a battle to even let me get this far just to say goodbye."

"At least you will be able to help me while I'm gone."

"Yeah, but I'm probably going to be grounded for a while, which will be a big drag on our ability to search."

"I know it will be tough. But you'll figure it out."

We were slowly moving to the ticket taker and I would soon be on the plane.

"Frankie. I'm really going to miss you."

He smiled at me. "Well, make this all worthwhile. Get to the Carnac Stones and find out why they have such a pull on you."

I threw my arms around him. "I will. I'm sure of it." I turned my face up to his and we kissed one last movie-like kiss. Just like Lauren Bacall and Humphrey Bogart right out of *To Have and Have Not*. I pulled away to see his eyes, and suddenly realized this was the kiss I had so desperately wanted from him back when I was waiting on the platform for the train to Seattle. How many years ago was that? It sure seemed like a long time. But it had been less than a week.

● ● ●

Agent Roberts sat in a chair on the far side of the seating area. He held a newspaper as if reading it, although his focus was on the group of people saying their goodbyes near the gate. He was glad he had an assignment again. He wasn't sure he would get another after telling Bull he hadn't eliminated the Simpson girl as ordered, and that she had gotten away from him at Pike Place Market. It was strike two after getting arrested at her house in Lake Oswego. He still couldn't figure out how she set up that trap.

But the CIA, or more accurately, Bull's little black ops part of it, needed him right now. Since she was still alive, Bull wanted him at the airport to make sure Melanie Simpson got on the plane. Not that she might pull something, but just to make sure. She was a smart girl and they had learned the hard way, she always seemed to have something up her sleeve. That's why they had already arranged for an operative overseas to book a room at her grandmother's place in England. Bull wanted to stay close and cover all the angles.

Bull also told Roberts to watch in case she gave the boys any sort of instructions for while she was gone. Roberts was pretty sure she had done just that by the looks of it. He was good at covert operations and could read body language. A lot of it was just the two love birds being all serious about missing each other. Very sweet. But when Frankie crossed himself, Roberts thought he could see a look on their faces that indicated more than just the longings of two hormonal teenagers. The Simpson girl must have told him something.

The boys, along with the other girl's mom, waved goodbye until the grandmother and two girls climbed the aircraft stairs and disappeared into the plane. Then they walked back down the concourse, probably headed to the parking lot.

Roberts followed them, folding his newspaper and tucking it under his arm as he went. He might be able to overhear something worthwhile, maybe even confirm his suspicion she had told Frankie something. The boys had dropped back behind the mother and were leaning toward each other talking in low tones.

He caught up to them without much trouble. He knew Frankie had seen him at the Simpson girl's house when he pretended to be from the University of Washington, but he had worn a disguise then, and was sure Frankie wouldn't recognize him now. He moved in close. They were in the middle of a discussion.

"Frankie, we're both grounded. How are we going to find that safe deposit box when we are stuck at home?"

"How long *are* you grounded?"

"Well, I turn eighteen in three years, so I'm guessing about that long. Mom can't do much once I become an adult."

"That's funny, but I'm serious. I probably won't be released from my shackles for a couple of weeks. I guess we'll have to be creative. All I know is I promised Mel I would try to find out where that key goes while she's gone. Now, I just have to figure out how to go about it."

Roberts continued to follow them until they reached the parking lot, but they didn't divulge anything more. He cut off to the side and stopped to think about what he heard. The key they were talking about was a new and *very* interesting development. It might lead to where the Orb is hidden.

This information about the Orb came from Miller. He had been working on Tom Richardson ever since they pulled him from the crashed van up in Seattle and secreted him away in a government medical facility. Miller figured out Richardson was the one who helped Roger Simpson smuggle alien material from the Roswell crash in 1947. But it was only after he gave Richardson a souped-up LSD cocktail, that Richardson dropped the bombshell about something called the Orb; some sort of gadget Roger Simpson received from a dying alien at the Roswell site.

Once Miller told Bull about the Orb, everything jumped into high gear again. This wasn't just crash material from the spaceship, but some sort of operable device. An item that obviously meant something to the dying alien. Who knows what advanced technology it might have that could put the United States well ahead of the Soviets? It might even be a weapon of some sort. And wouldn't that be something?

Bull was desperate to get this device. They needed to find it before it fell into enemy hands. He knew the Soviets would throw everything they had at recovering the Orb if they ever found out it existed.

This device could very well be over in England. Why else would Melanie Simpson suddenly want to go to Europe? Miller would be leaving today to run the operation over there.

On the other hand, this key might open a safe deposit box where the Orb was hidden. This new information would go a long way to put him in good stead with Bull, once he shared it with him. He also knew to wait until Miller was well on his way to England before he did. Then Bull would need *him* to run the operation on the boys and the key here.

But it also made him stop and remember something else he hadn't shared with Bull; how the Simpson girl had stopped his bullets in mid-air with her bare hands. He still couldn't believe it himself. Maybe he'd just imagined it. What other explanation could there be? His bosses would have thought him nuts if he told them what he saw.

He had to wonder, though, where that kind of power could come from if, in fact, it really did happen.

A Meal on a Bun

Lubbock, TX, May, 1947

Gloria

The Eat 'N Run sits right across College Avenue from the main entrance to Texas Tech College. That's in Lubbock. I've been working here almost two years.

Sal, the owner, has a bit of smarts about him. When he got back from Europe three years ago after serving in the war and this property came up for sale, he grabbed it. He grew up flipping burgers in a family business, so Sal understood location was everything.

A bell in the kitchen dinged and Sal called out, "Hey, Gloria. Order up."

Even though he owned the place and it was doing well, he loved to be the short-order cook. But he hated doing the books, so luckily our manager, Eulin Hastings, handled that chore. It kept Sal in a good mood, which was good for everyone.

When I first got here, Sal told me that he was the best short-order cook ever. He gave me a big smile and said, "So, why ruin a good thing?" Then he hired me on the spot. I was delivering burgers ten minutes later. It didn't take long to know he was telling the truth about his cooking.

College kids didn't tip very well, but the older men who came in easily made up for it. I've been running plates at burger joints for a while, so it didn't take long to figure out that a well-timed raise of the eyebrow could be the difference between a dime and a quarter tip. I had to put up with their drooling leers, but I'd learned to deal with them over the years.

Sal named this place the Eat 'N Run. Not the greatest name in the world, but definitely a fitting one. We lived by our slogan, "A Meal on a Bun at the Eat 'N Run." We offered up a really good and really cheap hamburger directed right at college students, always hungry and always in a hurry. Served with crispy fries and a tall Coca-Cola or frosty malt, the students flocked here in droves. Some of them pretty much lived here between classes and after school. I told Sal a couple of times that he should probably start charging rent to some of the kids who hogged the best booths.

Part of the reason was that Sal put in wallboxes when he remodeled the place; little jukeboxes in each of the eight booths at the Eat 'N Run. We also had a big jukebox in the corner for those who didn't have a booth. The college students loved dropping a nickel into the jukeboxes, and there always seemed to be a song floating in the air from when we opened to when we closed.

Right now, it was *Boogie Woogie Bugle Boy* by the Andrews Sisters. I almost had to stop every time I heard it. I could visualize the Andrews sisters dancing and singing from when I first saw them in the movie, *Buck Privates*, an Abbott and Costello comedy and a real kick in the pants.

That was years ago. I couldn't remember what town I was in at the time, or where I worked. But I remember going to a theater to see that movie, and having a few hours away from both my and the world's problems. All of America needed a release back then while the war raged on. We were fighting against the Germans and the Japanese, hoping that somehow we could win against such evil.

The Andrew Sisters song was so good that kids still loved listening to it today, even though the war ended a few years ago. I caught myself in that thought—the kids today. I'm only twenty-four. Barely older than them, but the last few years put me in a different category. Their life was one of study and excitement. Mine from seventeen until a year ago had been one of existence and coping.

I grabbed the plates from the pass-through and carried them over to a booth. "Here you go. A couple of cheeseburgers with Cokes." I set the plates on the table in front of two ravenous students who somehow managed to break themselves away from flipping through songs in the wallbox. They looked up at me as if I were the Archangel Raphael himself—healing their hunger and bringing them good health. But it didn't last long as they dumped ketchup on their fries and dug into the juicy burgers.

The little bell above the front door tinkled and I looked over. A tall, good-looking dreamboat of a man walked in and took a seat at the counter. Just then a Perry Como song came on and drifted from the speakers, *Prisoner of Love*. Now wasn't that some kind of timing?

31

I walked over to him and looked at my watch. "You're early today. Want some coffee?"

He stared up at me. His eyes penetrated deep into mine and held them. I tried to equal his stare and not blink. It was a game he liked to play every time he came in. His eyes grew more intense as it went on.

I finally blinked. I always blinked first.

He smiled at the win. "Now, Cookie, you know I would *love* a cup of coffee."

I rolled my eyes; a defensive maneuver against the draw of his. I went to the coffee station, grabbed a mug from the shelf, and took a moment to pour coffee into it. Why did he have such a hold on me? I strolled over and set the cup in front of him, trying not to show it so much.

He smiled and raised his eyebrows in a suggestive manner. "So." He stopped to let his eyes scan my body just long enough to make me feel uncomfortable in such a public place. "You're really quite the dame. What say we blow this place and find a little corner together somewhere?"

I heard a harumph from behind me and turned to see Sal watching us from the pass-through. "Gloria, is that guy bothering you again? You want me to toss him out?"

I turned back to the man, who had suddenly taken on a saintly look. "Naw, Sal. Not a bad thought, but a little late. That might have been an option a year ago before I married him and got pregnant. I'm kind of stuck now."

We all laughed, and Sal went back to flipping burgers.

I looked at Roger. "You're early. I don't get off work for half an hour."

"I know. But it just gives me that much more time to watch the mother of my child."

I leaned across the counter and gave him a kiss. "Very sweet. But ever since you found out I was pregnant, you have become obsessed with it."

He reached across the counter and touched my belly, which was just beginning to show in all of its four-month glory. "Just watching out for the family."

Roger pulled up to the house and parked the truck. We had stopped at the grocery store on the way home because we needed a few staples and something to fix for dinner tonight.

We got out just as Mrs. Delbert opened the front door. "Do y'all need some help there, kids?"

"Thanks for offering," I answered, "but I think we've got it."

She waved in acknowledgement and went back inside.

Roger handed me a bag of groceries. "I still can't believe we have this place. It's so perfect." He pulled another bag out of the truck.

We wound our way along the side of the house. It sat on the edge of a slope near the top of a low hill, along with other prominent houses of the Lubbock rich and famous. Lubbock was as flat as a pancake but did have a few places that were higher than the rest of town, this being one of them.

We lived in the daylight basement under the main house. Mrs. Delbert owned a very successful insurance company in town and had an expansive house. Our place covered the whole lower level. It was very nice and very private, and because it sat slightly above the rest of the town, we didn't have any nosy neighbors to worry about.

We had plenty of space, especially for when the baby arrived. Roger was already getting a room ready. We couldn't paint it blue or pink, because we didn't know which would be right, so we settled on a nice pastel green.

It really floored Mrs. Delbert when I first showed up at her door two years ago. I had grown up in this very basement apartment, living here with my mother. Mrs. Delbert was like a grandmother to me.

I was seventeen when I ran away. I spent the next five years wandering around the country, finding waitress jobs wherever I landed. It was only recently I realized how much of a mess I had been back then. I don't think I fully healed until I came back. All that time away, I wondered if my mom was still here in Lubbock. I finally got to the point where I had to find out.

When I first got here, I knocked on Mrs. Delbert's door.

"Gloria? Oh, my. Gloria, is that you?"

She was so excited to see me, she cried for nearly half an hour. Once she settled down, she told me my mom had left for England about six months after I ran away. She said Emilee had stayed here as long as she could, hoping I would come back. She even stayed for a while after receiving word her mother in England was deathly ill. Mrs. Delbert told me she eventually arranged passage as a nurse on a transport ship back to England. That was in 1940.

I felt both relief and guilt at the same time when she told me this. I wanted to see my mom again, but knew how hard it would have been. I don't think I overreacted to what my mother had told me that caused me to run away, but I could have handled it better. And now, I had no idea where she could be in England. She had told me about a family place where she grew up somewhere at the southern end of England near the Channel. But I was a teenager then and too busy with my own thoughts, so only listened with half an ear. I suppose I could have figured out where she lived if I really tried, but I think I used this as an excuse not to look.

Mrs. Delbert hadn't rented out the apartment downstairs. She kept it empty all that time, hoping one or both of us would return someday. So, she offered it to me. That was two years ago. I had been living here ever since.

I met Roger not long after I got my job at the Eat 'N Run. When Roger and I married, it made sense for us to stay at Mrs. Delbert's. She kept the rent low because she didn't need the money. And she knew it would help, what with Roger's college expenses, and the added cost of starting a family. It wasn't hard to see she was excited for us and the baby.

Things were finally going well for me. I had a good job and liked it. Roger was getting wonderful grades in his studies at the college. And after drifting around for so many years trying to recover from what my mother had told me, I felt like I was finally getting my act together.

The Offer

Roger

I picked up another fifty-pound bag of grain feed from the back of the truck and carried it inside to the rack where we store them. I dropped it on the growing pile. The late afternoon sun angled into the loading bay in a way that hit me every time I was near the opening. I needed a break from the sun and the workload.

I sat on a stool in the corner of the loading dock where I would be out of the sun and could catch my breath. I'm not in too bad of shape, but this was the thirtieth bag since I started unloading the delivery truck, and I was only half-way done. Plus, my wound from the war really hurt. It and I both needed this break. I took out a handkerchief and wiped the sweat from my brow.

It was late May and in the mid-eighties, but not as hot as Lubbock can get during the summer months. Still, it wasn't even close to the heat and humidity I experienced during the war. I massaged my stomach where the shrapnel had torn into me. It happened over in the Solomon Islands fighting the Japanese. I really thought I would have bought my ticket on Guadalcanal. That was rough, but things just got rougher. I picked up the shrapnel on Bougainville Island. 'Mud' and 'Blood' is what I called them; the nicknames for the two islands where I fought. That was the end of the war for me. I nearly died from an infection. There was some nasty stuff floating around in those jungles. It took me a year to get back to any good. But here I am and fitter than ever. The wound hardly ever gives me problems. But I had been doing a lot of lifting and turning—just what the scar didn't like.

Farmers Supply wasn't exactly the best place to work, what with all the hard labor involved, and lots of dirt and dust. I mainly worked here because Ken Cox, the owner, let me have flexible hours so I could go to college. It's tough to schedule all the classes I need at Texas Tech. Some are mornings, some afternoons, and usually at least one goes into the early evening.

I looked over to see the truck driver sitting on a cement wall, smoking a cigarette in the shade of a canopy overhang. I don't know if he was pulling my leg or not, but he said he couldn't help me unload due to union regulations. He just smiled every time I looked over at him. How am I to know if that was true or not?

"Sluffing off again, Simpson?"

I turned to see Dale, another worker at Farmers, and a real pain in the ass. I think he's jealous that I'm going to college, and will eventually end up doing something more liberating and rewarding. Whereas Dale has been here for eight years now and thinks he is a pseudo-manager, even though I heard he's been passed over for that position twice.

I found out he never served during the war. Maybe that also pulled at his craw. I don't know if he was too old or 4F. Doesn't really matter. But the fact that I did, and earned a Purple Heart, probably didn't sit well with him. He needed to prove himself in other ways. Like how he treated me.

He took a pickaxe from a section of tools and started to walk away.

"You know, I could use some help," I told him. "There's still another thirty bags in that truck."

He turned to me. "Oh, I'd love to," he said, a touch of sarcasm in his voice, "but dad gum it, Ken asked me to watch the storefront today and run things up there while he's away." He shrugged his shoulders, adding emphasis to the obvious deep sorrow he felt at being shackled with such responsibility. "It looks like you've got this job aced any-way."

He headed to the front of the store and then stopped and turned back. "Oh ..."

He seemed to start a lot of his sentences with 'Oh', as if to give his brain the few more seconds needed to form a complete one.

"... I nearly forgot. Some professor guy over at Texas Tech called for you a while back. I told him you were busy and couldn't come to the phone. I've been fixin' to tell you, but it just plum got away from me."

I stood and took a couple of steps toward Dale. He could get under my collar if he tried hard enough, and he was trying hard enough right now. I stopped myself and worked on my calm. I had a baby on the way and needed the money from this job. I wasn't going to let a jerk like Dale screw it all up.

I'm sure he knew this was an important call, what with it being from one of my professors, and to my work. I tried to keep my voice even, though knew right way I wasn't having much success. "Did you happen to get the professor's name? I have a few of them. It would be good to know which one."

"Well, you needn't have a conniption fit over it. Let me reckon on that a moment. I'm sure he gave it to me." He posed as if he were in thought. "Oh, Hilton, I think, like in the hotel. But I ain't quite certain."

"Could it be Holden?" I asked, trying to remain steady.

"Oh, might've been. But it could a been Hilton, like I said. Anyway, I told him you was busy and would call back on your break." With that, he turned and walked through the swinging door to the front.

I looked up at the clock on the wall. My break was coming up in less than twenty minutes. I wondered what Professor Holden would want that caused him to call here.

"Hey, Bud."

I looked over to see the truck driver flick his cigarette on the ground.

"I got more deliveries to make and that truck ain't unloading itself. I needs to get going."

I looked over at the thirty bags still on the truck. I had to get this done before my break. There was no way the driver would wait until after I made my call, and I wasn't about to work through my break. It would be tough to unload the rest of the bags in such a short time, but I didn't have a choice.

It took a little longer to finish than I hoped, but I still did it within my breaktime. I knocked and then opened the door to Ken's office. Sally at the front counter told me he had returned. Ken looked up and saw me standing in his doorway wiping my forehead with my handkerchief.

"Am I interrupting anything?" I asked.

His eyebrows raised when he saw my shirt soaked in sweat. "What in the Dickens have you been doing to get so lathered up?"

"I was unloading that feed delivery from Thompson Trucking."

"What, by yourself?"

"That's right."

"Where was Dale or Ted?"

"Ted was out on deliveries, and Dale said he had to mind the front of the store."

Ken studied a pencil in his hand, and then sat back in his chair with a sense of acknowledgment. "And Dale wonders why I pass him over for promotion."

"I hate to bother you, but I guess I got a phone call a little while ago from one of my professors at the college. Is it all right to return the call from your office? I couldn't take it when it came in because I had to finish unloading the truck."

Ken said, "Oh sure, sure." He stood. "I'll git out of here and give you some privacy." He came around to the front of the desk and then gestured to his chair and the phone. "All yours." He walked out the door and closed it.

I sat behind his desk, picked up the receiver, dialed the local switchboard operator, and asked her to connect me to the switchboard operator for the college. When she answered, I asked for Professor Holden's office. I heard a few clicks as she transferred the call. I hoped he would still be there.

"Hello, this is Professor Holden."

"Professor, this is Roger Simpson returning your call. I understand you tried to reach me here at work. Is something wrong?"

"No. Not at all. Actually, quite the contrary. I called because I decided to ask you to organize our upcoming summer field study expedition. And once I make a decision, I act on it."

I couldn't believe what I just heard. Juniors never got this assignment. It was always handled by a senior student.

"Hello? Are you there?"

"Oh. Sorry, Professor. I just needed a moment. I didn't expect this offer."

"Well, I've been watching you for a while. Ever since you majored in my program. Your grades are excellent, as they are in your other studies according to the professors to whom I have spoken. I was also very impressed last summer while observing your work at the Fingerpoint Cave site in Borden County. You have a great work ethic and a natural talent for archeology. I think you would make a great leader for our next expedition."

I stared at the desk, thinking of what he just said. I hadn't expected to hear such praise.

He continued. "Once I decided we needed a new site, my next step was to choose which of my students would put it together. After much consideration of the possible candidates, I kept coming around to you, even though you are in your junior year. Some of my senior students might not like it, but I also know you have the kind of leadership skills necessary for a successful expedition, and can probably handle whatever they throw your way." He paused for a moment. "The question is, will you accept the offer?"

I didn't hesitate. This was a great honor. "Yes, of course. Thank you so much!"

"Good. I hoped you would say yes. We will need to get together so I can give you the specifics."

We worked out a time I could come by and I hung up. I stood in the middle of Ken's office, a bit dumbfounded. Something like this would be huge for my future once I graduate. Part of the job would be to select where the expedition dug. The success of that choice and what we found would make or break the expedition, and my future.

Moonlight

Gloria

Moonlight filtered into the bedroom through gossamer drapes stirred by a slight breeze from the open window. It spilled onto the floor in flowing blue waves. I awoke to find myself standing near the window, my naked body awash in the moonlight.

I looked over to see my nightgown lying crumpled on the floor next to the bed. A dark and distant thought tried to work its way forward in my mind, but I quickly pushed it back. I didn't want to know what it might be.

My belly throbbed with uneasiness. I looked down to see it bathed in the waves of blue moonlight. I touched my slightly swollen tummy to feel the life inside. For a moment I worried that something had gone wrong with the baby. But everything felt fine. Why I would think such a thing was another reason I shut those thoughts out of my mind.

I looked over to see Roger still asleep in bed. One time, a few months ago, he woke to see me standing like this. We both laughed it off and agreed I must have been sleepwalking. Only, I knew differently.

I tiptoed to the bed, put on my nightgown, and carefully slipped under the covers. I lay on my back for a while, not able to sleep again. Sleep always evaded me after one of these incidents. I looked at the moon peeking through the drapes and it reminded me of something else. Another shape and a different brightness, somewhere hidden in the recesses of my mind. I shook off the thought. I had to. I knew where that thought would take me, and I didn't want to go there.

"Thanks, honey. Just what I needed."

I set a refreshed cup of coffee on the breakfast table where Roger had been working on his new project since early this morning. Actually, he'd been working hard on it all week, or at least as much as school and his job at Farmers Supply would allow. Books and maps and charts were spread all across the table's surface. It was Saturday morning. Normally a time to relax together, but today things were different because I could tell he was feeling the pressure of this new responsibility.

"How is it going?" I asked.

He shrugged and looked up in frustration. "I haven't come up with an expedition site yet. I don't want to do anything similar to the sites we have already excavated. It would be like I'm just being a copycat of what has already been done. I need somewhere fresh, with a new native society and culture for our field study, but I'm drawing a blank."

"Well, maybe what you really need right now is some brain food. I'll fix you a nice breakfast." I kissed him on the forehead.

A little later Roger looked up to see me holding two plates full of bacon, eggs, and country hash browns. He jumped up and pushed his paperwork to one side so I could set the plates down on the table, along with a cup of coffee for myself.

"This looks great, honey." He walked over and grabbed the coffee pot to top off his cup.

We ate in silence for a while, but I could see his worry. I wanted to help. "So, tell me. Why are you having such a problem picking a site?"

He chewed at his bite of egg and then said, "It's mainly because most of the places I've considered have been explored already. Professor Holden has run these expeditions for over a decade and has covered all of the native societies in our area. I need to find something new. Something that will stand out." He reached over and took my hand. "This is a big opportunity for me." He stopped, maybe to regroup his thought, then squeezed my hand ever so gently. "Actually, I should say a big opportunity for us. If this works out, it could help me land a good intern position once I graduate. Then I can work toward my Masters and maybe one day, even a Doctorate. And right now, it seems all of those plans ride on this one decision."

I sat back and thought for a moment, vaguely remembering something. I took a bite of bacon and wondered what it might be. What was it? It nagged at me from deep inside.

I suddenly sat forward. "Honey. Have you thought about over around Roswell?"

Roger stopped eating, perhaps surprised that such an idea would come from me. "What? Over in New Mexico? No. That's like close to two-hundred miles from here."

"Is it farther than other expeditions the school has undertaken?"

Roger focused on the notes and charts and textbooks on the table. "No. Professor Holden conducted extensive studies of the Yaqui Indians in Sonora, Mexico, and that's a long way from Lubbock. I just never thought about going into New Mexico." He looked at me, a bit confused. "What gave you that idea?"

I wondered the same thing. "I don't know. I must have overheard something about it."

The look on his face showed his interest but also held lots of questions. "Where would you hear such a thing?"

I couldn't come up with anything right away. "Hold on. I'm trying to remember." I could feel some thoughts working their way up, but also being held back. Like an internal struggle going on. I shook my head.

Roger finished eating and stood. "That's okay, but it's a good suggestion. I'll check it out." He motioned to my plate. "Are you done? I'll take it for you if you are."

I nodded, still confused by my feelings. He picked up our plates and took them to the sink.

When he returned, I grabbed his hand and pulled him into his chair. "I remember now. It was an Indian tribe, long ago, camped in an area above Roswell. Apache, I think."

Roger studied me. I could tell he wanted to believe me but needed a reason. "And you know this how?"

I ignored him. "Do you have a map of the area?"

He pulled all of his notes, maps, charts, and textbooks toward us. He worked through them, grabbed a map, and spread it out in front of us. "Here. This one has the area."

He ran his finger along the map but I pushed his hand aside and pointed to a spot. "Here. This is the place." My finger landed on an area of the map with some gullies and ravines as part of an old river bed, about thirty miles north-west of Roswell. "Here. This is where they had their camp. But it was a long time ago."

Roger studied me. His eyes flickered and then brightened. They shifted from uncertainty to some form of understanding, perhaps reading something in my face. Then he looked down at the map. He turned it to see it better. "How could you know this exact spot?" He looked up at me. "It has everything they would need for a campsite." His voice carried a sense of wonder.

"I'm not sure. Maybe some hunters came into the Eat 'N Run and were talking about the area, studying a map. Or it could have been at school. Remember, I was raised here. We could have studied the Apache in high school." I stared at the black coffee in my cup as if the clue could be found there. "You know how sometimes you see or hear something, and kind of forget about it. But then later, it gets drawn out?" I smiled at Roger. "That must be it."

"About an ancient Apache tribe over in Roswell?" But he didn't say this skeptically. It was more like he was trying

47

to connect the dots. "I'm amazed you could remember such a thing."

I leaned toward him so our faces were just inches apart. His breath washed against my face, full of anticipation. I focused on him. "Roger, I don't know where or how I came to know this, or what else I need to do to convince you." I took his hands and placed them on my chest. "I just know in my heart that this is the site you've been looking for."

His eyes studied every detail of my own, looking for signs of doubt. He didn't find any, because deep inside, somehow, I knew I was right.

He sat back. "Okay. You've convinced me. I'll take a look at it. If it works out, we should be able to put something together for late July."

"Why not July Fourth? It falls on a Friday. That gives you a three-day holiday to work with."

"The Fourth of July. A three-day weekend." He smiled. "It's as if you had this all figured out."

The Plan

Lake Oswego, 1967

Frankie

Mom and Suzie were getting dinner ready. I grabbed the phone from the table in the corner of the kitchen and snuck it down the stairs as far as the cord would let me go. I dialed Beanie's phone number. Luckily, he answered instead of his mom. I didn't feel up to dealing with Beanie's gatekeeper right now.

"Hello."

"Hey, Beanie. It's Frankie. Can you talk?"

"Hold on." I heard a muffled noise on the line before he came back on. He had a closet close to the phone he used for our clandestine calls.

"Okay, but keep it short. My phone privileges are kind of grounded too. So, what's up?"

"We need to figure out how to find where this key fits. And I'm not sure trying to do that over the phone is a good idea. We need to talk it through. Can you sneak out later?"

We had become really good at sneaking out of our houses without our parents ever getting wind of it. Beanie, due to his home environment, was a master at it.

"Sure. Later, when Mom is watching TV or something. I usually go to my room anyway to read comic books before I go to sleep. It just can't be long, because she always checks on me before going to bed. That's right after the late news."

"It shouldn't take long. We just need a plan. Meet me down at the lake around nine o'clock. Does that work?"

"Yep. I'll see you there."

I waited for Beanie at the picnic table by the water. On the way down, I picked up some small stones from the side of the road. I tossed one into the water every once in a while. A sliver of moon showed through the clouds above. It reflected off the lake water. The rings from my stones warped the reflection as they passed through its image. It hadn't rained all day, so I didn't expect it to start now. Especially since I could see some breaks in the clouds.

I heard the gate open and turned to see Beanie lumber down the stairs.

He came over, sat on top of the picnic table next to me, and said in a very British sort of way, "Well, Master Sherlock, have you found a solution to the mystery of the safe deposit box key?"

"What? Oh, that's a pretty good Watson." Beanie's ability to morph into a character had become a fairly normal thing to expect. "Well, dear colleague of mine, the first thing we need to do is take this key somewhere."

"Like to some sort of key specialist?"

"Or, maybe we can head down to one of the banks in Lake Oswego and see if they would know."

"Do any of them even have safe deposit boxes?" Beanie asked.

I tossed another stone into the water and watched the rings spread toward the moon's reflection. "I don't know. I guess it would be good to call around to see if any do."

"I hope you realize that even if they do, this key probably wouldn't fit one of them."

"Yeah. I already figured that out. Mel's family lived in Portland over by Berkeley Park back then." I looked at Beanie. "But it must be a bank somewhere in the area."

Beanie gave me a go-figure look when I said that. But then his look changed with a thought. "I hate to say this, but Mel's dad traveled all over the world. What's to say he didn't get a safe deposit box at a bank in some far-off Timbuktu country? You know, like in Nepal or some other place we would never, ever be able to get to?"

"I love your optimism, Beanie. You really know how to build up hope."

He shrugged. "I'm just saying, it's possible."

"Well, let's stay focused on what we can do, and hope for the best."

"Okay. Like I said, Sherlock. What's our next move?"

I thought for a moment. What is the best next move? So, okay, he wants me to be Sherlock Holmes, so why not use similar deductive methods to figure it out? "Let's take this to the simple truths. The first truth is we have a key given to Mel by Professor Lofton, who was holding it for her."

"From her dad," Beanie finished.

"Second, we all decided it fits a safe deposit box because of its shape."

51

"Right. I'm with you."

"And who would have the knowledge to tell us if that was true or not?"

Beanie frowned. "I don't follow."

"Okay. I'll ask it this way. Who knows more about keys than anyone else?"

I could see Beanie thinking for a while. "Key makers?"

I gave him a big smile. "Locksmiths. They know all about keys. A locksmith should be able to tell us loads about this key. Maybe even what bank it belongs to."

"Wow, Sherlock. You are good at this. So, we find a locksmith, right?"

"Yep. I'll look in the Yellow Pages when I get home. I'm sure there must be one in Lake Oswego." I tossed my last stone into the water and watched the rings attack the moon. "Do you think you can get away tomorrow? Dad will be at work and I think Mom and Suzie have shopping plans."

"Yeah. My mom is going to be out, too. I think some sort of bridge party with her friends."

"Okay. Call me tomorrow when she leaves. Then we can ride our bikes to the locksmith and see what he says."

"What about your car? Can we take it, instead?"

I shook my head. "Naw. My dad made a big show out of writing down the odometer reading when he grounded me. He would know right away if we took it."

Beanie nudged me with his shoulder. "Bikes it is." He slapped me on the back. "All the same, good show, old man. I like your plan, Master Sherlock."

Zimmerman's

Frankie

Zimmerman's Clocks, Locks, and Keys sat by itself in a little shop off Boones Ferry Road in Lake Grove. Beanie and I leaned our bikes against the side of the building and headed to the front door.

We originally planned on going to a place called Dwight's Locksmith Shop in Lake Oswego. We thought they would be the best ones to know about this key. Maybe because it had the word locksmith right in the name, whereas Zimmerman's seemed more focused on clocks.

But now we only had a small window of time. It had worked out perfectly that our parents were both gone at the same time, just as we hoped. What didn't work out perfectly was the weather, since it had rained hard all morning. The rain ended, but so did the thought of going to Dwight's. It was too far and would take too long. And we didn't want to think about riding two miles home in the rain if it started up again.

We decided on Zimmerman's, with the hope we could still make it back before our parents got home. We weren't sure if this Zimmerman shop would know much about safe deposit keys, but we had to give it a try.

We walked in through the front door, and it felt like walking into time itself. Clocks of all shapes and sizes covered the entire store. Little ones on tables. Tons of them hung on every available inch of wall space. Some had glass domes with little moving balls. Big ones stood guard on the floor, and very expensive ones sat in a glass countertop case just in front of us. Every one of them ticking. We were surrounded by ticking; and every clock had exactly the same time on it: 10:54.

We stood just inside the door for a moment, not sure what to do. We didn't see anyone. Beanie walked over to a little clock on a table and said, "Check this out, Frankie."

He leaned down and batted his eyes. I looked to see Betty Boop in all of her sexy splendor as she held a small, round clock.

I gave a bit of a sigh. "Let's try to keep focused here, Beanie."

A voice from somewhere said, *"Ich dachte, ich hätte Kunden gehört."*

We looked as a man stuck his head out from a little doorway at the back of the store. He had a kind of Albert Einstein appearance, with white hair that flowed out from his head in all directions as if someone had just rubbed a balloon over the top of it. He walked over. I could see he was small and stooped, and wore an old wool sweater even though this was still summer. A pair of odd-looking glasses dangled on the end of his nose. They had thick lenses. Maybe he used them while repairing watches or something.

"Can I help you, *Jungen*?" He obviously spoke another language and had a fairly thick accent. I think it could have been German. Or maybe Swiss, considering all of the clocks around the place.

I stepped forward. "We hope so. You obviously know a lot about clocks, but you are also a locksmith, right? I mean, you work with keys too, don't you?"

"*Natürlich.* Of course I do. I wouldn't have it in my shop's name if I didn't."

Beanie jumped in. "You will have to excuse my friend's inability to see the obvious. He sometimes gets caught up in the minutia of things."

I frowned. "Thanks for all the help, Beanie."

"My name is Mr. Zimmerman, but you should have already surmised that unless, of course, you are still caught up in minutia. I run this little shop. How can I help you?" He walked over to the countertop display case and waved a hand over the top. "Perhaps a present *für deine Mutter oder deinen Vater*?"

I looked at Beanie and then at Mr. Zimmerman. "I'm not quite sure what you just said, Mr. Zimmerman, but we need your help. We have a key and we don't know what it goes to. We think it's a safe deposit box, like at a bank or something."

"Yeah," Beanie added. "We're hoping you ought to know what it fits."

Mr. Zimmerman gave us a confirming look. "*Ja.* I most likely could tell you. The majority of safe deposit keys have a code or stamp on the head that gives indication as to the bank, or at least the manufacturer who could then identify the bank. It is a safety mechanism should the key be lost."

"Then you would definitely know," Beanie said.

He gave us a look like he had more important things to do than talk to teenagers with no plans to make a purchase. He tapped at the glass countertop with his fingertips in a way that suggested he was getting a little annoyed. "Then, it would be a big help to actually see the key. You do have it with you, *ja*?"

He held out his hand.

"Oh!" I reached into my pocket, took out the key, and placed it in his palm. "Sorry."

His eyes lit up for a quick moment. He held the key up and studied it for a while. "But in this case, I am afraid to say, I cannot tell you such information. There is no coding on this key for a bank."

My shoulders slumped at his words. I didn't know what to say.

But Beanie did. He leaned toward Mr. Zimmerman, gave him a secretive look, and whispered, "So, what's the deal, Mr. Z? Would you have to kill us if you told us?"

Mr. Zimmerman chuckled at Beanie's comment, and set the key on the glass countertop. "*Nein*, nothing like that. It's just that this key —"

All of the clocks suddenly tolled. Thousands of gongs and chimes and coo-coos, all battling to destroy my eardrums. A quick glance around the room showed it was straight up eleven o'clock.

Mr. Zimmerman kept talking and pointing to the key, but I couldn't understand a thing he said, all of it muffled by the loud dings and clangs. It was as if he didn't even notice the clocks blaring away.

They continued to toll. I looked over at Beanie and shouted, "Why didn't we come here at one o'clock instead of eleven?" I put my hands over my ears to try and save my hearing.

Beanie did the same. It looked like he was counting under his breath. "… eight … nine … ten … eleven."

The clocks stopped, all at once, as if on cue. We lowered our hands.

"I'm sorry Mr. Zimmerman," I said. "We didn't hear that last part."

"*Ich sagte*, that this key doesn't have any bank coding on it because it doesn't go to a safe deposit box. *Es ist ein uhrschlüssel*, a clock key."

I was stunned. From the get-go, we had all thought it went to a safe deposit box. None of us even came close to thinking it would fit something else.

"Like one of your clocks here?" I asked.

"*Nein*. Not one of mine." He picked up the key again and looked at the head using his magnifier glasses. "This is a Kieninger key. The Kieninger Company is one of the world's best manufacturers of longcase clocks. They started back in 1912 in *Deutschland*. You call it Germany here in the United States. Kieningers are well-made and very expensive. This key fits a one-of-a-kind Kieninger."

I didn't understand. "What is a longcase clock?"

"They are pendulum clocks. Here in the United States, you call them grandfather clocks. I prefer the original terminology—*langkoffer*, or in English, longcase."

I could see he was thinking about something. "What is it, Mr. Zimmerman?"

He was deep in thought and tapped the key against the glass countertop in an absentminded sort of way. "Why are you so anxious to find this clock? What do you feel is so important about this key?"

I didn't know how to answer. What do I tell him? "Uh, well—"

"It fits a hidden compartment," Beanie cut in.

I gave Beanie a look. He had to be losing it to tell that to Mr. Zimmerman.

He nudged me in the ribs with an elbow and continued, "Yeah. You see, my father found a crashed alien spaceship a while back. One of the dying aliens gave him an object which we understand can save the world. We think the object is hidden in the clock. So," he said, as he tossed on his biggest smile, "can you tell us where it is so we can save mankind?"

Mr. Zimmerman's face transitioned from one of feigned interest to a blank stare that lasted uncomfortably long. I was sure Beanie had just blown it. Then Mr. Zimmerman burst into deep-welled laughter and slapped the countertop with his hand. "That was good. *Sehr gut!* I love young people's imaginations. But also, a perfect reason why I shouldn't share such information."

"Hah," Beanie exclaimed. "I bet that's more because you can't figure out where the clock is?"

I looked over at Beanie and kicked him under the counter. "Sorry, Mr. Zimmerman. My friend sometimes has social grace issues."

Mr. Zimmerman glared at Beanie for a moment and then slowly regained his composure. He turned to me, maybe thinking I was the sane one in our group of two. "Well, I wouldn't be a very good horologist if I couldn't figure that out now, would I?"

Beanie raised his eyebrows. "You work with plants, too?"

Mr. Zimmerman gave out a little laugh. It seemed to break the ice. "No, *mein junger Mann*. That would be an herbologist. Horology is the art of clock and watchmaking. And I happen to be a master horologist."

He leaned on the counter to get closer, and held the key out in front of us. "You see, I believe this key goes to a very unusual longcase clock. It has special markings that I have not seen associated with any other Kieninger clock. And you are correct in your statement earlier. Most clock keys are meant to open the front cabinet and to wind the clock. This one, as you said, is a second key, with the specific purpose to open a hidden compartment within the clock."

He took a small tool from his shirt pocket. It looked a lot like something a dentist would use. He pointed to a little stamp on the head of the key. "This imprint identifies it as such. The Kieningers only made a few of these. Mostly special requests. Which makes this a very interesting key."

Things were getting really crazy weird. "Could you tell us where the clock is?" I asked.

"*Nein*, I think not."

"But what about the markings?" Beanie said. "Aren't they like with the keys for bank deposit boxes?"

"Not quite the same thing. Banks do such things for financial reasons. There is no similar need for longcase clocks."

Beanie tossed on his broadest smile and said, "But you do know, don't you, Mr. Z? Mister Master Horologist."

"It's really very important," I added.

"I am a busy man. And on top of that, I don't know that I should even tell you. I am sure it will only lead to trouble. I have a few years under me and know those looks on your faces. *Unruhestifters.* Troublemakers. You should go now. I need to get back to work." He took a few steps toward his office.

"But the key," I said. "We need it back."

He turned to me, the key still in his hand, and held it up. "This key? I know the clock and its owners. I will be happy to return it to them for you."

Beanie and I looked at each other. What just happened?

I gave Mr. Zimmerman my most pleading look. "Ignore what Beanie said earlier. It's really important we find out what's in there. We're on kind of a quest. That's why we were given the key. We're supposed to get whatever is in the compartment. Once we do, we won't need the key anymore. You can have it then."

He stepped back over to us and stood there, once again tapping the key on the glass case, sizing us up, considering what I just said.

"Pretty, pretty please," Beanie decided to toss in. Like this would make all the difference in the world.

Mr. Zimmerman seemed to be working all the angles. He finally sighed and said, "*Sehr gut.* After all, it seems that whoever was charged with this key, awarded it to you. Therefore, whatever is in that compartment, the key has intended to be yours. Though, let it be on your own heads. *Ich habe ein schlechtes Gefühl dabei*. In other words, I have a bad feeling about this. Nonetheless, once we have completed your quest, I will retain the key afterward. Agreed?"

"Sure. No problem," I said.

"Is the clock close? Is it in Portland?" Beanie asked.

"No. It is not in Portland, but you could say it is close. At least I would. You see, the minute you handed me this key, I knew to which Kieninger longcase it belongs. Simply because there are no other keys like it in the world. I know the parent key, the one which winds the clock, and they are a match. *Ein set*, so to speak. But only a few are aware of the existence of this second key; created to fit a hidden compartment within the clock. A compartment *I* have seen."

Beanie nearly broke my rib when he gouged me with his elbow. "You've actually seen the clock and the compartment?"

I wanted an answer to a more focused question. "How did you find out about the hidden compartment?" I asked.

Mr. Zimmerman threw his little stooped shoulders back and proudly stated, "This is not only a masterfully built timepiece, but a masterful piece of art as well. Whom might you assume would be called upon to repair and maintain such a priceless longcase?"

Beanie and I just looked at each other. We were definitely thinking the same thing. What are the odds? One in a zillion?

He held up the key so all three of us could focus on it. "I am sure this is the long-lost key to that hidden compartment, and it has found its way home through you."

The proverbial hairs on the back of my neck stood on end.

Mr. Zimmerman laid the key on the counter. "So, *Jungen*, are you familiar with Timberline Lodge?"

Timberline

Frankie

I was about to answer him, but Mr. Zimmerman held up a finger before I could, to indicate I should wait. Then he walked to the back of the store and disappeared. A moment later he came out with a large book and placed it on the countertop between us. It kinda looked like one of those books someone would display on a coffee table, but a lot older and bigger.

He asked again. "Timberline Lodge. Do you know of it?"

I said, "You mean, like up on Mount Hood?"

"*Ja*, the very one. And what might you know about its history and the WPA?"

Beanie and I looked at each other. I had been up there once with my parents. We went inside the lodge, but only for a quick look around, and then we ate lunch at the Cascade Restaurant. I think they did it just to mark it off their list. Maybe because friends had recommended it. But we weren't skiers, so it didn't have that draw. And I knew Beanie didn't ski. I'd have seen the cast on whatever appendage he broke if he had ever tried to go down a snowy mountainside strapped to a couple of flat sticks.

63

Beanie answered for both of us. "Wasn't that part of the New Deal?"

I looked over at Beanie. "You mean you actually listened in history class?"

He shrugged. "I got caught unawares once." He turned to Mr. Zimmerman again. "But what does the lodge's history have to do with our key?"

Mr. Zimmerman's eyes lit up. "Everything." He took a proud stance again. "I am not only a master horologist but also somewhat of an historian regarding timepieces." He swept his hand across the top of the book he had brought out. "This is a tome of the great clocks of the world. A rather wonderful work I am happy to share with you here, and to which I contributed." He slowly flipped through the pages, stopping once in a while to admire a particular clock. "It's been a while since I have leafed through it. What beautiful clocks."

He stopped and patted a page to which he had just turned. "Ah, yes, here we are. You see, a great depression happened at the end of the twenties. Many, many people were out of work. President Roosevelt put together what he called the New Deal. Basically, it was a program to get the unemployed back to work on federal projects. Your Timberline Lodge was one of them."

I wasn't following. "And that has what to do with our key?"

He swung the book toward us so we could see the photograph. It showed a big clock, intricately designed. A weird looking guy stood next to it, no doubt the clockmaker. The photo showed him only from the knees up, next to the clock.

It looked like the clock was set into a huge chunk of wood. Maybe from a tree trunk. Not one with bark and such, but one of smooth, polished wood.

The picture must have been from when he had just finished it. He looked to be kind of young, maybe in his thirties. He wore a vest over a long-sleeved, striped shirt and a wide, dark tie. He must have used some sort of goo on his hair because it was all slicked back.

Mr. Zimmerman pointed to the man. "*Das ist* Otto Kieninger, the long-lost son of Joseph Kieninger, founder of Kieninger clocks. He grew up in the business and learned everything about it. But he had a falling out with his *Vater* in the mid-1920s and came to America. It was only a few years later that the stock market crashed and the Great Depression hit. The clock business he started collapsed, *er war fertig*, finished, and soon became one of many millions of unemployed.

"It wasn't until the Federal Arts Project came along through the WPA, that he found gainful employment within this program. Otto soon became known for his expertise in clocks and mechanisms. When the construction of Timberline Lodge became a reality, Otto was sought out as the master of his craft to build special clocks for use in the lodge. Clocks that would be in tune with the environment. And, as it turns out, his being there helped them solve a problem, the result of which was this longcase clock. He worked closely with other masters of their craft, wood carvers and metalsmiths, to create what you see on this page."

"And this is it? Our clock?" Beanie asked, running his hand over the photograph. "Wow. It's so cool looking. I can't wait to see it in person."

"Well, the picture doesn't do it justice. It is quite an amazing clock."

"Yeah, thanks, Mr. Zimmerman," I said. "You've been a big help." I picked up the key from the counter and put it in my pocket.

He smiled, in a funny sort of way, as if there was more to be told, but was waiting for something. I brushed it off. Now that we knew where to find the clock, we had no reason to hang around any longer. Mission accomplished. And, judging by any one of the thousands of clocks in the room, it was time to head home so we wouldn't get caught.

"We'll turn the key over to you as soon as we get whatever's in the compartment," I told Mr. Zimmerman, then nodded to Beanie and headed for the door.

"I assume you have transportation. Maybe a parent can take you? The lodge is over sixty miles away."

We stopped and turned to him. I said, "We'll figure something out."

"And how will you find it?"

Beanie and I looked at each other. I don't think either one of us quite knew what he meant.

Beanie asked, "What, the clock? You just told us where it is."

Mr. Zimmerman closed the book and looked at us. "The compartment. The *secret* compartment. How will you find it?"

Beanie walked over to him and said, "We'll find it, Mr. Z, now that we know where it is. And the clock's big, so how could we miss it?" But there wasn't a ton of confidence in his voice.

It made me think, how would we find it? I stepped next to Beanie. "What are you getting at, Mr. Zimmerman?"

He gave us kind of a disheartened smile, like one would give to someone who doesn't quite get it. "The compartment is *versteckt*, hidden. Something *versteckt* is not meant to be found. Or, at least only found by certain individuals with privileged knowledge."

"And that would be you, I suppose?" I asked.

His face took on a serious look. "Only a few people are aware of a key to a hidden compartment in that clock. One was Otto Kieninger, who by the way, disappeared not long after finishing the clock, and has never been seen again. One would also be me, of course. And the other would be whoever holds the key." He focused in on me. "And that, *Junge*, is you."

Beanie sheepishly raised his hand. "Umm. Hello. I'm here, too."

I ignored Beanie, and focused on what Mr. Zimmerman just said. "What. Me? But I—"

And then I caught myself. There was no sense in bringing Mel into this as the one who actually received the key. He didn't need to know about her. Not at this point, anyway. And, after all, Mel had given me the key, so there was some truth to what Mr. Zimmerman just said.

He continued, "As I said before, I am not interested in what might be found inside the compartment, if anything is in there at all. You boys are welcome to it, since it appears whoever gave you the key intended the contents to go to you. My only request, which isn't a request at all, is you turn over the key when we are done. *Verstehen?*"

I was good with that, but then it hit me. "What do you mean by when *we* are done?"

"I mentioned transportation. Even if you were able to get up there, you would have no idea where to look for the compartment."

"What are you getting at?" I asked.

"I will take you. This is an offer you need to accept. I can gain access to the compartment and help you retrieve the contents. Then, you will give me the key."

So that was it. He wanted to be there when we opened the compartment. Maybe he wanted to see what was inside. Or, maybe he just wanted to be there to make sure he got the key from us as soon as we were done with it.

He smiled and looked off into the distance, then back to us. "At some point in the future, I will make an announcement that I have discovered an unknown key to a hidden compartment in this famous clock. It will certainly spike this horologist's notoriety with my colleagues." He gave us a wink. "Old men need to find their thrills in different ways, now that they are no longer virile young men such as yourselves."

And it could be that, also.

"Hold on a minute, Mr. Zimmerman. I need to discuss this with my associate." I nodded to Beanie and we took a few steps away, turning our backs to Mr. Zimmerman.

"What do you think?" I whispered.

"What do you mean, what do I think? How else would we get up there? Your car? And how are we going to work that out? Even if we got away with taking it, they'd see the extra miles on the odometer. I think we have to go with him. It will be tough enough just figuring out how we can get away for a few hours without our parents knowing."

I told him what Mel suggested with Captain Thornton, then added, "But he isn't back from vacation yet. I called the police department because I wanted to feel it out. To see if he would give us a ride. But they said he wasn't back yet. I think they are worried about him."

Beanie said, "This is our best bet, anyway. I'd rather go with Mr. Z than to trust our beloved Captain Thornton. He'd probably want to know what we got out of the compartment. And Mr. Z just said he didn't care what it was."

On rare occasions Beanie could actually make sense, and this was one of them. "I guess you're right."

We went back to Mr. Zimmerman. "Okay. We're in. You can drive us. We, uh, just have a little issue with figuring out when we can get away together. Are you willing to work with us on that?"

"*Natürlich*. I will need some time to review my notes on my work with the clock. I have not been up there in quite a while." He took something from the pocket of his sweater and handed it to me. "My card with my phone number. Call as soon as you can get away. For this, I am willing to close my shop."

I took the card and slipped it into the back pocket of my jeans.

"Oh, and by the way, *Jungen*, the hidden compartment is inside the pendulum housing, so it would have been interesting to watch the two of you attempt to gain entry since the case itself is locked. The staff at Timberline are not in the habit of handing out the key to just anyone. But," he patted his chest, "as the caretaker, it is a natural thing that I should need access to the housing for maintenance." He looked at us, knowing we had no other choice. "So, *wer sind gut, ja?*"

Beanie and I grabbed our bikes from the side of the building and walked them to the street. I looked up to see dark clouds overhead. "We'd better get home before it starts to rain."

Beanie said, "Am I alone here, or is it kind of weird that we just happened to go to probably the only guy in the entire world who knows what that key fits?"

"No. That didn't escape my thoughts either, even though I am drowning in minutia." I tossed him a sarcastic smile.

Beanie chuckled, but then went serious, which doesn't happen very often. "Now we just have to find a way to steal a precious few hours away from our wardens without their finding out."

"I have no idea how we will pull that off, but we need to figure something out. Let's hope we can."

I pushed off on my bike, but Beanie stopped me. I looked over at him and saw he had gotten even more serious on me. "Have you thought about how Mel's father managed to get access to that compartment?"

"No." And I hadn't, until now. Just how did he get access to a very public clock and not only know about a hidden compartment inside the housing, but also have the key in his possession to open it? One more mystery in a tall stack of mysteries that had been mounting up ever since we found out Mel's father had been at that UFO crash.

● ● ●

Roberts had followed the boys to this funny little shop and parked across the street. Now, he watched them kick onto their bicycles and ride down Boones Ferry Road. They cut across a store parking lot and onto Bryant Street. No doubt headed home before they got caught sneaking out.

Here was another interesting little turn of events. He looked at his watch. The boys had been in there for nearly half an hour. They must have found out something important about the key.

He started his car, drove over to the shop, and parked in the lot. He got out and headed to the front door of Zimmerman's Clocks, Locks, and Keys. Now, it was just a matter of finding out what the person inside told the boys.

The Proposal

Lubbock, 1947

Roger

It was another hot day, and racing up two flights of stairs had its effect. Sweat beaded on my brow, and my shirt clung to my back between my shoulder blades. I reached Professor Holden's office and stood outside the door to catch my breath. I checked my watch. It was six minutes after two, which means I was six minutes late. Oh well. Not much I could do about it now. I pulled a handkerchief from my pocket, wiped at my forehead, smoothed my hair into place, and opened the door.

His secretary, Mrs. Arthur, looked up from typing. "Hello, Mr. Simpson. The professor has been waiting." She said this in a 'put me in my place' sort of way to let me know she wasn't happy I was late. "I'll inform him you are here." She pressed an intercom button on her desk. "Professor, Mr. Simpson has arrived."

"Let him know I will be a minute."

"Yes, Sir." She turned to me. "The professor is just about finished up. He will be with you shortly." She nodded to a couple of chairs in the corner of the waiting area and went back to typing.

I took a seat and laid the manila folder on a small table next to me. The reception area served three offices: Professor Holden, Professor Patton, who taught geology, and Professor Schmidt, physics. Mrs. Arthur was the secretary for all three.

A fan stood in one corner of the room and oscillated back and forth, sending a cooling breeze over me each time it swung in my direction. Much needed relief. The professor had the prestige of an office on the third floor, but with that came the heat filtering up from below. I might have preferred a cool spot in the basement somewhere. There had been talk of installing some form of air conditioning system in the buildings, but that was all still in the works. It would be very expensive and the funding still needed to be approved.

A buzzer sounded on Mrs. Arthur's desk. She pushed a button and said, "Yes, Professor?"

"Send in Mr. Simpson."

"Yes, Sir." She nodded to me. "You can go in now."

I knocked on the door, opened it, and walked into Professor Holden's office. His desk sat close to a set of windows overlooking the commons. Stacks of paperwork covered its surface. An array of artifacts was strewn across the stacks, acting as paperweights. A fan in the corner, just like the one in the reception area, worked hard to keep the room cool. The artifacts worked just as hard to keep the paperwork from blowing out the open windows.

Professor Holden looked very much like a professor should look. He sported a white shirt and dark blue tie under a double-breasted jacket, which he wore even though the temperature in the room must have been close to ninety-degrees. Still, I couldn't see a single bead of sweat on his brow. Black, wire-rimmed glasses sat on his nose. He had a long, narrow face with a prominent forehead from a receding hairline that made his face look even longer. None of this distracted from the nature of his dignified appearance. In fact, it probably made him even more so. And he always had an aura about him of substantial knowledge.

He looked at the folder in my hand. "Is that the proposal?"

"Yes, Professor." I stammered a little. I was nervous. "I need to apologize for being late."

He waved me off and held out his hand.

"This is your copy." I handed it to him. "I hope you like it."

He took the folder and motioned to a chair in front of his desk. "Sit."

The folder consisted of about fifteen pages and included the proposal, four maps, and an expense budget. One of the maps showed what I believed to be the migratory route of the native people in the proposed study.

He opened the folder and scanned the contents.

I looked around the room. I had been in here a few times, and always found some new artifact I hadn't noticed before. I made it a game to guess where it had been found, and to which native people and period it belonged. I never thought to ask him. He always appeared to be really busy.

For the times I had been in here, it seemed I was in and out before I knew it.

The professor looked up from the proposal and asked, "New Mexico, near Roswell? Tell me, why there?"

I let out a nervous laugh. Probably because it was such a big risk. This proposal would be a whole new direction for an expedition. Most of the professor's work in the past had been centered in the surrounding areas of Texas or in Mexico.

"I thought we should look outside of the natives we have studied already in this area. The location I have selected is known to have been used by the Mescalero Apache. The *Mashgalé-neí*, which they call themselves in their native tongue. It translates roughly to 'People Close to the Mountains'.

"They covered a wide area of Arizona, New Mexico, the panhandle of Texas, and down into Mexico. There were different bands of the Mescalero. I believe the one in this area would be either the *Natahéndé* or the *Ch'laandé*."

"Yes, I am familiar with the *Natahéndé* of the Northern Panhandle, though we have never studied them."

"Then as you probably know, the Mescalero were a nomadic group, going north in the summer to hunt buffalo, and south in the winter to gather *agave parryi*, commonly referred to as the Mescal plant. In their native tongue, they called it *Astaneh*. It was a staple food source for their diet. Thus, the name given them by the Spanish when they arrived in the area—Mescalero Apache."

I pointed to a location on the terrain map. It was a dry river bed in a hilly area consisting of gullies and ravines on the edge of an otherwise flat desert landscape. An area that could provide water, shade, and protection from the wind. "This is a point where two arroyo riverbeds merge. I believe this area would have been a perfect location for their base camp from which to gather the agave."

He looked at the proposal again and studied the maps. "Yes, I can see how this area could be the location for such a camp. The mountains are not far off, so there would be abundant deer and other game to be hunted in the area. And during that time of year, it looks like a steady stream of water would be available."

I felt a sense of relief and the thrill of acceptance. "I set the date for July Fourth. It happens to be on a Friday this year. That gives us a three-day holiday for those with jobs, without taking too much time away. I talked to a core group of your students who can be there for the duration. That will be Wednesday of the preceding week through the following Tuesday. I wanted to make sure they were available to do this. Our core group will pack up the equipment and leave on Wednesday, with a stay overnight in Roswell. Then we can get an early start on Thursday, which will give us time to find the best site for a base camp. Once we have the camp up and running, we will conduct a large-scale reconnaissance survey of the area using the transect method.

"If we have time and identify sites with a higher density of artifacts on Friday morning, we can conduct intensive surveys of those areas, and collect artifacts for examination when you and the others arrive later that day. The three-day weekend should give us plenty of time to establish whether this site is worthy of further study."

"July Fourth weekend. I think that will work out well." He set the proposal and maps aside and reviewed the cost analysis. "This looks to be within our standard budget for such an expedition. Who is in your nucleus?"

"I'll take Williams, Donagle, and Brentwood as the core group to get things ready."

"A good team." He looked at me with some concern. "Williams and Brentwood are seniors. It won't be an issue, their taking directions from you?"

"No. I put out feelers to see if they would be okay with that, and to make sure they could get the time away. I didn't go into details, but they were excited about the expedition, and about studying a new native people."

"Good." He closed the folder, set it on his desk, and placed a stone Zuni badger fetish on top so it wouldn't blow away. He gave me an affirming look. "Then you had better get to work. We only have a little over a month until the fourth."

The Tartan Lounge

Roger

I walked into the Tartan Lounge and stood near the entrance until I could get my bearings. Always a necessity when transitioning from the bright evening Texas sun into a club where the lights were low and the shadows deep.

"Hey, Roger. Over here." An arm waved to catch my attention. It came from a booth in the back.

I could tell by the voice it was Billy Donagle. We were both juniors at Texas Tech and had become friends because of all the classes we took together.

I walked over. He was sitting with Roy Williams, Steve Brentwood, and Stu Furman. All seniors. The four of them did a good job of filling up the booth, so I grabbed a nearby chair and sat at the end of the table. I placed a folder on it in front of me.

A waitress came over. "What will you have, honey?"

I looked up to see a pretty brunette on my right. She wore a black apron tied around a very tiny waist. It had tartan accents. So did the lounge. Red and black. Texas Tech colors. We were only a few blocks away from Jones Stadium.

"I'll take a glass of Lone Star," I told her.

She left to get my beer. The rest of the group already had a beer.

"Well, isn't she the peaches," Roy said, checking out her caboose as she left.

Roy came from South Carolina and never failed to let everyone know it through the slang he used and the accent of his voice, but he had to really work at it because Texans were just as proud of their colloquial dictionary, and much of the two were similar. Billy, Steve, and Stu were all native Texans. I grew up in Oregon, so sometimes felt like I was in another country for the way they talked down here.

I looked around the table. "Thanks for coming." All four were students of Professor Holden, working on degrees in either anthropology or archeology. I called them together hoping they would buy into the details of my plan. If I could swing them, especially the seniors, then we would be all set.

"So, what's the big fuss all about, Simpson?" Stu asked. "And nice try on being late so you didn't have to pay for our beers. But this ain't my first rodeo, so I told them to run a tab for you. After all, you called this shindig."

Stu, plain and simple, was a hothead. The kind of guy who could have a full glass of beer in front of him, and still be half-empty. For that same reason, I needed to try to win him over or he could cause trouble. But he would have definitely caused trouble if I didn't invite him to this meeting, and he found out about it later. Probably my biggest strike with him though, was that I'm a northerner.

"Not a problem, Stu. Sorry I'm late. I had to close the shop and a customer held me up for a while." The waitress set a glass of beer in front of me. I looked up at her. "You might as well bring a pitcher. I'm sure we'll need it."

"On your dollar?" she asked. "They started you a tab. Is that what we're doing?"

"Yes. Thank you." I turned to the guys again. "As you know, Professor Holden offered me the job to put together our field study for this summer."

Billy jumped in, "Isn't that a hoot? How'd you manage to pull that off?"

Stu gave a mocking chuckle. "Yeah. I'm wondering the same thing, being a junior and all. What are you, kin of his or something?"

Steve and Roy nodded to show they also wanted to know.

"No, I'm not kin. And I have no idea why he picked me. He said he liked my work ethic, and that I was doing well in my classes. All of us were at Fingerpoint together last summer. Maybe you can figure it out. All I know is he said he liked how I handled myself and what I did there." They didn't look convinced. "Really, guys, I have no idea. But he offered me the opportunity and I accepted." I looked at each of them in turn. "If he had offered it to you instead, would any of you have turned it down?"

Roy answered for all of them. "Course not. We all woulda loved the opportunity just as much as you. So, why the gathering?"

"I met with the professor on my proposal." I tapped the folder in front of me. "He's given it his stamp. Now, I want to go over the expedition with the four of you to get your perspectives on it."

I opened the folder, took out a folded map of the area, and set it aside. "I'll show you this in a minute." I handed a copy of the proposal to each of them. "Look this over first. I'd like to know if any of you have knowledge of the area or the Mescalero Apache."

Roy jumped in, excitement in his voice. "I lived over yonder until I came to Texas Tech. I'm an Air Force brat. My dad is stationed at Holloman Air Force Base. I went through high school in Alamogordo. I know the area pretty well, including the Mescalero Reservation just a smidge to the northeast."

I looked at him. "I heard you were from over that way. I thought you might have some insights on the expedition. I'm interested in what you think of it. Same for all of you."

They studied the proposal for a while in silence. It was two pages and I'm sure they were digesting every word of it.

Steve spoke first. "The Mescalero are a nomadic tribe. How do you propose to study them? It's not like there would be a settlement with structures such as the kivas we have excavated at other sites?"

"True to that," Roy added. "They never really settled down. At least, not until we forced them onto the reservation back in the late eighteen-hundreds. While at the base, I went to the Mescalero Reservation a number of times. I was fascinated by their culture. I think that's what got me interested in anthropology." He brightened with a thought. "Did y'all know that Geronimo and Cochise were Apache? Those Apache were fierce fighters, with some pretty kick-ass guerilla tactics."

"That's one of the reasons I want to study them," I said. "They have a rich history. But because they were nomads, no one has really conducted a study like I'm proposing."

Steve said, "Well then, quit messin' around and tell us where you're going with all this."

"I propose we establish the style and dating for the arrowheads and pottery we find at our site, then see if we can match it up north and locate their summer camp." I held my breath as they absorbed this idea.

Stu cut in. "How you gonna tell the difference between bands of Apache? There were a bunch of them all over the area as far as I understand. I don't think it can be done."

I looked to Roy, hoping he would have something to say. I knew it wouldn't matter what I told Stu.

He did.

"Actually, there *are* differences between the bands of Apache," Roy said. "I've seen arrowheads in the museum on the reservation recovered throughout the area, from before they were forced together. The differences are minor, but they are there. Probably due to who made the arrowheads for that specific band."

"What," Billy asked, "like pissing on a fence post to mark your territory?"

We all laughed, except Stu.

Roy said, "Well, that's one colorful way to put it. But I think more like differences in handwriting. Each band had

82

their own way to form arrowheads. I'm afraid that none of the arrowheads at the museum would be of help to us, since they were never logged in properly as to their location of origin. But this indicates there may be enough of a difference that we could distinguish a specific Apache band."

I finished the thought. "If we can do that, then we should be able to trace their migratory path to their northern camps through the arrowheads, and any other artifacts we gather. I believe this would be the first of such a study."

Roy hollered, "Shee-it, Roger. That proposal is finer than a frog hair. It's worth a shot." It was funny how he could be all scientific one moment and then a true South Carolinian the next.

I looked at Steve. I had Roy locked in. I knew Billy was with me. And I could already tell what Half Empty was thinking. I wanted Steve on board before Stu said a word. "What do you think, Steve?"

"I guess we can shake a stick at it. If we pull this off, it could become an important find for Professor Holden."

Stu grabbed his beer and downed it, letting out a long belch before he slammed the glass back on the table. He looked at the others. "I think Roger is all hat and no cattle. There is no way I'm hitching up my horse as part of his team." He picked up his copy of the proposal and tossed it on the table in front of me.

"Then why don't you git?" Billy suggested, giving Stu a look. "No sense hanging around if you don't like the weather, 'cause it ain't going to change."

"I'm fixin' to, if you will get out of my way."

Billy nearly landed on his butt as Stu pushed his way out.

Stu stood and looked down at me. "I don't want a thing to do with putting this together if that's what you wanted me here for. But I sure do plan to be there. It will be fun to watch this expedition crash and burn." With that, he strutted to the front door and pushed his way outside.

Steve gave me a look of reassurance. "Don't mind him. He's broke bad. Mostly all bark. Roy and I will talk to him later and make sure he doesn't pitch a hissy with the professor, and create a ruckus."

Billy cut in with his observation. "Stu is two-faced. Sucking up to the professor with one side, and talking down to those he doesn't like with the other."

I smiled at the conviction on their faces. "I never expected him to go for it to begin with, but I had to give him a chance." I took the map and opened it. "I'm hoping you three will help me put this together. Can I count on you?"

All three smiled and nodded. Billy said, "Sure. I think we can hang our hats on it. Speaking of which, we may be here for a while. It's Wednesday and that means steak bite night. I think we best get ourselves a big order of deep-fried steak bites and French fries, and a whole vat of bar-b-q dippin' sauce. I can't wait to smear some of that sauce all over your map."

I laughed and motioned for the waitress, and then we all picked up our glasses and clanked them together. Steve said, "Well, let's git r done!"

London and Beyond

Isle of Wight, England, 1967

Mel

Katch and I explored the ferry. I mean, how could we not? This was the new Portsmouth to Fishbourne ferry that just started up a few years ago. Emilee told us about it as we boarded.

It left Portsmouth Harbor half an hour ago, and now we were only a few minutes from the Fishbourne Ferry Dock on the Isle of Wight. Emilee stayed in the lounge. She had taken this ferry a few times since it opened, so let us explore on our own, though there wasn't a lot to explore because the ferry wasn't very big. Certainly not like the ones I had seen on Elliott Bay in Seattle.

The weather was clear but a little cold, especially with the breeze from the ferry chugging along as we crossed the strait between the mainland and the island. The brisk air stung my face and the salty smell of the ocean invaded my nostrils. It reminded me of when I stood outside the Virginia Inn that morning in Seattle and the same bittersweet smell of the ocean there.

We walked up to the front of the ferry to watch the island slowly approach.

"This is just so crazy," Katch said. "Only a few days ago we were in Lake Oswego with no idea we would now be on a ferry practically halfway around the world." She looked over at me, her eyes bright with adventure. The breeze played with her raven hair and her cheeks glistened pink from the cold. Well, as much as the luminous, bronze skin of her Hopi-Indian descent would allow.

"I know. But lately, I have come to expect the unexpected."

Katch laughed. "You got that right." She suddenly quieted down and became reflective, then reached over, grabbed my hand, and nodded toward the island. "Look. That's the Isle of Wight. You have generations of ancestors on that island. You must be excited."

I gave her a curt little smile. It was the best I could do; the excitement tempered by my worry of facing the unknown.

I thought about what we had seen so far. We landed at Heathrow Airport absolutely dead tired. I didn't think about the time change, but Emilee said we were about eight hours ahead of whatever time it was back in Lake Oswego. And after a ton of hours in the air, I didn't even know what day it was.

We took the train to London. Emilee arranged for us to stay in a really nice hotel downtown for a few days so we could get over what she called jet lag. I think I slept for about ten hours that first night.

The next day we insisted she take us to see Trafalgar Square and the London School of Economics she had attended. When we first met, she told us about herself, including that by going to LSE, as she called it, she happened to be in the square right when Eglantyne Jebb was handing out those flyers about the starving babies in Germany. That got her involved in their Save the Children organization, and through them, eventually ended up in Russia. If she hadn't done that, she never would have met my grandfather and I wouldn't have been born. So, as far as I was concerned, it all started in Trafalgar Square.

The Square met all of my expectations. It had tons of statues: Lion statues, men on pedestal statues, one with King George on a horse, and a thing called Nelson's Column. The column was really tall and I guess it had Nelson on top, but he was so far up there it was hard to see him. There were two cloverleaf-shaped ponds with statues of naked figures surrounded by jumping fish. They were made out of a metal that looked green, maybe due to being in the water, but were all the more beautiful for it. These were things I had only seen before in art and history books. All of this felt strange and new. Trafalgar Square seemed to be the center of London itself.

In fact, everything about England was strange and new. The English all spoke with accents like Emilee, but some were really hard to understand. And there were lots of brand-new words for old things that Katch and I would need to learn. Over here cookies were called biscuits, French fries were chips, an elevator was a lift, and the restroom was called the loo.

The buildings were made of stone and really old, whereas most of the buildings back home were wood and comparatively new. The London double-decker buses were a real kick, and the taxis were all black and called Hackney Carriages or cabs, and many of the drivers wore uniforms.

The hardest part of it all, was getting used to the driver being on the wrong side of the car. And the fact that they drove on the wrong side of the road was even worse. It's not like I didn't know they drove like this. I'd seen my share of James Bond movies. But actually being here and sitting in the car brought it to life. It took me a while to get used to it. I kept thinking we would hit another car, being in the wrong lane and all, especially when turning onto another street. I'm glad I didn't have to drive. I would have gotten into a wreck for sure.

We were close to the Isle of Wight now, so we headed back inside and sat next to Emilee.

She said, "I've arranged transportation to meet us at the dock. It is only a few minutes ride to Brightwood Manor."

"So," Katch asked, "why is it called a manor?"

Emilee gave her a thoughtful look. "No one has ever asked that before, so I've never really thought about it. I just think of it as home."

But it made me wonder. Maybe this was another word difference, where manor here meant house. I remembered back when she first arrived in Lake Oswego, she had told us about the Harris Family Tree. I guess there was an Earl in the family long ago, and the Harrises had been on the island for a long time. She said she had a house and ran it as a bed and breakfast. We had never heard of that before. She said it had a few extra rooms and she rented them out, providing breakfast in the morning for all who stayed there. But I don't ever remember her calling it a manor. Now I'm as curious as Katch as to what that could mean.

A cab waited for us at the ferry station. The driver loaded our luggage into the boot, as they call car trunks here. And another good example of a new word for an old thing. He also placed some luggage in the front passenger area. The three of us sat in the back, Emilee on my left and Katch on my right.

The houses along the route were made of stone, just like the buildings in London. And the English seemed to love their stone walls and hedgerows, which lined our route. We passed through a place called Wootten Bridge, I guess because we crossed a bridge there. Why would they name a town after a bridge? But then again, I came from Lake Oswego, which was named after a lake. So, maybe it wasn't that strange after all.

Once out of Wootten Bridge, we were in the countryside. Large oak trees with scraggly branches appeared next to the road along the way, but there wasn't a single fir tree anywhere to be seen. No wonder they built their houses from stone.

We went through a town called Newport. Emilee said it was the largest town on the island. The streets were very narrow and the buildings were made of … yep, stone. They

89

were three stories high with shops below and flats above. That's what Emilee called the apartments above the stores. I thought the town looked very quaint. And that's a word I doubt I had ever used before in my life.

Emilee turned to me and said, "We only have a few miles to go." I could see the shine in her eyes. She was very excited to share the family home with me. I really didn't know what to expect.

I watched the countryside pass by. It was hard to see much, other than the tall hedgerows. But I could tell we were really out in the country now. We came to an area of low, rolling hills. The hedgerows became smaller and sparser, giving us a view of fields swathed in bright green grass. Some had pastures with horned sheep, thickly covered in mottled brown and tan wool. Sleek and beautiful horses grazed in other pastures.

I think some sort of crops grew in other areas of the countryside. I recognized patches of corn, and some fields looked like they were covered in wheat ready for harvest. Only a few houses were spotted along the road. Emilee told us they called this the Downs. Whatever that meant.

We came over the top of a hill and soon the area was heavily wooded on either side of the road. We drove through a ravine, the banks steep and covered with some sort of leafy plant, a few ferns, and lots of ivy. The cab slowed. We passed a quaint (there's that word again) stone building with a thatched roof.

"Here we are," Emilee said.

The cab turned onto a graveled driveway. It was marked with a short but stocky stone pillar on the right. A sign on it read Brightwood Manor. A low stone wall curved in from the other side. The driveway looked long. I could just barely see some buildings through the trees in the distance. They looked huge.

Emilee's voice filled the air with excitement. "Welcome home."

Brightwood Manor

Mel

We drove up the driveway and an old structure slowly revealed itself through the trees. Katch nudged me and whispered, "I thought Emilee said she no longer owned a castle."

It wasn't exactly a castle, but now I had my confirmation that a manor was a whole lot more than just a house. It sat in an 'L' shape, with two buildings attached to each other. The closer one, as we approached, was larger than the far one. Both were huge, had three stories, seemed to be very ancient, and sprouted more chimneys than I could count. The whole structure was, of course, made of a grayish stone, much of it old and pockmarked. But other than that, the buildings looked to be in very good shape.

I sat there, stunned, and stared out the window as we drove along the first building. I didn't know what to say. I had to look past Emilee to see it. I glanced at her, but the look on her face didn't provide any answers to all of the questions suddenly forming in my mind. Maybe this wasn't her place. How could it be? She ran a bed and breakfast … just a couple of extra rooms. I knew the place had to be nice looking, but nothing like this.

The driveway curved around a large field on our right and then continued beyond these buildings. There appeared to be another smaller structure farther down the road. I couldn't see it very well. Maybe that was Emilee's place, and we had to go past this huge mansion to get there.

But we didn't keep going. The cab continued past the larger building, pulled around the next one, and stopped at the front door.

"Here we are," Emilee said, her voice very cheerful. But I only felt trepidation. Before I could say anything, she was out of the cab and giving instructions to the driver regarding our luggage.

Katch and I sat there and looked at each other.

"Can you believe this?" she said, her face completely awestruck.

I shook off the feeling of shock that hit me the moment we turned up the driveway. I said, "Did you see the sign on the post when we entered? This place really is named Brightwood Manor."

She laughed. "Okay. So, I was wrong when I called it a castle. But it might as well be one. It sure isn't just a house."

We slid out on Katch's side, so the cab was between us and the manor. It gave me a moment to take it all in. I stepped away from the cab and heard the crunch of gravel under my feet. The entire road seemed to be made of light brown chipped rock. Nothing paved here like the roadways we drove in on.

A long, very old stone wall followed the roadway to our right, starting at the manor and continuing all the way to the building off in the distance—the one I thought might actually have been Emilee's house.

Now that we were directly outside this part of Brightwood Manor, there was even more to it than I first thought. I could now see an extension that ran parallel to the parking area. It was long and seemed to maybe have been added at a later date. The house was also made of gray blocks of stone, but it had to be really old because most of the face of the house was weathered and aged. I mean like a centuries-old kind of aging.

Little spires stuck up at the corners of the roof and on the tip of the gables. The roof shingles seemed more modern, kind of like what they used back home. There were three chimneys on this house alone, all constructed of red clay brick.

Windows made of little glass panels mounted within white wooden slats were everywhere. Ivy-like plants grew up the face of the building. A tall rosebush stood near the front door. It seemed proud, and showed it through a covering of lovely white roses fully in bloom.

Emilee stood next to it at the entrance, talking with a woman. By the way they spoke together, it looked like she worked for my grandmother. She appeared to be a little older. Her graying hair sat in a bun and she wore a simple but stylish dress. Her shoes were black with short heels. She looked very business-like, but at the same time there was a pleasant, almost matronly look to her face that would put most people at ease immediately. Emilee motioned us over. We walked around the cab and joined them.

"Mrs. Bea, this is my granddaughter, Melanie."

Mrs. Bea curtsied.

Emilee put her arm around Mrs. Bea. "She is my house-keeper, which here in England means much more than it does in the United States. In other words, she runs this place, and I thank my stars every day for her."

Mrs. Bea blushed. "Your grandmother gives out praise too easily. I am only as good as the mistress of the house." She nodded to my grandmother, then turned to me again. "Welcome to Brightwood Manor, Miss Melanie. The whole of the staff bubbled with excitement when we found out about you. It is a pleasure to make the acquaintance of Mistress Harris' granddaughter and future heiress to the estate."

That last statement hit me. Heiress to the estate. It sounded like a title, and one with a lot of responsibility attached to it.

Emilee made an indication toward Katch. "And this is Kachina Gallo. Melanie's very close friend."

Mrs. Bea curtsied once more. "And a pleasure to meet you as well, young lady." She looked to me. "It is always good to have a trusted advisor along on your journeys." She turned to Emilee. "With your permission, I shall resume my duties."

"Yes, of course," Emilee said. "We can go over operational details after I help the girls settle in."

"It is so good to have you back, m'lady. I will prepare a report for you, then." With that, she disappeared inside.

Emilee turned to us. "Well, what do you think?"

She laughed when she saw the look on my face.

"I think this is a little more than a place with a few rooms you offer as a bed and breakfast," I said.

"Well, when you get down to the brass tacks of it all, not really. Maybe a little bigger than you might have imagined. But that's pretty much what it is. A bed and breakfast. Guests sleep here and eat breakfast here. I'm not sure what else it might be called." She laughed again.

"A mansion," Katch said.

Emilee looked the estate over. "Well, it is rather large, I agree. But I have lived here for much of my life, so I don't think of it in that way. I definitely understand your perspective, though, when compared to your home in the States."

"No kidding," I told her.

She took my hand and pulled me out onto the driveway and farther away from the house. The three of us walked a little way down the road; the one I thought might lead to her house.

"Down there is the carriage house. Of course, we don't have horse carriages anymore in the true sense, so we use it for our autos and equipment."

Katch's eyebrows went up as her eyes widened. She grabbed my arm, pulled me close, and whispered into my ear, "You have a carriage house."

I nudged her with my shoulder. "Stop."

Emilee continued, "Down from that is the caretaker's house. Here to our left, on the other side of this wall, is our Victory Garden. That's what I still call it, anyway. Long ago, when I came back to England after having left Lubbock ..."

She looked at me, then continued. "When your mother ran away, well, I was lost." She suddenly swept me into her arms. A slight tremor ran through her body. She pulled back and looked into my eyes, sharing a deep sadness in her own. "Just as I felt when I thought I might have lost you a few days ago." She took my hands and squeezed them briefly, maybe as her assurance that I was actually here.

She put an arm around my waist and one around Katch, and slowly walked us down the road toward the carriage house. "I've told Melanie this, but I would like you to know as well." She looked over at Katch. "I stayed in Lubbock as long as I could. I tried everything to find Gloria, even hiring a private investigator with the help of Mrs. Delbert. But then I had to come back to England because mother became very ill, and the war with Germany had started."

An opening appeared in the tall stone wall to our left. She walked us through a wide gate and into the garden area.

"When I got to Brightwood Manor, I immediately organized the grounds staff to plant a Victory Garden. It was the thing to do in wartime. But it also meant so much more than that to me. It gave me a point of central focus." She lowered her head for a moment in thought. A whirlwind of emotions overtook her face, decades of them, now finally released to flow out of her. "There was already a small garden here and lots of flowerbeds. I had them expand the area for vegetables and herbs, and remove most of the flowers. Somehow, I think, this was how I atoned for my being gone for so long, and for what happened with Gloria. It was good to see things grow and bear fruit when I felt so lost of meaning."

She walked us deeper into the garden, which seemed very large. Rows of crops were set in stone-framed beds.

Grass walkways ran throughout them. "Of course, now everyone here calls it the Kitchen Garden, but it will always be the Victory Garden to me."

In that moment I truly felt a connection to Emilee. A sense of common purpose which flowed through me as a wash of emotion. After all, we had both lost my mother, just in different ways.

I wondered what Mom would have thought of it all. And that's when I realized, for the first time, my mother knew nothing of this place. Perhaps Emilee had told her about the estate. But she never saw it. Maybe things would have been different if she had.

I thought of how similar their histories were. Just as my mother had run away from Lubbock, Emilee had run away from here as well. The black sheep of the family, as she had put it. Pregnant and unmarried, she never came home. Not until her mother was near death. They had both run away from family. And now I was here, the piece to connect it all back together.

Silence held us for a moment longer, and then Emilee turned around and walked us back toward the manor. She directed us past it to a spot where we could see the other, larger building.

"That is the East Wing of Brightwood Manor and where our guests reside. I understand we have about eight guests at this time. Some of whom, Mrs. Bea tells me, are Americans just arrived from the States yesterday. We should make plans to meet them at one of the breakfasts." She shrugged. "I think for now, that is all for the outside. Let's head in and get you settled."

She took my hand and walked us back to the smaller building. She opened the door and ushered us inside. "We call this Little Brightwood."

Little Brightwood

Mel

We walked in the front door to what looked like a dining area. The floor had an area rug under a rustic, wooden dining table. Under the rug, some sort of gray flagstone flooring showed, looking very old. A large, ornate cabinet sat against the wall, showing a display of painted plates. A fireplace at one end of the room waited for winter to arrive.

Emilee said, "The original house was built in the 1600s and sits where an old monastery used to be. Those with knowledge think it existed back in the 1300s. The estate is around eighteen acres or so. Part of it consists of our world-class botanical gardens behind the manor."

She turned to us. "This estate is in a very special location as there is a spring that bubbles up from a chalk aquifer in our garden area. It forms a brook that meanders through our little town. Be sure to wander around the garden while this weather holds. It really is quite something to enjoy."

She swept the room with her hand as if she had done this many times before. "This is the entryway, and acts as our dining room as well."

She went to our right and into another room, signaling us to follow. We walked into a big living room with a fireplace at the far end. The floor was covered with old rugs detailed in fancy designs. An array of comfortable couches and lounge chairs filled the room. A small table and four chairs stood near where we entered.

"This is our living room. I enjoy a good book here by the fire on cold nights. You can see how bright it gets during the summer when the sun is out."

Three sets of windows covered the wall facing the driveway and let in lots of light. The room felt very comfortable, almost like you would see in an expensive lodge somewhere. But this was Emilee's home, and now mine … if I wanted it to be.

To our left stood a set of French doors. "What's out there?" I asked.

"Let us go see." Emilee put her arm through mine and ushered me into the room. "This is our sunroom, which also leads to our patio and botanical gardens beyond."

The room was ablaze with light. There really were no walls, only windows. The sun shone brightly through them, and lit up the interior as if in a huge welcome to us. The room had similar, comfortable furniture to that of the living room, only lighter in color to match the atmosphere. I looked outside to a deck where a couple of umbrellas shaded two wooden tables with chairs.

"We are still working on updating some of the rooms throughout the house. After all, they didn't exactly have electricity or proper plumbing back in the 1600s. Much of the manor was shut off by my ancestors, as the rooms were not needed.

"I am the first to open it to the public as a bed and breakfast. But I waited until Mother passed before making such an announcement." She leaned over to us and whispered, "I have no doubt many of my ancestors rolled in their graves at that decision." She laughed. "Well, I've always been the black sheep of the family."

I laughed, too. I couldn't help it. I had just thought about that.

She looked at me. "You're not exactly pure yourself, you know."

I nodded. "You've got that right."

She gave me her perfect smile, and continued. "But there has been no sign of disgruntled ghosts yet, I am sorry to say." Then she leaned in closer and said, "Now, wouldn't that bring in the clientele?"

She directed us back through the living room. "Let's finish the tour. I can fill you in on all the details later, but I am sure you would love to get settled in." With that, she led the way.

Katch was taking this in with a look of total amazement. "Settle in? I don't care how tired I am. I want to explore every inch of this place."

"Maybe this is just a dream," I told her. "It's really too good to be true."

"And this is supposed to be the little house," Katch added. "I wonder what the big one looks like."

I thought again to my mother and how I wished we could have shared this together. She never even let me know I had a grandmother. I only found out after she died. I knew the reason, and to a certain extent, understood it. But it was still hard to accept the fact she completely cut ties with Emilee. Even though this was all very amazing, for that reason, there seemed to be a shadow hanging over it all.

Emilee walked us through a couple more rooms. "This is the kitchen. Feel free to use it whenever you get hungry. Lots of food in the fridge, bread in the pantry, and our famous jams and jellies, which are absolutely to die for. Fix whatever strikes your fancy." She walked us into a little dining area. Maybe a place for breakfast.

Then she pointed to a door at the end. "That is Mrs. Bea's quarters. She insisted on the room since it is so close to the heart of our operations."

I turned to Emilee. "What? She lives here?"

"Well, of course. And so do the servants."

Katch grabbed my hand and turned me so I could see her. She threw her nose in the air and said in a very snobby sort of way, "Your servants."

She gave me a look when I didn't react. I didn't know what to think at this point. Was this a good thing or a bad thing—being an heiress to all of this?

Emilee waited for us to catch up and then directed us to a door on our left. I got the feeling she had done this tour a whole bunch of times before. "Now, for the upstairs."

We walked up a stone staircase, worn down by footsteps over hundreds of years. They wound up to the next level. We came to a landing with a hallway going in either direction. The steps continued to the top level, but we stopped here.

"There are five bedrooms on this level. Two of them are still being remodeled." She pointed to our right. "I hope you don't mind my taking the liberty of assigning rooms to you." She looked at Katch. "Yours is down this way." We went to our right and stopped at a door. "This is my room. I took it over from Mother after she passed. It's what we do through the generations." She pointed down another narrow hallway that angled off from where we stood. "This way."

She led us to a door at the end. There was another door to the right. She opened it. "Kachina, this is your loo. I wish it was adjoining, but it is the best I can do. However, we have fully remodeled it. I hope it is to your liking."

It wasn't very big but served the purpose.

She opened the door at the end of the hall. "And here is where you will stay," she said.

"Oh, my God." Katch walked into the room. She ran over to the big queen size bed and threw herself on top of it. The bed had a thick, white, down comforter and she sank into it on impact. She sat up quickly. "I can't believe it. This is my room?"

It was the most amazing bedroom I had ever seen. Some of the walls were angled, due to the design of the house. And there were roughly cut wood beam accents here and there, similar to some I had seen in the living room. Delicate end tables framed the bed with wonderful lamps on them that tossed their light out as if showing themselves off. And they were. I would be if I had been a lamp in this room.

Katch ran to the window and looked out through the little panes of glass. "It has a view toward the carriage house and the vegetable garden. It's such a beautiful view. I can see off to the countryside. What did you call it?" She turned to Emilee.

Emilee smiled. "The Downs."

"Yes, the Downs," Katch repeated. "Green, rolling hills as far as I can see. There are even sheep off in the distance."

"And did you happen to notice the fireplace?" I asked.

She turned to us, ran over to Emilee, and threw her arms around her in a hug. "Emilee. This is so amazing. I feel like I have just entered a fairy tale."

I wondered if maybe we had.

Emilee hugged her back. "I am so glad you like it." She turned to me. "Now, let's have ourselves a look at Melanie's room." She took my hand and walked us down the hall, pointing to more doors on our right. "There are two more bedrooms and two bathrooms here, but in remodel. I don't rent out any of the rooms in Little Brightwood as it is my home." Then she turned to me, squeezed my hand, and corrected herself. "*Our* home. But, on the rare occasion when friends wish to spend their holiday here, I will have these rooms available so we can be close."

Which made me think I would also have a place for my friends to stay when visiting, if I ever had to move here. I dropped that thought like a brick. I didn't want my head to go in that direction right now.

She opened a door at the end of the hall. "This is the room I grew up in. Now it is your bedroom for as long as you wish to stay."

I walked into the room. It wasn't as big as Katch's bedroom, but still very nice. It had a similar, billowy bed cover, and accent tables and lamps that otherwise might only be found in antique shops. Two windows looked out onto different parts of the estate. I paused at that word, 'estate'. Wow, I never thought I would have such a word in my vocabulary. Certainly not when it applied to somewhere I might call home.

This room also had a fireplace. Emilee saw me checking it out.

"Back when Brightwood Manor was first built, fireplaces were the only source of heat. Wherever you see a chimney outside, there is a corresponding fireplace on each floor." She pointed to a wall. "We now have proper electric heating installed, but in the colder months, a nice fire really cozies up the room."

I walked to a door at the far corner of the room and opened it. I thought it might be a closet. It was a bathroom. I turned to Emilee.

"Some rooms have an adjoining loo. Your room happens to be one of them."

I walked in. The floor had white tiles with little black squares where the corners came together. The sink stood on a pedestal, with a small white cabinet next to it. And a beautiful porcelain bathtub, set on clawed feet, stood opposite the sink.

I turned back to the room to see my luggage in the corner, having already been brought up.

Emilee walked over to me, gave me a hug, and kissed my cheek. "I'm sure you need to get settled in." She looked at Katch. "You two make yourselves comfortable." Then she looked at me. "After all, this is your new home, if you would like it to be." With that, she went out the door and down the steps.

Katch and I looked at each other.

I walked to the door and closed it, then strolled back over to Katch. "I don't know what to say."

"I do. You are an heiress. A little over a month ago, you were practically an orphan about ready to be dumped into a foster home. Now you have a whole family history that goes back hundreds of years on this island. Not to mention having this eighteen-acre estate, which means you are probably freakin' rich."

"I didn't ask for this." And I hadn't, and I wasn't sure I wanted it. I didn't ask for anything that was happening to me right now. And there was just too much going on to add this to the mix.

Katch looked at me, frustrated. "Oh, lighten up." She pushed me onto the bed, and jumped onto it next to me.

"How can I? We came here so we could get to the Carnac Stones, not inherit an estate."

Katch propped herself up on one elbow and said, "Well, I know what Beanie would say about that. He would be very precise and articulate." She made a Beanie face and screamed, "Aaaagggg!"

I tried to smile, but didn't get there.

"Oh, for God's sake." She leaned over me, took my shoulders, and shook them. "Get over it."

Her eyes went wide and she imitated Beanie again. "Aaaagggg." This time I found it funny, more from the look on Katch's face than her interpretation of Beanie. I couldn't help but get caught up in it and join in. She did it again and

I screamed with her. As I did so, I felt my tension drop away. Then I quickly put my hand over my mouth to restrain myself. I didn't want Emilee or the staff to wonder what was going on.

Katch rolled onto the bed next to me, so we were side by side, and looked at the ceiling. We giggled until our sides hurt. It felt good to laugh again. It had been a long time.

"How unbelievable is this," Katch finally said. It was more of a statement than a question.

How unbelievable was any of this? What would be next in destiny's plan? The slow reveal of my many layers. And the next, I knew, would come at the Stones of Carnac. As soon as we can figure out how to get there. And I hadn't a clue as to how we would pull that off.

—

The Expedition

New Mexico Desert, July 4, 1947

Roger

The sun dipped in and out of white, puffy clouds that had formed throughout the day. A searing heat penetrated the back of my shirt every time the sun appeared. A typical afternoon, in the desert, in July.

Roy and I were bent over a dig site we discovered yesterday while conducting a general survey of the area. Once we focused in on this spot, we found a few arrowheads, along with other artifacts we believed were from the Mescalero Apache. Hopefully, either a *Natahéndé* or a *Ch'laandé* band.

To while away our time, Roy told me about living in the area and how much he enjoyed it. "We spent a lot of time at our cabin up by Alto Lake." He used his trowel to point to the southwest. "It's over that way, just north of the Mescalero Reservation in the Sierra Blanca Mountains. We had a lot of fun times there hunting and fishing. The cabin's fairly rustic, but my mom fixed it up pretty nice. So, it's comfortable."

"Why do you say rustic?" I asked.

Roy used his trowel to emphasize each point. "No phone, no electricity, and no indoor plumbing. The bathroom is an outhouse. Dad did manage to get a well dug, so we do have the convenience of a water pump in the kitchen. I heard they're building a development up on the plateau, so maybe we'll get all of the conveniences soon."

Just then someone called to us from above.

"Roger. Roy." I looked up to see Steve on the hill above us. "Someone's coming."

We finished up what we were doing, marked and bagged our artifacts, and then climbed to the top of the hill. Steve pointed toward a cloud of dust off in the distance indicating vehicles approaching.

"Must be the professor," Steve said. "He's about due."

We headed back to camp and got there just as three vehicles pulled up. Billy was in one of them. I had sent him with my truck to wait for Professor Holden at the rendezvous point, so he could lead them to our base camp.

The other vehicles were trucks, their beds full of equipment. Four men got out. Professor Holden looked around and then walked up to us. "The camp looks good. How is it going otherwise?"

Roy answered. "We have some promising finds. Let me show you." He directed the professor toward our research tent.

Professor Holden turned to one of the men who arrived with him. "Professor Fielding, will you join me? We could use your expertise." He looked at the other two, who were students. "Stu, why don't you and Nick get our tents and gear set up?"

"Sure, Professor. Sounds like a plan," Stu answered.

I pointed to an open area of the camp we had left for them. "We have a spot for you over there."

Stu ignored me as if I didn't exist. I could tell by the look on his face he would do everything he could to screw up my expedition.

Roy called to me. "You coming, Roger?"

"Yeah. I'm on my way."

Roy and I spent the remainder of the afternoon walking the professors through the survey areas we had identified so far. We discussed our strategy for the next few days. It was early evening by the time we were done.

We had eaten a late supper and were in the process of cleaning the dishes. Billy and I drew KP duty because we were both juniors and the rest were seniors and professors.

We were nearly finished cleaning up when Stu walked over. "Glad to see you found your calling, Simpson."

I ignored him. It wasn't worth spending energy on Stu right now. I handed Billy the last dish to dry. We needed to get these done. I worried about the growing storm off in the distance. It had been building for a while. The wind had changed, and now it looked like the storm had plans to head our way.

Stu walked around the table so he could face me. "You've managed to pull the wool over the professor's eyes so far, but I still know you are all hat and no cattle. I can't wait for this to blow up in your face."

"Why don't you git, Stu, and leave him alone?" Billy said. He dried his hands on the dish towel and tossed it on the table.

I looked at Stu. "What you really should be concerned about, is this place blowing away." I pointed toward the storm in the distance. A flash appeared in the dark clouds indicating a lightning bolt somewhere deep inside it. A moment later, thunder rolled across the landscape. "You see that? You know how bad these summer storms can get. And it looks like it's headed our way. Why don't you help Nick check your tents and gear to make sure everything's secure?"

Stu grinned at me in an offish way and flipped a quick salute. "Yes, Sir. Mr. Boss, Sir. Right away." He performed a quick military turn and strutted off.

I looked over to see Roy and Steve coming from our dig site. Steve walked up to us. "Everything is good down there. We spiked a few tarps over the dig area. It should hold in the storm. But it sure 'nuff looks like this one is going to be a real toad choker."

"Thanks for doing that," I said. "It sure does."

I wondered about our sheepherder tents. Big ten-by-tens with heavy, canvas-walled sides. They were built to handle severe weather. That's why we used them. I just hoped they had been secured correctly.

"Billy, did you check to make sure our tent is staked properly and the tie-downs are tight? Steve's right. We're going to get some serious wind and rain by the looks of it."

"Yep. I did that before dinner, as well as anything else that might fly away. It's all good."

112

I studied the oncoming storm, which was quickly approaching. "I hope so because it's definitely getting itself all worked up and ready for a visit."

A lightning bolt raced across the center of the storm leading the roar of a giant thunderclap. The dark clouds brightened in that same spot and an object broke from them, trailing a flaming blue-steel tail. We all watched in awe as it angled toward us.

It hit the ground behind a rise of hill about a mile away and tossed up a huge plume of dirt and debris into the air.

"What was that? A meteor?" Billy asked.

The dirt settled and a reddish glow showed on the horizon.

"It didn't look like one to me," I said. "It looked more like a man-made object."

We hurried over to Professor Holden and the rest of the students, who were surrounding him and peppering him with questions.

"No, I have no idea what it was," he told everyone. "But right now, that storm is what we need to think about. It's nearly on top of us." He looked at me. "Is everything secure?"

"Yes, we've checked. The camp is battened down as best as we can get it."

"What about the thing that crashed?" Roy said. "Shouldn't we investigate, whatever that was? It might have been a plane. People could be hurt."

"No one is going out there tonight, in the dark, in that storm," the professor said. "We can send a small party out tomorrow morning."

The storm was almost overhead. A few fat raindrops splattered the area around us.

"Get to your tents and ride out the storm inside," Professor Holden ordered. "It won't be long until it hits us."

Everyone disappeared into their tents.

Billy headed for our tent. He turned to me when he saw I wasn't with him. "You coming, Roger?"

"Yeah, in a moment." I looked in the direction of the crash site. The rain and wind intensified. Drops hit my face and shirt. Big drops, exploding on impact. It was darker now, with just a sliver of orange in the west indicating where the sun had set.

I didn't know what had crashed, but I was pretty sure it wasn't an airplane. I watched as the dim glow of the crash site faded out, hidden now by a sheet of rain dropping from the intense storm between it and our camp. A lightning bolt flashed across the sky, delivering the roar of another thunderclap. I used the light to study the terrain, and marked my bearings in the direction of the object. I planned to leave as early as possible in the morning. I didn't know what had crashed, but was sure of one thing—I needed to be the first one there to find out.

Dawn

Roger

It was pitch-black inside the tent when I woke up. I rolled onto my side and reached out to a table near my cot, fumbling around to find my flashlight. My fingers bumped into it. I found the switch and flipped on the light, shining it on my watch. The dial read four-fifty in the morning. It wouldn't get light until closer to five-thirty. I rolled onto my back, flipped off the light, and was immediately enveloped by darkness again. I thought of going back to sleep, but knew it would be hopeless. Something was pulling at me.

Billy rolled over and his snores sounded from the other side of the tent. He snorted and then rolled over again, quieting.

I tossed off my blanket and swung my legs over the edge of the cot. There was a slight chill to the air, leftovers from the invading thunderstorm and rain. I ran my fingers through my hair a few times, an absent-minded way of bringing me to my senses. I walked to the tent opening, unhooked the tie-downs on the flap, and peeked outside.

The storm had passed long ago and a few thin strips of clouds floated across the sky. White ribbons accenting the pearled moon above.

I stepped outside and the silence of the desert night immediately wrapped me in its blanket. A great display of stars splayed out across the vast universe above me, as if it were a star-lit orchestra in full performance; a concerto wrapped around the Milky Way, with the nearly full moon the conductor, playing into the night. I felt thrown by this line of thought, so took a few more steps away from the tent in order to get an uninhibited view of the sky above.

Where did this urge to look up come from? My head has always been buried in the earth, not turned to the stars. I spend my time digging with my hands and a trowel; dusting away time with a camel hair brush, looking for that special piece of history buried in the dirt, hidden by centuries. Why up, now?

I went back into the tent and lit a kerosene lamp on a table near my cot. I searched for my pants and put them on, and then my socks. I shook my shoes to make sure nothing had made them their home. Scorpions and tarantulas love such recesses. Satisfied there would be no surprises, I put them on. I knew I needed to find that crash site. I felt it call to me and had no idea why. Just like I had no idea why my eyes had suddenly turned to the stars.

I looked for my satchel. It had everything I needed. I always made sure it was packed with energy food like jerky, nuts, and hard cheese, along with a compass, first aid kit, and all those things we learned to carry while in the Boy Scouts.

Billy stirred. "Roger, what are you doing? What time is it?"

I looked over to see him shade his eyes from the lamp-light.

"It's early. I can't sleep anymore. I'm going to the crash site."

He waved me off. "Are you plumb crazy? Wait until it's light out. You could get hurt or lost. Or step into a hole and break your ankle."

"Go back to sleep, Billy. I'll be fine. Come find me when it's light."

I turned the gas down on the kerosene lamp until the flame died, and threw the strap of the satchel over my shoulder. I stepped out of the tent, closed the flap, walked over to the mess area, and picked up a canteen. A large vat of drinking water sat on a table. I filled the canteen, clipped it to my belt, and set out. The moon provided enough light that I could have used it alone, but decided to flip on my flashlight, maybe to prevent Billy's prediction. I swung the beam back and forth across my path and headed in the direction I had fixed in my mind last night.

It had been about half an hour of difficult hiking. I should be getting close. The first indication of the sun showed on the horizon. Though it was still a while before it would be up, the light it did provide was enough so that I could turn off my flashlight.

I crossed a riverbed, which still had a trickling stream of muddy water from last night's storm. I climbed the other side and crested a hill to see the sheer rock face of an arroyo on the far side of a wide gully. I carefully worked my way down into it.

The rain from last night's storm still held in the soil, so I had to be careful, but I knew it would quickly be absorbed by the thirsty terrain once the sun shared the horizon. The muddy stream I had crossed earlier would be dry by midday, with very little sign of having been there at all. Such is the way of a New Mexico desert.

More and more of the area became visible in the growing light. Then I noticed some sort of object against the base of the rocky arroyo wall and a deep gouge in the ground leading up to it. That must have been where the object hit before it struck the wall. I was still a distance away, so picked up my pace. I wondered what this thing could be. I reached the gully and walked toward the crashed object. That's when I saw the bodies.

The Site

Roger

Three bodies lay on the ground on the other side of the craft. They didn't look human, but they did look dead. I walked around the ... spaceship? I guess that's what it was. No other explanation. I could see a big gash in the side. I stuck my head through the opening. Nothing looked familiar. No steering wheel or foot pedals, or knobs of any sort. Nothing even close to what you would see in a car or the cockpit of an airplane. Everything inside looked smooth and futuristic. There were four seats, unoccupied; all as if they were made for child-sized occupants.

I picked up my pace. The object resembled a plane more than anything else. But in that same thought, it was nothing like a plane. It had a silvery luster to the fuselage, but not like the metal used in airplanes—something different and more advanced. The sheen seemed to have a waning energy to it. Perhaps, just now dying, but still showing what it might have been when fully operational. Well, at least in this thin light, that's the feeling I had.

There were no airplane wings, but instead, little extensions or nubs stuck out where regular wings would be. They curved toward the front, giving it somewhat of a crescent shape. I couldn't imagine how a craft like this could fly. Maybe it was an escape pod.

Material from the spaceship was strewn across the area. Little pieces and bigger ones. I took some material from the ship where the side had gashed open: thin, foil-like material; some components, electronic-like of some sort; and spaghetti-size filaments, loose and limber and appearing to be made of something similar to quartz. I added all of these samples to my satchel.

There were I-beams also. I picked some up and put them in my bag. I noticed symbols on them, and it dawned on me this could be writing from another world. I gathered other materials of different types and shapes and put them all in my satchel. I was no longer collecting artifacts from the past, but artifacts from the future. Then I thought about the definition of the word as I had read it in a copy of National Geographic magazine when younger. It was the very thing that got me interested in archeology to begin with: 'An artifact is an object made by a human being'.

I chuckled a little, which surprised me, considering what was in front of me. But I couldn't help it— 'Made by a human being'. Well, that will need to change, won't it? It rang so true of our myopic view of the universe, and our possessiveness of it. Humankind's self-indulgence and self-infatuation. All soon to be blown wide apart.

I then turned my attention to the bodies. Two appeared to have been thrown from the ship. They were torn and broken. I think the third one had crawled out. It had some injuries, cuts, and gashes, but not as bad as the other two. I went to it and leaned over the body to check on it, just in case it might still be alive. It wasn't. It didn't move, appear to be breathing, or have a pulse—though I wasn't sure it would have any of these things when alive. I just didn't know. But for all outward appearances, it looked to be dead.

I suddenly realized I referred to the being as 'it', because nothing indicated the gender. Not as we use to identify such in humans.

I inspected the body closer. It looked human-like, in that it had the shape, appendages, and makeup of a human body. The similarities stopped there. The body was maybe only a little over four feet tall, though I doubted it was a child. Children wouldn't man a spaceship like this. And the face looked adult, as much as I could tell for an extraterrestrial—for that was what I decided it must be. It had on a silvery one-piece suit and matching silver boots. There were four fingers on each hand, thin and long for its size. Its skin had a slightly grayish tinge.

I studied the head, which was much too large for the body. There were only small indentations for the ears, nose, and mouth. As if these beings never used them anymore, so through evolution they were slowly disappearing. It had large, jet-black, almond-shaped eyes. I noticed a clear, oval covering had dislodged from one of them.

I kneeled down to get closer. It looked like a lens of some sort. It made me think of an eyeglass lens, but softer, very thin, and shaped to go right on top of the eye. I took a tweezer from the side pocket of my satchel, and delicately removed the lens. I held it up and studied it. As I did, I could see through it, and everything through the lens appeared brighter than the otherwise darkness of the pre-dawn morning. Almost like it was already daylight. I pulled a plastic sample bag from my satchel and dropped the lens inside. I took the one from the other eye and did the same. I didn't know what these lenses were, but the technology around just these eye coverings was mind-blowing. It made me wonder how advanced these aliens were.

I decided I should recover the lenses from the other bodies. I went to the two damaged aliens and removed the lenses from them as well. After I was done, I looked around the site.

It was then I noticed a fourth body in the distance on the ground. I hadn't seen it before because it was hidden behind a big juniper bush. I walked over and kneeled down next to it. I was about to remove the lenses when the alien turned its head and looked at me.

Contact

Roger

Human entity, do not fear me.

I jumped back. The alien had clearly spoken, but its mouth never moved. Still, I heard the words just as plainly as if it had.

It focused on me. I could see into its eyes. Whereas before they were just black and flat, now they seemed endless. Then I realized it wasn't me seeing deep into the alien's eyes, but the alien's eyes penetrating deep into mine.

You are relaxed. Unafraid. There is no danger to you here.

An overwhelming sense of compassion flowed into me from the alien, followed by a feeling of relief. My fear from before dissipated. I moved closer.

Everything turned to curiosity. I studied the being, as it studied me.

"I sense you are in pain. Are you dying?" I asked.

No, but I am very weak. It stopped for a moment, got up to a sitting position, and then looked in the direction of the spaceship. *What is the status of the others?*

"All three are dead."

As I thought. I have been unable to read their biological indicators.

I scooted in closer so we were eye to eye and touched his arm. "I'm sorry for your loss."

Do not feel this way. We long ago learned to control such emotions. Though your words are appreciated, they resonate differently than our observations of Earthlings. Humans are more inclined to show a lack of empathy toward each other, rather than a sense of compassion.

How true a statement this was. We had just finished a world war where millions died, many of them needlessly slaughtered, and used nuclear weapons to end it.

The alien took my hand; his touch rubbery and cold.

You have arrived here to understand this: the universe is interconnected. Much like the web spun by the arachnids you call spiders. Tap a thread, and it vibrates to the farthest points of the web. So it is with the web that ties our universe together.

The alien paused. I tried to figure out what he could mean when he said I had arrived here to understand this. Like I was meant to be here.

The universe is in a state of chaos. The web is vibrating. It has been this way for generations of time. It vibrates here on Earth as well, but the signs are ignored by the leaders of your planet.

"Why are you telling me this?"

Long ago, after the chaos began, a prophecy came to our council. It told of a biological entity known as the Intrepid One. A life form that could still the threads and end the chaos. We have sought this entity throughout the galaxies. We do not know from where or when it will come, so have kept vigil through the eons.

A thought hit me and I didn't like it. "You don't think I'm the one, do you?"

We believe you are the conduit by which to find the Intrepid One.

"Conduit?" I sat back and tried to take this all in. How could such a thing be even close to true?

The threads of the universal web are comprised of energy. All galaxies, stars, and planets are intertwined through the energy of the web. Signs have directed our ship to this point, just as you have been directed here.

"But you crashed. You're dying."

We knew nothing of this before it happened. Such is the mystery of the universe. We have been guided here. Our lines were meant to cross, regardless.

"I don't understand." And then I thought about how Gloria and I had decided on this site for the expedition, only a mile away. And how I was drawn to get here, and be the first to do so. Could it be true?

Help me lay to the ground again. I am too weak just now to sit up.

I put my hand on his back and held his arm as he laid down. He turned his head to me.

Know this, as we now do. You are the conduit to the Intrepid One.

He stopped and turned toward a hill opposite us.

Another human being approaches. He has been directed here to assist you.

The alien removed an object from his side, and held it out to me.

Prophecy directs us here to pass this on to you, as the new charge. Use the device to follow the lines of energy within your world. It will lead you to discovery.

I reached out and the alien placed it in my hand. A sense of exhilaration overtook me as soon as I felt the object's touch. It measured about five inches high by three to four inches wide. It was oval-shaped, with the lower end wider than the top; like the shape of an egg, but not quite. I turned it in my hand to see it was thinner when looking at it from the side rather than from the front—or what I guessed to be the front. It had a dark blue, shimmering nature to it. Almost as if I could see, when I really concentrated, a fluid movement below the hard outer shell. I thought of energy in motion, for some reason.

The sun had risen now. Its rays skimmed the crests of the hills above, though the gully remained in shadow. We sat in a delicate state of illumination that the object, this device of some sort, seemed to be absorbing. Like a highly polished mirror without a single reflection; absorbing, rather than reflecting light.

"What am I to do with this device?"

You will know.

The alien took over my mind, implanting information about the device and its relation to the universe. Not through telepathy, but more like a transfer of knowledge. I wasn't worried or scared, just intrigued and amazed. I could feel the alien's presence as it explored the neurons of my cerebrum, filling it with little pockets of information, tucked into places I could tell had never been used.

The alien stopped and I looked up to see a man coming down the hill toward me. I put the device in my satchel. He ran over and kneeled on the other side of the alien.

"I thought it was a child," he said. "But as I got closer … well, I still don't believe it."

"He's dying," I told him. I realized I just said 'he'. Ever since we first communicated, I couldn't think of this alien as an 'it' any longer.

The alien turned his head toward the man, who had a look of shock on his face. Then, just as I had, the man relaxed. I was sure he and the alien were communicating via telepathy, though I wasn't part of this communication.

We turned when we heard a voice in the distance.

"This way. Over here."

Billy, Steve, and Stu came over the top of the same hilltop as I had. They hurried down the hill toward the spaceship. They hadn't seen us yet because the juniper bush blocked us from their view, just as it had with me earlier.

The alien reached out and touched my hand.

Others will soon be here from your military. They must not capture the device given you. Share none of this with anyone. Only this man, as he is here to help you.

There were so many questions, but time was running out. The others had made it down the hill now, with loud exclamations over what they saw. Some looked into the ship, while others checked out the bodies. Those with knapsacks were placing crash material in them. I knew it was only a matter of time before Stu would see us.

Billy shouted, "Hey, someone's coming. Look." He pointed down the gully to where it fanned out to the flat of the desert in that direction.

We could see a cloud of dust in the distance being kicked into the air, alight from the rising sun. A lot of dust.

It had to be a bunch of vehicles. Probably from the military, just as the alien foretold. I grasped the alien's hand and shared an unspoken understanding, then let go.

The man and I stood. I grabbed his arm and pulled him aside so we were a few steps away from the alien. I didn't want the others to see him lying there.

"What's your name?" I asked.

"Tom, why?"

"I'm Roger. I need your help." I shoved the satchel into his arms. "You have to take this and get it out of here."

I worried we were running out of time. "Please! Hurry! Before whoever is coming sees you. I'm with those other men. We're an archeology group with a big camp not far away. I know they'll spot it. We won't get away. I won't be able to get the satchel out. You're the only one. We can't let them take this!"

Tom stared at me. "What's in it? Why is it so important?"

I shook my head. "We don't have time." I thought for a moment. "There's a place where we can meet. My team ate there when we stayed in Roswell overnight. It's called Katy's Cafe. 118 N. Main Street. Meet me there a week from tomorrow, Saturday. At noon. I can explain more then. Please go. And hurry."

Tom took the satchel and nodded. He looked at the alien, and I could tell they were communicating one last time.

Tom turned to me again. "Okay, Roger. I'll see you in a week." He put the satchel strap over his shoulder and ran back the way he came. He started up the hill and was quick to work his way over the top to where he soon disappeared from view. I looked at the others. I don't think any of them noticed him leave. I moved toward the other students and away from the alien.

A firetruck came into view from the gully opening and stopped when it caught sight of the spaceship. Some of the firemen got out and headed toward us. Even from here, I could see the disbelief in their eyes.

One walked toward me, looking around. "We had a report of a plane crash. What the hell is all of this?" Then he saw the alien bodies. "Oh my God."

The military showed up next. Two jeeps and a couple of canopied trucks. They came to a sudden stop next to the firetruck.

Men in military uniforms with carbine rifles quickly jumped out and surrounded the area. Some raced to the top of the hills to stand watch. I hoped Tom made it without being seen.

An officer got out of the lead jeep and walked toward the crash site. He took a moment to study the spaceship and the bodies around it.

He pulled the firemen to the side, spoke to them, and they soon left the site.

A sergeant directed the soldiers to collect us into a group. The officer walked over and addressed us in a loud and commanding voice. "I am Lieutenant Colonel Unger from Roswell Army Air Field. This is now a military operation of the utmost secrecy."

He motioned to his sergeant nearby. "Sergeant Benning and his men will escort you to one of our Jimmy trucks where you will climb in, sit down, and remain silent. Not a word between any of you. Once at our base, you will be questioned and debriefed."

Sergeant Benning took everyone's knapsacks. I was so glad Tom had gotten away with my satchel.

Lieutenant Colonel Unger slowly strode past us, and carefully studied each one of us as if we were his soldiers assembled for inspection. His voice went ominous. "I will tell you this now. If any one of you leaks a single word about what you have seen here to the public, it will put you and your families in grave danger."

Visitors

Isle of Wight, 1967

Mel

I see snippets of hard stone, grayish to brown in color. At first, they are distant and vague, but soon come into focus. As they do, I see they are not stones honed and cut to set upon each other like those of Brightwood Manor, but are large, roughly quarried, flat-faced, and standing upright. Each of them is taller than me. The gaps between the stones are filled with rocks and dirt, so no light gets in. The whole thing is crudely built. Huge caps of flat rock make up the ceiling. It is a room of stone, wide and deep. Some of the stones appear to have shallow carvings on them.

I am standing just inside the entrance. At the far end, a fire of intense, blue flame glows. It pulls me to it. There is no tinder or kindling under the fire. Just packed earth, as with the rest of the room, where centuries of footsteps have set the floor to the hardness of the surrounding stone. The base of the flame dances inches above the ground, swirling upward to reach flickering fingers of crimson-gold darting about at the top.

A boy is there, or I could say, a man. He looks to be at the cusp of transition from one to the other. About nineteen or twenty. He is tall and thin and carries a wisp of brown hair on his head that reminds me of the fingertips on the flame.

"Hello, Melanie," he says. "You need to see this."

He beckons to me and points to a stone at the end of the room. His green eyes shine with information.

I look at the stone, its flat surface facing me. On it are three symbols. Circles. Unlike the other shallow carvings in the room, these are in relief. As if the stone has been carved back from them, rather than they being carved into the stone.

No … not circles. They are reshaping before my eyes, becoming more pronounced. I look closely and they are glowing; just a light yellow at first, like that rare maple leaf in autumn on the edge of turning from pale yellow to white. We walk toward them and with each step, they grow more intense—from pale yellow to a deeper hue, and then to reflective gold.

I recognize the symbols now, and their position. I have seen them before. Stars. Three stars at an angle, the top one slightly off line and measurably separate from the other two.

I walk up and reach out to touch them, as if they want me to.

I am alone now. The blue flame grows in size and intensity, and encircles me. I am in a whirlwind of blue flame.

It feels cool and welcoming.

The flame dissolves, and now the stones themselves swirl around me. They also disappear and I am surrounded by countless pinpoints of light—now floating in the vastness of the universe. I look over to see a nebula in the shape of a horse's head in the distance, and then the three angled stars of Orion's Belt.

It is then I hear his voice. "Welcome home, Melanie."

Slowly it fades from me, like that yellow autumn leaf fading to white. I transition to a wakeful state, and then it is gone.

● ● ●

I opened my eyes to morning light filtering in through the windows. My bedroom faced west, so the sun didn't make it in. Instead, it reflected off the trees outside to cast the hint of a promising day throughout the room. My mind wandered to the room itself, and thoughts of how it had been Emilee's room so many years ago.

Someone knocked at my door. It opened and Katch peeked in.

"Time to get up, sleepy head." She came over and sat on the bed.

I brushed my hands across my face. "I'm up. Just not out of bed. I've been laying here thinking about this room, and how it had been Emilee's. It didn't hit me until now, but this is where she was first visited."

I sat up and pushed a few pillows behind my back.

"You never told me that," Katch said.

"Oh. I didn't?" I looked at one of the windows. "Emilee said she was about seven years old, so it had to be this room where the aliens first visited her. She said they came through a second-floor window. And I mean *through* the window. It wasn't open." I took Katch's hand and held it for reassurance. "It has to be this room."

She squeezed my hand. "Wow. That's kind of freaky."

"Yeah. Tell me about it."

Katch let go and walked over to one of the windows. "Do you want to sleep in a different room?" She looked outside as she ran her fingers along the base of the frame, almost as if to test whether it was solid and firm. "Or, you can share mine."

"I already thought about that, but I don't think it would make a difference where I was if they wanted to visit me."

"Or take you," she added.

I scooted down in my bed and pulled a pillow over my head. "You really didn't need to say that out loud." I peeked at her from under the pillow.

Katch turned to me. I could see she was working through something. "What made you think of this now? We've been here at the manor for three days."

"I don't know."

She came over and sat on the bed again, pulled the pillow off, and studied me. "Do you think they could have visited you last night?"

A moist film appeared on the surface of my skin as soon as she said this; a clamminess that tells your body when something is terribly wrong. It rolled into a chill, and I shivered.

Maybe Katch was right. But my mind had a way of avoiding such worries whenever this happened. "I don't know. I'm not sure if it's because I can't remember, don't want to remember, or maybe it's both. I've thought of similar experiences, but they're no more solid than visions floating in a fog way off in the distance."

"Do you want to remember?"

I shook my head. "No, I don't. I think I'm like my mom. It scares me too much." Then something just came to me. "Although, in some of my dreams, if that's what they were, I think there was a boy. I always felt safe when he appeared."

Katch's eyes lit up. "A boy? Like a hot, dreamy boy?"

I sat up and slapped her arm. "Not like that! Something else. Though, I'm not sure exactly what."

"Well, we'll need to figure it out eventually."

I shook my head. "What we need to figure out now, is how to get to the Carnac Stones. I was all excited when I decided to come to England because it was so much closer than Lake Oswego. But now that we're here, how do we get all the way across the English Channel and a big chunk of France to get there? Between the time we spent in London, and here, it has already been over a week. We don't have much more time."

"Yeah, we had no idea how complicated it would be."

We both sat in thought for a minute.

I took out my locket and showed her the one side. "Why would the Carnac Stones be on this locket?" I asked. "After all, it's the whole reason I decided to come here."

"We've talked about this before. There has to be something to it," she said. "It's too much of a coincidence for your dad to have been at the Stones, and for them to also be on a locket your mother had."

I opened the locket and looked at the pictures of my dad and mom. Then my eyes brightened. "I never showed you this." I removed my dad's picture and took out the memory foil I had put behind it.

Her eyes brightened as soon as she saw it. "You kept some?"

"Yeah. Before I left for Seattle. I hid it in my music box, just in case. Which was a good thing, because I lost the rest of it." I leaned into her and whispered, "We will always have proof aliens exist, and of what my dad witnessed."

Katch took the foil, crumpled it up and dropped it onto the bed to see it unfold without a wrinkle in it. "I wonder how it does that. What kinds of technology do they have if they can make something like this?"

I looked at my mom's picture. The token was just barely visible behind it. I popped her picture out. "There's something else you haven't seen. I hadn't thought about showing this to you before now." I took it out and handed it to her.

"What is it?" she asked. She had a look of wonder in her eyes. She studied it and then turned it over. Her eyes went wide. "I recognize these markings on the one side."

I nodded. "They looked familiar to me, too. But I couldn't figure out what they were until I got the book out about Betty and Barney Hill."

She grabbed my arm. "Oh, my God!"

I took the token from her and pointed to the planets and lines on it. "They match the map Betty drew when she was abducted."

"From the one the leader showed her, right?"

"Isn't that the craziest thing? Why would they be on this token?"

Katch grabbed it from me again. "And why is it cut in half, like a jigsaw puzzle?"

"You mean like half of it is somewhere else? I don't know."

She handed it back. "Someone must have the other half."

"That's what I figure. But who?"

I put the token and foil back in their places, covered them with the pictures of Mom and Dad, and snapped the locket shut. "It's a big mystery, isn't it? Just like the rest of this."

"One we will hopefully solve," Katch added.

I held up the locket. "Or, *it* will solve for us." I tucked it back into my shirt.

Katch looked over at the clock on the table and then stood. "We'll figure it out. But right now, you need to get up and get ready. Emilee told us last night we are having breakfast with the guests at the big house this morning, re-member?"

"Oh, yeah. What time is it?"

"Seven." Then she used her best British accent. "Break-fast shall be served promptly at eight."

"You've been hanging around Beanie too much."

"Well, I miss his quirky weirdness. Maybe that's it."

"I miss Frankie, too." I threw the covers off. "Okay. I need a quick bath."

Katch walked into the hallway and called back to me, "Come knock on my door when you're ready."

"Okay, as soon as I wash all these questions away."

Black Pudding

Mel

Katch and I went down the stairs to the main level and into Little Brightwood's breakfast room. We found Emilee waiting for us at the table, drinking a cup of tea and reading a newspaper.

She looked up when we entered. "Oh, there you are. Good then; perfect timing." She took a last sip of her tea, set her cup down, stood, walked past us and onto the landing of the stairwell.

Katch and I looked at each other.

"Where are you going?" I asked. "We just came from there."

She turned to us. "Come on. About face, and follow me." She took a set of keys from her purse and unlocked a door on the stairwell landing. Though I had noticed it before, I hadn't really given it much thought. Maybe a broom closet or something.

"We keep this door locked most of the time. It connects Little Brightwood to the main house." She opened the door and motioned us through.

We walked into a huge room two stories high. One end was a wall of windows overlooking the front of the estate.

The other also had windows, but they were on either side of an enormous, white fireplace. Burgundy floor-to-ceiling drapes accented the windows. The walls were wrapped in wainscoting almost shoulder high and painted a medium gray. Large paintings of the English countryside, in gilded frames, hung along the walls.

Emilee swept her hand through the air. "This is the Great Room of the main house. We use it for large gatherings, wedding receptions, a concert once in a while, and events of that nature."

She continued to a doorway on the far side of the room. Katch and I followed along, still gawking at the grandeur of it all when she turned to us and said, "Careful now, watch your step."

She led us through the door and down some wooden steps to Brightwood Manor's breakfast room. A long wooden table sat in the middle with seating and place settings for ten. Some house guests relaxed in comfortable chairs by the windows. Others stood around the room in little groups. All eyes turned to us as we entered.

Mrs. Bea came in right then from what looked like a kitchen. "Good morning, Lady Harris and her charges. We are ready to serve, if you so wish."

Emilee said, "Right so, Mrs. Bea, that sounds just ideal." She turned to the guests. "Thank you all for choosing Brightwood Manor for your visit. Mrs. Bea and the staff are renowned for their breakfast offerings. After all, breakfast is the proper meal of the day, if you plan to make a good start of it."

She walked to the head of the table. "Please allow me to seat you, and as I do, I shall perform the introductions." She looked at me and Katch. "This is my granddaughter, Melanie Simpson, and her good friend, Kachina Gallo. They are from a state called Oregon in America." She motioned to me. "Melanie, please sit on my right, and Kachina, I'll have you next to her."

She turned to an older woman. "Mrs. Caldwell, let's seat you on my left. Mrs. Caldwell is a regular with us when on holiday."

She turned to a family of four. A mother and father with a young boy and girl. They looked to be about ages eight and ten. "These are the Sutcliffes, here to enjoy our warm and wonderful beaches. Mr. Sutcliffe, I would be honored if you would anchor the other end of the table. The children can sit next to Kachina, and Mrs. Sutcliffe can sit on your right." She looked at me and said, "The Sutcliffes are from the East Midlands area of England."

She turned to the remaining couple. "Mr. and Mrs. Martin, that leaves you to sit between Mrs. Caldwell and Mrs. Sutcliffe."

We all took our seats.

Emilee turned to me. "Mr. and Mrs. Martin are the Americans I told you about. They are here for a few days as part of their European holiday."

"Where are you from?" I asked.

Mrs. Martin answered. "We are Midwesterners. I grew up in Kansas and Frank is from Iowa. We met while attending Iowa State University."

Just then Mrs. Bea and the servants came in with plates of food for each of us. I could immediately see this would very much be the proper breakfast Emilee had made for me back in Lake Oswego: eggs, sautéed mushrooms, fried to-matoes, Heinz beans (for Emilee said no other beans would do), rashers (bacon), bangers (British breakfast sausage), fried bread slices, and the dreaded black pudding that nearly made me throw up.

I leaned over to Katch and whispered, "Watch out for the little round things. You really don't want to know what's in them."

She shook her head in question. "Why? What *is* in them?"

I shrugged. "Okay. You asked. It's pig's blood, pig's fat, and oatmeal pressed into a beef intestine casing and boiled to solidify. Then they slice it and fry it until it turns black."

She gulped. "Oh. Thanks for the warning."

Everyone attacked their plates, including the Sutcliffe family, who seemed to have no problem gobbling up the black pudding.

"Are you young ladies going to tour England while you are here?" Mrs. Caldwell asked. "I'm from Leeds, a wonder-ful city up north in West Riding of Yorkshire. You must come and explore Roundhay Park. Just superb. And the buildings, galleries, and museums on The Headrow are a must-do."

Emilee leaned toward us, "Mrs. Caldwell is a social cor-nerstone in her community, and the self-appointed ambas-sador for Leeds. For that reason, I believe her only goal in coming to Brightwood Manor for holiday, is to grab up my tourists and Shanghai them to the north."

Mrs. Caldwell answered. "I am caught holding the smoking gun. So, now that I have been laid bare, what say you girls?"

I was trying to figure out how to give her a polite no, when Katch answered, "When we arrived, we stayed a few days in London. That was really nice." She gave me a side glance. "But actually, I've always wanted to see France."

I picked up on where this was going. "Yes, Katch and I have been talking about it. We recently covered the Carnac Stones of Brittany as part of our Celtic studies in history class. They are so mysterious. We'd love to see them."

"I wasn't aware of this," Emilee said.

I turned to her and tried to show a face of innocence. "It came up this morning while we were getting ready. We've been here on the Isle for days now, with visits to Newport and Compton Beach. We thought of what else we'd like to do if we could spread our wings. That's how a visit to the Carnac Stones came up."

"Well, isn't that interesting," Mr. Martin said, looking over at me. "Mrs. Martin and I are headed to France as well. Not, per se, to the Stones…"

He paused and studied me. Maybe sizing me up. It was a strange feeling, and it made me think that something about him seemed very familiar.

"What did you call them?" he asked.

"The Carnac Stones," I answered.

Something in his face did seem familiar. No. Not in his face, but in the *look* on his face. I felt like I had seen it somewhere before.

"Ah, yes. The Carnac Stones." He took his wife's hand and patted it with his other. "We had originally planned to see the beaches of Normandy. D-Day and all that. What American wouldn't? Then on to Paris and a visit to the Louvre, and a date with the Mona Lisa." He looked at me again. "But these Carnac Stones ... mysterious, you say. They sound fascinating. Tell us more about them."

Where was this going? I sure didn't want this couple to get into the mix. Then, in the next moment, I thought maybe this could be how we get there.

"There are something like 4,000 stones, all in straight lines. They go on for miles. Most of them are tall, much taller than a man. And very heavy. No one can figure out how they got there." I turned to Katch. I didn't know if I should go on.

She took over. "The reason we know about them, like we said, is because we studied the Celts. These stones predated even them. No one knows who put them up. Some say they go as far back as 4,500 BC."

I finished the thought. "And were brought from quarries as far as 30 miles away."

Katch continued. "Scientists who are now studying them, feel the Stones may be aligned in a mathematical sense, and to summer and winter solstices."

Mrs. Martin cut in, "My goodness, you two girls do pay attention in school. How impressive, and so Nancy Drew of you both." She looked over at Mr. Martin. "Perhaps we should take them. After all, it is a mystery to be solved."

Katch and I shared an excited look. Maybe we just found our way to the Stones. But in the same thought, I lingered on the last thing she said, and boy, she sure hit the mark.

Long Distance

Mel

"I've never had Cornish Game Hen before," Katch said.

I giggled. "It tastes like chicken."

We were just finishing up dinner with Emilee after spending most of the day trying to convince her to let us go to the Carnac Stones with the Martins.

Emilee laughed. "Well, I guess in all respects, that is probably what they are—little chickens. Or, at least their distant cousins."

"Where in England are they raised?" I asked.

Emilee laughed again. "You would think with such a British-sounding name they would be a United Kingdom product, but they are not. They come from your States. Imported, of all things. And are now all the rage in fine home dining these days. Since we first tried them, I have made sure we have some on hand for such occasions as this."

Mrs. Bea came into the room to pick up the plates. "Will there be anything else, Miss Harris?"

Emilee turned to her. "Yes, I'd fancy a cuppa. Could you be a dear and freshen up some tea for us?" She looked at the little clock on a side table in the dining room. "We'll take it in the living room."

146

"Yes, ma'am," Mrs. Bea answered, and returned to the kitchen.

"What do you mean, by such occasions as this?" I asked.

Emilee gave an affirming nod. "Ah. You caught that. Let's go into the living room." She stood and led the way.

Katch and I followed. Emilee went to the side table near her favorite armchair and picked up the phone. Not just the handset, but the whole thing. She worked the telephone's wall cord over the top of the chair and brought the phone to the small sitting table. Four chairs surrounded it.

She noticed us looking at a puzzle in the middle of the table. "Ah. Mrs. Bea has a penchant for puzzles."

She stood there holding the phone. "Well, sit down."

Mrs. Bea appeared with a tea set, placed it on Emilee's side of the puzzle, and left.

Emilee repeated herself. "Sit."

We did as we were told.

Emilee placed the phone on the table so it was pretty much in front of me.

She sat down and said, "I'll prepare your tea." She picked up the teapot and poured three cups.

"You're acting very odd," I told her.

Her only reaction was a smile as she made the three cups to each of our liking with milk and sugar.

The wall clock above the fireplace struck seven and sent its notification in a melodic tone, with six more to follow.

My curiosity took over. What could this be all about? I looked at the phone as if it were the solitary clue.

Though I had seen it before, I took it in with new interest. It was very British and very ornate. It had a white porcelain base with colorful hand-painted floral patterns, and sat on four little feet like the claw-foot tub in my bathroom.

It had gold accents on the handset and cradle. The handset was also porcelain with painted floral designs. The part you talked into curved up so it would be directed at the mouth. This wasn't just a phone; it was a work of art.

And just as the wall clock sang its tone for the seventh time, the phone rang and startled me. I looked at Emilee expecting her to answer it. It rang again. Instead, she took her time to place cups of tea in front of me and Katch.

On the third ring, Emilee nodded to me. "Well, aren't you going to answer it?"

"What? Me?"

It rang one more time. Did I have a choice? I lifted the handset, feeling it was more like a big question mark, rather than the phone's receiver. I put it tentatively to my ear. "Hello?"

"Mel. Is that you?"

My eyes flew open and I leaned onto the tabletop. "Frankie?"

I felt Katch grab my arm. I looked over at her and raised my eyebrows to show my surprise. She matched my look as if staring into a mirror.

Emilee smiled her big smile. "I thought you two might miss your lads, so I arranged this call. I'll take my tea to the other room to give you some privacy." With that, she stood and left.

"Yeah, it's me, Mel."

I leaned into the handset, wanting to fall into the sound of his voice.

Frankie continued. "This is crazy, right? Emilee made this all happen. Beanie is here, too."

I looked at Katch. "It's Frankie." As if she didn't already know this. "And Beanie is with him." Katch's eyes lit up. I motioned for her to get closer to me so we could both listen. She scooted her chair next to mine and leaned against me, ear to ear.

Frankie's voice sounded wonderful. "She pulled this together yesterday with a call to my mom. Set it up for right now. Had to do it that way since it's ten o'clock in the morning here. Mom said it would be like seven at night there. Is that right?"

"Yes, we just finished dinner. Oh, Frankie, you won't believe this place. It's huge, with never-ending rooms, and sits on eighteen acres with a big, beautiful garden. It's like a palace. Remember when Emilee said her family once lived in a castle? Well, this isn't quite that, but to Katch and me, it comes really close. I can't wait for you to see it someday."

"I'm sure I will," he answered. "It's probably already planned out by the stars." Silence held the line for a moment. "By the way, does this mean you're rich?"

"I guess so. I never really thought of it that way."

"I have no doubt the Queen will probably anoint you before you leave, and I'll have to start calling you Lady Melanie."

"You should be calling me that, regardless."

"Good point. By the way, how is it going? I mean, getting to the Stones?"

Katch and I gave each other a look. "We're still working on it. But we may have figured out a way."

"It's been well over a week. You don't have a whole lot of time left."

"I know, but we think we have it worked out. At least we managed to put the thought in Emilee's head. Now we just need to convince her."

"What do you mean?"

"An American couple is staying here. They offered to take us."

"Isn't that kind of risky, going with strangers?"

"Yes. But we have no other choice. My hope is that either Emilee lets us go with them, or feels obligated to take us herself. Though that would present a whole new set of problems by having her there with us."

"Sounds like you've worked the regular Mel magic on this."

"I hope so." I wanted to change the subject to what they were doing. "Can you talk, or is your mom hovering around?"

"Yes, I can talk."

"Are you sure?"

"Yeah. Mom gave us some space. She's in the sewing room with Suzie, and Dad is at work. We're good."

"Can you tell us what's happening there? Have you figured out the key yet?"

"Mel, you won't even believe this. I mean it's just crazy weird. We took the key to a guy named Mr. Zimmerman. We didn't even plan to go to his shop to begin with." Frankie paused, maybe to collect his thoughts or something.

"You know this whole destiny thing? I'm beginning to believe it's true. If we hadn't gone to see Mr. Zimmerman, we never would have found out what the key fits."

"You figured it out?" I couldn't believe what he just said. Katch and I gave each other a quick glance at this big news.

"Mel, I haven't even gotten to the crazy part yet. This key fits a hidden compartment in a huge clock up at Timberline Lodge on Mount Hood."

"It fits what?" How could this be true? "We always thought it would be to a safe deposit box. How did you manage to figure that out?"

"I know. That's what's so weird about it. We never would have, if we hadn't gone to Mr. Zimmerman. It's like he recognized the key right away, and what it fit. Beanie and I have talked about it a bunch. It couldn't just be a coincidence."

"Straight-up, bad-ass dharma," I heard Beanie say in the background.

"Have you gone up there?" I asked, excited to know. "Up to Mount Hood? Did you find out what's in the compartment? Was it the Orb?"

"No, we haven't. There's still a little issue with being grounded, if you remember."

"Oh yeah, I forgot about that."

"So, we are stuck for now. While you two wander the world, we sit here in chains."

"Yeah, I'm sure your life is pure hell." Then I remembered something. "What about George? Have you called him to see if he will take you?"

Frankie didn't answer right away. "He hasn't made it back from his vacation yet."

"Oh. He's been gone a while. I'm surprised he'd take that much time off."

"Yeah." Another pause. "I'm not sure what the deal is there. But we have a plan B."

"What is it?"

"Mr. Zimmerman offered to take us. We arranged to call him as soon as Beanie and I can figure out how to get away. We think our grounding should be up soon. We'll go with him then, if we can't sneak out before that."

"Do you trust this Mr. Zimmerman?"

"About as much as you trust the American couple, but neither one of us have much of a choice, do we?"

"You're right. Just be careful."

"You, too." The line went silent for a moment. "Gee whiz, Mel, there's a lot more I'd like to tell you about this whole thing with Mr. Zimmerman and that clock. And I wish we could have hours to talk about what's going on there. But we've already been on the phone for a while. It wouldn't be fair since this is on Emilee's dime, and it's probably costing her bigtime."

I hadn't thought about how much this call would cost my grandmother. I remembered back to when I tried to call Major Keyhoe at NICAP in Washington, DC, and how expensive that would have been. I never made the call because I didn't have enough money. This must be costing a fortune.

"Okay. You're probably right. We shouldn't talk much longer. But I'm so glad to hear your voice. I miss you so much."

"I love you, Mel."

"I love you, too, Frankie. I'm going to turn the phone over to Katch so she can talk to Beanie, okay?"

"Yeah, sure. Just don't hang up before I get a chance to tell you one more time how much I miss you. In case you haven't figured that out yet."

Katch pulled at the receiver, anxious to talk to Beanie.

I held it just long enough to say, "I have, but it wouldn't hurt to hear it one more time."

RAAF Base

Roswell Army Airfield, 1947

Roger

I stared out the barracks window at a couple of oak trees, some scrub brush, and a huge expanse of New Mexico desert. That's about all I could see. The barracks didn't have any windows facing the base.

I thought about what had happened to me at the crash site with the alien and the device, and the responsibility given to me. I knew I couldn't share it with anyone here. We all had enough on our hands anyway; probably because we were the only people in the world, outside of those who showed up from the military and fire department, who knew life existed outside our planet.

We'd been here for some time. The barracks we were in sat away from the rest of the buildings. It was small, with eight bunk beds, an area with tables and chairs, and a latrine. All Army issued. They must have put this building here for such situations. In order to keep prisoners separated from the rest of the base. Like a jail without bars.

Once we arrived, we were ushered into a facility and interviewed individually to gather information on each of us. They wanted to know my full name, age, address, spouse, kids, relatives, job, and school. Pretty much anything and everything about me.

After that, we were unceremoniously dumped here, and told not to talk about what we saw. Billy lay on one of the lower bunks, his arm folded across his eyes. I doubted he was asleep. Probably more like wondering what would become of us. Steve appeared from the latrine sporting a wetted-down towel around his neck.

It was mid-afternoon and a blistering day. We tried to open the windows, but could only move them a few inches. They seemed to be blocked, apparently so we couldn't crawl out and escape. Two fans were mounted high up in the end walls, at the apexes of the gabled roof. One pulling air in, and one pushing it out. But it appeared to have no effect on the stifling air inside.

Stu paced the room like a caged lion, the areas under his armpits dark with sweat, perceptibly growing. "I don't get why they can't let us go. Y'all know we ain't done nothing."

No one said a word.

The door opened and we turned to see Professors Holden and Fielding walk in. I was surprised to see them. They hadn't been at the crash site, so why were they here?

They were followed by two MPs with rifles. Four soldiers carried a bunch of duffle bags into the room and set them against the wall. The bags were our personal belongings from camp. The MPs and the soldiers left. They closed the door and I heard it being secured.

"Why are you two here, Professor?" Steve asked. "What's going on? And why is our stuff here and not at the camp?"

The professors walked over and sat at one of the tables. I could see they were spent.

"A group of soldiers came to the camp first thing this morning," Professor Holden said. He pulled a handkerchief from his pocket and wiped his brow. "They had us pack up everything and escorted us here. When we asked about the four of you, they said you were here at the base as a matter of national security."

"But, what's with our stuff?" I asked. "Why did they bring it here?"

"Pick a cot," Professor Fielding said. "We're going to be here for at least a day." Beads of sweat rolled down his forehead. He took a napkin from a holder on the table and wiped at it, then added, "Maybe longer. I think it depends on what we tell them. So, the truth is our best bet, and anything short of that," he looked around to make sure we all understood, "could prolong our stay."

Professor Holden nodded. "Don and I figured out that whatever it was you came upon, they want to clean up every trace of it before we are released."

"That's why they brought us here," Professor Fielding added. "They want us together so we can get our stories straight on keeping quiet."

Professor Holden stood and addressed us all. "We know something unusual crashed into the desert last night. It isn't hard to figure out what it was, based on what has happened since."

"That thing that crashed," Stu blurted, "was a flying saucer from outer space. There were dead aliens! We're supposed to keep quiet about that?"

Billy shot up from his cot and glanced nervously toward Stu. "We ain't supposed to talk about it. Don't get us in more trouble than we already are."

Stu waved his hand at Billy to shush him. "I can talk all I want. What they goin' to do about it?"

Professor Holden took a step toward Stu. He quickly glanced around at all of us, but addressed Stu directly. "We will not be saying a word about this to anyone. Those of us from the camp were not given much information about what you saw, but we were told the importance of keeping it quiet."

I suddenly realized something that concerned me. "Professor Holden, where are Roy and Nick? Why didn't they come in with you?"

"They're still being questioned about our expedition and why we were there."

"But they weren't at the site. They didn't see a thing," I said. "Why would they be questioned?"

He continued, "You know the military. No loose ends. They wanted to interrogate us first, before bringing us here. They had questions about the four of you. What you are like, your personalities, and things of that nature. But mostly they wanted us to know how serious this all is," again looking at Stu, "and to keep our mouths shut."

A sergeant stepped into the room with two MPs. "I'm Staff Sergeant Williams. I need Steven Brentwood and Stuart Furman to come with me."

Stu and Steve looked at each other.

Stu, a bit defiantly, said, "What for?"

Professor Holden told him, "They need to ask you some questions. Go with them and comply with their demands."

Stu and Steve walked over to the door and were escorted out by the sergeant and MPs.

I pulled Professor Holden aside. "What do you think is going to happen now, Professor?"

He shrugged. "For one thing, our expedition is over. I've been told in no uncertain terms, that we are to wipe this trip off the books, and destroy any documents relating to it."

"What?" I was shocked. "We need to finish. Maybe we'll have to come back. But why can't we complete the expedition?"

"They don't want a trace of it to remain anywhere. In other words, it never happened. And the area around our worksite is now cordoned off, and will remain that way for a long time. We wouldn't be able to come back and finish anyway."

I shook my head. "But, Professor?"

He gave me a very serious look. One that told me to pay attention. "Roger. I know how hard you worked on this. But it's over. It never happened. Years from now if anyone tries to look up this weekend and what we were doing, all they will think is we were enjoying a nice barbeque with friends on the Fourth of July weekend in Lubbock, and nothing else. That's how it needs to go down. Period."

The Lieutenant

Roger

An MP escorted me into an interrogation room. A table sat in the middle with a chair on either side. There were no windows. A single metal lamp hung by a cord from the ceiling centered above the table, its exposed bulb the only light in the room. The MP motioned for me to sit in the chair on the far side of the table, facing the door. "Wait there." He walked out of the room.

I didn't like the fact I was being questioned last. They had taken Billy not long after Stu and Steve. Roy and Nick had come into the barracks soon after. They all eventually came back, one by one, and none of them said a word about what had taken place. I did get a furtive side glance from them once in a while; like they knew what was ahead for me. Whatever did happen with them, I could see how seriously they all took it. Even Stu.

I tried not to think about why I was last, but I had some ideas. Like the fact it was my expedition, and I was the one who picked where we went. Or, that I was the first on the scene of the crash, and had been there for a while before the others finally arrived. That certainly could have come out. But I hoped it wasn't because someone saw Tom take the

159

satchel and get away. I didn't want to face what repercussions that would bring, if in fact, they had figured it out.

A moment later a lieutenant stepped through the door and closed it behind him. He was young and of medium build. His uniform showed crisp pleats and sharp lines. His garrison cap sat perfectly angled on his head. He wore his uniform in a way that showed he was well aware of the stature it gave him. His eyes blazed with intelligence and purpose.

He didn't come over right away. Instead, he stood by the door and studied me for a moment. When he finally did come over, he sat down and placed a folder on the table. "I am First Lieutenant Burnham. It is my job to ask you questions, and it is your job to answer them truthfully." He studied my face and I could feel his eyes working to penetrate my thoughts. "Just so we understand each other, I *will* know if you are lying."

I tried to be non-committal in my look: not scared, or excited, or worried, but maybe just a bit curious.

Lieutenant Burnham opened the manila folder. It had a small stack of papers in it, already typed up. I could see this as he turned each one to review what was on it. He took his time, never looking up while he did so. My guess was these had to be notes from the other interrogations. My curiosity and apprehension grew as to what could be on those pages. Maybe that's what he wanted, to set worry into motion within me.

He studied the last page, holding it up to read and giving it emphasis by doing so. I could see the ink of the typeface through the back of the paper. He picked up the other pages, put them all together, sorted them into order, and stacked them into a neat pile before closing them in the folder.

He sat back in his chair and took his time to read me. I think he was looking for body language giveaways. I tried to stay non-committal. It was my only defense, and I hoped it would work.

He took out a pack of cigarettes and lit one. "Do you smoke?" he asked, offering me the pack.

"No," I replied. I didn't want to say more. I could feel him hoping I would.

He put the pack in his pocket and called to the door. "MP."

The door opened. "Sir?"

"Bring me an ashtray."

"Yes, Sir."

He took a puff and studied me while he blew it out. The bluish smoke spread in a thin cloud, settling like a thermal layer within the heat of the room.

"You're right in the center of this whole thing, aren't you, Simpson? You picked the spot, ran the expedition, and you were the first one to the crash site."

I didn't move a muscle. "What? You think I had it all planned out for the spaceship to crash right at that spot?"

He chuckled. "No. But it's still quite a coincidence, isn't it?"

I didn't comment.

The MP darted back in and set an ashtray on the table, then left just as quickly.

The interrogation went on for hours, and the ashtray slowly filled with cigarette butts. It hadn't taken long for my shirt to be soaked with sweat, and my hair damp with it. I had a white handkerchief, embroidered with my initials. Gloria gave it to me as a Christmas gift last winter. I had now used it to wipe my brow so many times, it sat in my hand, limp with moisture. It became my focus when Lieutenant Burnham would leave.

He often left the room, and would be gone for long periods of time. When he did return, an air of newfound knowledge would sweep in with him. As if he had just received a flash of important information at the very moment he opened the door.

But all he did was ask the same questions over and over again, in different ways—with different words or emphasis—but they were always the same questions, just wrapped up in new packaging; searching for cracks to appear in my answers.

It scared me, though. He wouldn't give up, and I wouldn't give in. He had started out somewhat matter-of-fact. But as time went on, his demeanor became more aggressive. He accused me of lying, which I was doing, of course. He knew it and I knew it. But I wasn't going to tell him a thing. Then he dropped the bombshell.

He lit another cigarette and took a puff. He blew the smoke in my direction. "I've been waiting for you to divulge this, but since you won't, I will." He leaned in close, a cunning look taking over his face. His stale, cigarette-tainted breath washed against me. "Tell me who the man was that got the satchel out, and how to find him."

My eyebrows twitched up. I couldn't help it. He surprised me. How did he know this, and when did he find out? Had he known all along, and if so, why wait this long to spring it on me? But in that same instant, I knew the answer. Because he got the reaction he wanted. Just a little reaction, but one that proved he was right.

He sat back and smiled with his win. "You were known to have taken a satchel to the crash site, but it was nowhere to be found when the soldiers arrived. We heard from more than one of your colleagues that you are never without it. But you didn't have it on you when our troops arrived. And it wasn't in your tent or among your belongings, either."

He flicked his cigarette ash onto the top of the butts stacked high in the ashtray. "You were seen at the crash site with another man, not from your expedition. Why don't you tell me about him?"

I knew not to answer, silence being my best friend right now. I just continued to stare at him, wondering who had seen us and told the lieutenant.

"It isn't hard to figure out you gave him your satchel and worked with him to smuggle it out. Tell me where he is. We need to recover that satchel." He leaned forward. "Let me explain it this way. The two of you are loose ends that need to be tied up. We have no doubt your satchel is packed full of material from the crash site. And we will do everything and anything necessary to recover it."

I kept quiet. I couldn't see how anything I said would be of help to me. For the simple reason that I couldn't tell him the truth.

He waited. Thick silence added itself to the layers of stale smoke in the room.

He put out his cigarette and looked at me. His face became even more serious. "So, Mr. Simpson ... there is a Mrs. Simpson, am I correct?"

I leaned forward and glowered at the lieutenant. "You leave my wife out of this."

"I also understand she is pregnant. Congratulations. Yes, we also found that out. We found out much about you and your wife, Mr. Simpson. And how you stay with Mrs. Delbert."

"Don't you dare threaten us. And don't you dare touch my wife." My body shook at the thought. Sweat rolled down my face. I dabbed at my forehead with my handkerchief.

Lieutenant Burnham looked as if he had suddenly been possessed by some terrible evil. "Then maybe you should understand how serious this matter is, Mr. Simpson. And how far your government will go to keep this event under wraps. The only thing standing in the way of our mission's success, is you and the material the two of you managed to sneak out of the site. This is a matter of national security of the highest order. So, carefully weigh your options, Mr. Simpson, with strong consideration for the safety of your wife and child."

My mouth went dry. It didn't help that my requests for water were denied. I hadn't had a drop the whole time in here. Still, my hands felt clammy, and a cold chill flowed through my body, even in the dire heat of the room. A bolt of anger shot through me. I shook with the thought of his threats to my family. It absolutely scared me. Just the look on his face. Like he took pleasure in it.

I didn't know what to do. I made a promise to the alien. He shared with me the importance of the device. I gave a fleeting thought to turning over the satchel and alien material, but keeping the device. Just as quickly, I knew that wouldn't fly. It would show I had lied. They would guess, and correctly, that I kept some of the alien material for myself. I would be in no better position. My only way out was to keep at my lie.

Besides, what could they actually do if I didn't turn over the satchel? I had no idea. Would they really hurt my family? I didn't want to take the chance to find out, but there wasn't an option. No matter what, I couldn't give it up. I was the guardian of the device now, at least until I can get it to the Intrepid One, whoever that might be. Keeping it safe had now been instilled in me as resolutely as if it were a vein of quartz embedded within a mountainside of granite.

I stared right into the lieutenant's eyes and said, "I don't know what you're talking about. Someone apparently gave you bad information. Maybe to save their own skin."

He pounded the table with his fist, bouncing the ashtray off of it to clatter across the floor. Cigarette butts flew everywhere and ashes floated to the ground.

The MP barged into the room. "Is everything all right, Sir?" He looked at the mess. "You want me to get an orderly to clean that up?"

"No." Lieutenant Burnham waved off the MP, still looking at me. "Mr. Simpson has graciously offered to take care of it."

He left. Lieutenant Burnham motioned to the floor. "Well?"

I walked over and picked up the ashtray. Then got down on my knees and worked my way back to the table, picking up cigarette butts and putting them in the ashtray. I placed it on the table. When I tried to rise, he shoved me back down with his foot. "You're not done yet. The ashes."

I looked at him. "How am I supposed to clean those up?"

He shook his head. "Not my problem. Lick them up if you have to."

All I could think of was my handkerchief, so I took it from my back pocket and slowly scooted the ash into a pile. I slid the mess as best I could into my hand and dumped it onto the ashtray. Gray streaks of ash still showed on the floor.

The lieutenant picked up the ashtray and dumped the contents onto the floor again. "Start over. And get it right this time."

I repeated the same steps as before, but this time I wiped at the streaks with my handkerchief until the damp sweat within it had absorbed the remaining ash, and the floor looked pristine. I folded the hanky once and rubbed at the gray soot on my palm to get it off as best I could, then folded it again and stuck it in my pocket.

"Good," he said, then stood. "Now, I'm going to get something to eat. And guzzle down a big glass of ice tea."

He motioned nonchalantly with his hand in my direction. "So, you stew on things for a while." He walked to the door. "Get used to this, Mr. Simpson. We won't let you or your wife rest until we get that satchel." Lieutenant Burnham opened the door and started to walk out, then turned back. "Oh, and one more thing. It's a big desert out there. People can easily disappear in it."

Confession

Isle of Wight, 1967

Mel

It was the day after breakfast with the Martins, when they offered to take us to France. Katch and I were having tea with Emilee in the sunroom at Little Brightwood. She sat in an armchair. Katch and I sat on a couch angled next to her. Soft rays of sunlight filtered into the room.

"You do know I can't have you traipsing around Europe with the Martins, don't you? I would be absolutely bonkers to allow such a thing."

I leaned forward with the most pleading look I could muster. "But Emilee, the Martins are leaving today, and they offered. How else are we going to get there?"

She took a sip from her cup; I think to let me wonder if she was considering my plea. But she wasn't. "Although they have been wonderful guests, I know nothing of them. It is just not going to happen."

I sat back against the soft cushion of the couch, but it might as well have been made of thorns for the pain I felt with her answer. I looked over to Katch. She seemed just as dejected as I did, her brow furrowed in disappointment.

Emilee placed her cup on a small table between us. She studied me for a moment. "You really are set on seeing these stones, aren't you?"

My hopes shot up. "Yes. We would love to see them."

She took on the look of a detective digging for an answer. "And, just why would this be so important? You never mentioned them before yesterday."

I shot a side glance toward Katch. She threw me a shrug, kind of like an 'I don't know what to say' shrug.

I thought for a moment. What do I tell her, if I tell her anything? I knew there were certain things I couldn't tell her because it could put her in danger. But I decided I needed to tell her something. "My dad was there. I want to see them because he was studying the Stones."

Emilee's eyebrows raised at that bit of news. Her right one a little more quizzical than the left. Like they were in an argument on what to say next.

"Does this have anything to do with the Orb?" she asked.

I was stunned. "What? You know about it?"

"Yes. Frankie told me back when you ran off, and about the material from the crash site. I'm glad he did. It allows me to understand much about you that was missing, and a part of why you acted as you did when I told you about the visitors. There were many things in play that you hadn't shared."

I suddenly felt very guilty. "I know. I'm sorry. I just couldn't."

I had kept this from her because it all seemed to be wrapped in bright red paper with the word *danger* emblazoned in yellow all over it, and something ominous inside; something that pounded away at the wrapping. I didn't want Emilee anywhere near that package when it finally exploded and whatever was inside came rushing out. I knew one day it would.

Emilee leaned over and patted my knee. "That's all right. Water under the bridge, as they say. Did your father have the Orb at the Stones?"

"Yes. I found that out."

"Then I guess I would understand why these stones were of interest to him, and to you. It has to do with the Orb." She thought for a moment, then asked, "How is it you knew he went there with it?"

"I saw a film of him. A professor showed it to me when I went up to Seattle. He worked with Dad. They went to study the Carnac Stones together because they knew the Orb has something to do with them."

"Ah, I see," Emilee finally said. "You know I haven't pried as to why you ran away to Seattle. Now, perhaps, you have just given me the answer."

"Yes," I told her. "And it was amazing to see the film of him. Now I want to go to the Stones and stand where he did. It's one of the last places he went before he died."

"Do you have the Orb now?"

"No," I told her. Katch and I both shook our heads. "We don't know where it is."

"But are looking for it?" Emilee added, as if to finish my sentence.

"It's not at the Stones, if that's what you're thinking," I told her. "At least, not that I know of."

"Still, you must get there. I understand now."

Emilee sat in thought for a moment. Then a shine took to her eyes and a thin smile to her lips. Just a slight upturn at the corners of her mouth. The kind of smile the wearer doesn't even know came to them. Subtle, but there, because of a plan developing behind it.

She reached across and took my hand. "Okay, then. I think you should go. I have an idea. Let me see if it bears fruit. If so, it will be a way for you to get to the Carnac Stones, and in a safe way so I won't have sleepless nights of endless worry."

Katch and I beamed at each other.

"Really?" I asked her.

"Well, it's not set in stone, yet."

Then we all laughed at her pun.

"Give me a day," she said.

The Arrangement

Mel

Katch and I were returning from a walk in the botanical gardens. We had come to taking long walks every morning through them to enjoy the beauty they held.

It also allowed us to perform the smudging ceremony. Katch taught it to me back in Lake Oswego, not long after we met. In her Hopi culture, it is standard practice to cleanse your spirit and your surroundings through smudging using the smoke from burning sage. Katch liked to smudge daily, at least as things and the weather permitted.

The first time we performed the ceremony together, she told me it was important to gather the sage yourself. She said, "You must be sure it is picked correctly. The sage plant must be thanked for the offering, and only be used in a good way, with good energy for cleansing. And the Creator must be asked to bless its harvest."

Such things are all about respect. She and her grand-mother go to a place in eastern Oregon every year to harvest a type of sage plant worthy of such rituals. It's the same sage we just used for our smudging ceremony this morning.

The first time we wandered into these gardens to find a good place to perform the ceremony, I don't think either of our mouths ever closed, propped open by the wonder of it all. The whole garden area was well cared for, and as ancient as time itself. Worn flagstone paths, brick walls, archways, iron gates, and stone bridges were covered in ivy and layered with moss. Flowering plants and delicate, shade-bearing trees filled the gardens. One day we discovered the stream Emilee told us about, and found it really did bubble up from the ground.

We walked into the sunroom to see Emilee in the living room, sitting in her lounge chair and talking on the phone. A steaming cup of tea sat on the table next to her.

"Yes, brilliant. Just brilliant. Thank you, Helen. I'm sure Eddy will be a wonderful guide. Thank you for arranging this." She hung up just as we entered the room.

"Who was that?" I asked. Maybe it had something to do with our getting to the Stones.

"A dear friend of mine." A broad smile took to her face. Her pearly white teeth accented her equally lit-up eyes.

"Is it something about the Stones?" Katch asked.

Emilee clapped her hands together as if she were a giddy schoolgirl. "Yes. As a matter of fact, it is."

Katch and I jumped into chairs facing her.

"What?" I asked.

She didn't answer right away, as if purposely building our anticipation.

I groaned. "Come on, Emilee! What is it?"

"I have made arrangements so you can visit the Carnac Stones. I felt you needed a guide, and so I wracked my brain wondering who might be right to do this, as well as available on such short notice. I would take you myself, but it is imperative I attend to things here, having been gone so long already. There were not a lot of options. Then I thought of Helen and her son, Edward. Though, he goes by Eddy."

Katch and I looked at each other at the news of an Eddy.

I wasn't so sure about this. I leaned close to Katch and raised my eyebrows in question to this news. "A boy?"

Emilee leaned toward us, making up the third of this newly formed, intimate group. "As a matter of fact, Eddy is a young man, twenty-one to be exact. He is a student at Oxford University and has just finished his third year working toward an integrated Master's Degree. As with you in America, it is holiday school break here in England, so classes have been suspended for the summer. I knew that to be the case and hoped he would be available as your guide and guardian. Helen has been instrumental in arranging such."

"I don't know," I said. "Even if he is twenty-one, are you really going to send us with a guy?"

"He isn't a *guy*, but a young man. There is a difference. I have known Eddy since he was a small lad. Helen assures me he has grown to be of the highest moral integrity. We have confidence he will take good care of you. And, what's more," she said, as she leaned even closer, "is last summer he and his class chums were in Brittany, France for summer study, and had indeed visited the Carnac Stones." She leaned back and slapped her knees. "How much better could it be?"

I had to wonder. No one can be as perfect as this Eddy sounded.

I looked at Katch. "What do you think?"

She sat back, folded her arms, and morphed into her interpretation of Beanie. "Hmm, let me weigh all the options before us." She looked up at the ceiling and then tapped her shoe on the flagstone as if in thought. She turned to me, flowed back into herself, and said in her best British accent, "Well, this does seem to be the best choice of the lot."

Emilee laughed. "Very good. Your accent is near perfect."

"I've been practicing."

I guess that was it. "Okay. It sounds like a plan." I looked at Emilee. "So, when does this happen?"

She stood with purpose and said, "He will be here the day after tomorrow, first thing in the morning. Now, I have lots more to do, and more arrangements to make. You two head upstairs and decide on what to take. And keep it simple. You shall only be there for a few days."

Pavlov's Dog

Lubbock, 1947

Gloria

I refilled a couple of teenagers' Cokes from the pitcher I carried. This whole idea of Monday Madness, where we give away endless glasses of Coke like we offer endless cups of coffee, was beyond me. Maybe Sal couldn't see these kids had hollow legs. All the same, I guess it worked because the place was packed, even though it was late afternoon and normally a slow time for us.

I wasn't scheduled to work today, but told Sal to let Martha have the day off and I would take her shift. She had mentioned something about needing it off, and I needed to keep busy while Roger was on his expedition. Sal didn't like me working so many shifts, what with my being over five months pregnant and all. But I felt fine. All the same, thank goodness Roger would be back tomorrow.

"Order up!" Sal shouted as he rang the bell sitting in the pass-through.

I went up to the window. "One or the other will do, Sal. I can hear your voice, and I can hear the bell. Seems a little redundant to do both." It's not like I hadn't told him this a thousand times.

Sal nodded, but in a way that showed he wasn't really paying attention to me. He had been watching the two men staked out in one of our booths. "What's with those two suits, anyway? It's like they're camped out over there. And all they do is swill our free coffee."

I looked at him and said in my best bouncer voice, "You wants I should toss them out on their keesters?"

He laughed. "I'd like to see that. I bet you could, even pregnant like you are. But, nah. It's not how we do things at the Eat 'N Run. Otherwise, we'd have to toss out half the kids who come into this joint."

I glanced over at the two men. One was short and stocky with a big head and small ears. The other was taller and more on the lanky side. Quite the odd couple. They were both dressed in identical black suits, white shirts, and black ties. They also shared the same serious look, like they couldn't dig up a laugh between them. A couple of fedoras sat on the table. The men appeared to be young, maybe in their early thirties. They hardly talked at all and when they did it wasn't more than a whisper.

"I'm just wondering if they plan to barricade themselves in that booth until we close." Sal said. "They've hogged it most of the day."

I looked at him. "You want me to ask?"

"No. No sense in that. I'm just curious."

"Well, we'll find out eventually. They'll leave when they leave."

I grabbed the plates sitting in the pass-through and walked them toward a booth occupied by two drooling Texas Tech students. I could see Pavlov's Dog syndrome had struck again. This place was like a laboratory for his experiment of classical conditioning. When the bell rang, the dog drooled, expecting food. Same thing here. Every time the bell rang in the pass-through, I could see it immediately in the faces of those waiting for their food. I have served a lot of Pavlov dogs during my two years at the Eat 'N Run.

The front door opened. I turned and saw Roger walk in. My heart raced at the sight of him, and my body went flush with excitement. I quickly placed the burgers in front of the students and ran over to greet him.

"You're back early." I threw my arms around him, gave him a big hug, and then smothered him with kisses.

"Hi, sweetie. How's my wife and kid?"

I finally managed to pull myself off him long enough to answer, "Missing you like crazy." I kissed him again and asked, "Are you hungry?" But I didn't wait for an answer. "Of course, you are." I put my arm through his and dragged him over to the counter. I felt him wince.

"You're limping. Did you hurt yourself?"

He smiled. "No, I'm fine. It's nothing."

I pointed to a stool. "Then sit." I called to Sal, "Get this wayward traveler a big juicy burger and some fries."

Sal looked out the pass-through. "Welcome back, stranger. Gloria has been a pain in my ass while you were gone."

I laughed. "Yeah, because *someone* needs to keep you in line."

I turned to see Roger's reaction, but he wasn't playing along. Then I noticed how pale he looked. I put my hand against his forehead. He felt clammy.

"Roger? Are you all right?"

I couldn't get him to make eye contact. He seemed anxious and kept shooting quick glances toward the two men in the booth. He finally looked at me. "Oh, sorry, Gloria. It's been a long day."

"Are you okay? You don't look well."

He gave me a half smile. "Just really tired. I'll tell you all about it later."

I studied him for a while, wondering what could have happened for him to be like this. I finally said, "Okay," but didn't really believe him. I walked around to the other side of the counter. "Would you like a Coke, or maybe some coffee?"

"A Coke sounds great."

I took a glass from below the counter, topped it with ice, and filled it from the Coke machine. "Weren't you due home tomorrow?"

"Yeah, we cut the expedition short. It didn't make sense to stay. Like I said, I'll fill you in later."

I set the Coke in front of Roger and studied him. He definitely had a paleness to him and there was something odd about how he said that. And his eyes showed there was a whole lot more to those tiny, little sentences than he was letting on. Things weren't adding up.

I tried to cheer him up. "That's okay with me. I've been missing you bunches. I don't have a problem at all with your getting home a day early."

A couple of kids waved to me from a table against the wall. I could see they were about to pass out from dehydration, and were desperate for a refill.

"I'll be right back."

I grabbed the pitcher of Coke, walked over to them and refilled their glasses, then made my way around a few other tables to check on them.

The bell rang. Sal shouted, "Order up, Gloria."

I headed back to the pass-through and shot Sal a look on the way. He laughed. I placed the burger and fries in front of Roger, grabbed a bottle of Heinz ketchup, and set it by his plate. I leaned on the counter and gave him a dreamy look. I wanted to distract him from whatever seemed to be bothering him.

He smiled. "You definitely are a sight for sore eyes. I'm glad to be home."

"You look pretty clean for just getting back."

"I stopped at our place to drop off my gear. Mrs. Delbert came out to greet me and told me where you were. I was a sweaty, dirty mess, so I took a shower and put on some clean clothes. I wasn't about to come in here looking and smelling the way I did."

"I truly do thank you for that," then leaned over and kissed him.

I got a half-smile in return, which really wasn't like him at all. He was having a hard time getting the ketchup out of the bottle. His hands shook ever so slightly.

I took it from him, grabbed a fry from the plate, and stuck it into the bottle opening to get the flow going. I pulled out the fry and shoved it into Roger's mouth. He laughed as he nearly choked on it.

I giggled. "I'm glad to see you didn't leave your sense of humor out on the high desert after all." I tapped on the end of the bottle and ketchup flowed onto his plate. "See. A person learns a few things working at one of these burger joints. What would the world do if we waitresses didn't have such lifesaving little secrets?"

He smiled. "It's so good to see you."

"Good?" I stiffened my shoulders to show my protest. "Just *good*? That's it? Is that the best you can do?"

He didn't say anything for a moment. "Sorry, I'm tired and a little distracted." He shot another quick glance toward the two men. "How long have those guys been here? They sure look out of place."

"Most of the day. And Sal and I have been thinking the same thing."

"Have they asked you about anything? Maybe about me?"

I gave him an odd look. "Why would they ask about you?"

Roger shook his head and didn't answer. Instead, he took a bite of his hamburger. He was obviously avoiding my question. It made me wonder what those two guys could have to do with Roger. I decided to drop it, but still, I wondered if I should be worried.

But I was definitely worried at how pale he looked, almost on the verge of being deathly ill. I also knew if I said anything to him about it, he would just deny it.

I did a run through of the tables while Roger ate. I filled glasses, took orders, and bussed dishes. Then I grabbed the coffee carafe and walked over to the two men. They had become more animated now. Where before, they had been sullen and laid back, now they were leaning across the table and whispering up a storm. They stopped when I approached the table and filled their coffee cups.

"Will you gentlemen need anything else?" I asked.

They looked up at me with a set interest in their eyes.

The smaller one answered. "No, Ma'am. We're sittin' pretty for now."

Something about the way he said that sounded odd. I nodded, gave them a big smile, and walked away. Maybe I needed to look at them in a more discerning light.

Unveiled Threats

Roger

I chewed on a bite of my hamburger and struggled to swallow. My mouth went dry the moment I saw the two men in the booth. They were so out of their element. I knew why they were here. There could only be one reason. Me.

I took a drink of Coke to moisten up the bite, and then swallowed. I had hoped for some recovery time, but it looked like that wasn't going to happen. Not with those two here. My head swam with the exhaustion of what had happened over the last two days. I needed to hold it together a little longer.

I watched Gloria as she worked her rounds. A chill hit me when she stopped at the men's table. She gave them a big smile as she filled their cups.

When I told Gloria it had been a long day, it wasn't a lie. At six o'clock this morning a bunch of MPs barged into our barracks and rousted us out of bed. They made us hurriedly dress and pack our gear. Then they took us to our trucks, which were all ready to go. Billy rode shotgun in my truck. We were escorted off the base by two MP jeeps, one in front and one at the back.

The temperature must have been eighty degrees when we left. Our trucks were loaded down with all our equipment, and the going was slow. After an hour of driving, I pulled to the side of the road and asked Billy to take the wheel. I couldn't focus anymore, and worried I might have an accident.

The trip took over five hours on bumpy, dusty roads in nearly ninety-degree heat. Neither of us said a word about what had happened all the way home. I tried to sleep, but it was impossible. After what Lieutenant Burnham did to me, my knees ached and throbbed from being jarred around on the rough roads.

When we got to Lubbock, we dropped off the expedition gear at the college. Then I said goodbye to Billy and headed home. I wanted to see Gloria.

When I got home, Mrs. Delbert came out and told me Gloria had taken someone's shift at work. Maybe that was for the best. It would give me a chance to get myself together before seeing her.

Mrs. Delbert helped me take my stuff downstairs. She saw how I looked and that I could barely walk, so insisted I stay home. I thanked her for her concern. She left, probably knowing I would ignore her request.

I sat on the bed and took off my clothes. It was a struggle to even take a shower. I could barely walk and felt completely drained. It took me a while to get dressed. My legs had turned to rubber and I couldn't stop my hands from shaking. There was no way I would see Gloria in this shape. It took the better part of two hours to settle myself down. I thought about staying home to get some sleep, but I desperately needed to see my wife. I needed to make sure she was safe. And, she was the only solid thing I had right now, what with everything that had happened. I also used the excuse that she would be unhappy if I didn't see her right away, and it might lead to a lot of questions I didn't want to answer.

I held my hands out and tried to steady them. It made my thoughts fall back to the two days we were detained at the Air Force base. I wasn't allowed to return to the barracks with the others on Saturday. Lieutenant Burnham had other ideas. He kept me in that room. My interrogation lasted all through the night and into the next day.

The lieutenant worked me over pretty hard. He liked doing this and it showed. Things became rougher and more threatening. An MP brought in a floor lamp with a bright bulb set into the middle of a big, round, metal shade. They pointed it directly at my face and turned off the overhead light. Everything around me went black, other than that blinding light shining in my eyes.

Lieutenant Burnham made me kneel on the hard concrete floor for long periods of time with my wrists bound behind my back. Knees aren't made for such abuse. I know because as an archeologist, I studied the skeletal structure of homo erectus and homo sapiens. When kneeling on a hard surface, the kneecap is jammed against the femur bone. Not a good thing. The pain becomes excruciating.

It didn't take long for my legs to shake from the pressure. The lieutenant walked around me, asking the same question over and over and over again in a dozen different ways, "Where is the satchel and the material?" I think I memorized every possible variation of his question.

And I always gave the same answer. "I don't know what you're talking about."

He continued his threats against Gloria, and the baby as well.

The few times they allowed me to sit, I couldn't get up. My knees were shot and my calves had turned to putty. I had to use the seat of the chair to work myself onto it. And just as I felt a bit of recovery, I was forced onto my knees again. They screamed the moment they touched the floor. When Lieutenant Burnham wasn't in the room, an MP stood guard. I wasn't allowed to get up or move around without permission.

They were good at this, so didn't leave any truly visible signs of bruising or physical damage. There was some redness and swelling around my wrists. The wraps that bound them were firm, but made of soft material for just that reason. When I undressed, I found that large, red welts had formed on my kneecaps. My joints were visibly swollen; bursitis had set in. I worried that I might never be able to walk properly again.

The kneeling was terrible enough in itself, but the psychological torture intensified it. The constant badgering and threats. Water denial. Sleep deprivation. Torrid heat. And sitting in a dark, windowless, sweltering room with that light constantly shining in my eyes.

I lost all track of time. When they finally let me out, I was surprised to see most of Sunday had passed. They took me to our barracks, pushed me inside, and closed the door.

The guys were spread out amongst the cots and tables. Neither of the professors were there. They must have been given different quarters. Everyone looked at me. Steve, Nick, and Stu quickly turned away. Maybe they felt guilty. I knew much of the information used against me had come from them. Only Billy and Roy ran over to help me to my cot. I dropped onto it, too exhausted to care, and immediately fell asleep.

"Hello, Mr. Simpson. Welcome home."

I had been so wrapped up in my thoughts, I didn't notice the two men come over and stand right behind me.

"Mind if we sit?" the shorter one asked. He didn't wait for my answer. He took the stool next to me and tossed his hat on the counter. The other, taller man took a seat on my other side.

"I hear you had a wonderful stay at one of our finer government institutions."

It now hit me that what Lieutenant Burnham said was true. They wouldn't let this go. Not even for a moment. I felt weak. The room swirled. I worked hard to keep from passing out. Maybe I shouldn't have come. But then, I didn't know these two men would be here.

I needed time to recover and to think. I picked up a fry, dipped it in ketchup, and shoved it in my mouth. I chewed slowly. Why would they do this here? I was way too tired and worn out to even come close to an answer.

Maybe the bigger question was who are they—FBI? CIA? An amusing thought came to me, and I had to chuckle. They were probably CIA. After all, the FBI deals with United States citizens, whereas the CIA deals with foreigners. I'd have to guess that alien beings from another planet would be considered foreigners.

I turned to the man who spoke, deciding the best defense would be a good offense. I needed to hide how depleted and scared I felt. "Can I help you guys? You seem to be lost. The Eat 'N Run doesn't look like your regular kind of place. Maybe I could direct you to the cafeteria at the Lubbock Federal Building. That seems more your style."

He just stared at me, then leaned in so Sal couldn't overhear what he said. "You're a bit glib for a man in your situation, Mr. Simpson."

I matched his stare. A bead of sweat rolled down the side of my face. "And what situation would that be? It's like I told your friend, Lieutenant Burnham. I don't have any material, so don't understand why you are still bothering me."

The man on the other side said, "Hey, Bull. Are you getting this guy? He's a hoot."

Bull laughed, then said in a low voice, "Those at my agency are masters of deception, lying, and misinformation, Mr. Simpson. It therefore comes naturally for us to read such things in others. Such as yourself."

I kept my eyes locked on his. "And…"

"We want that material, so—"

He suddenly stopped.

Gloria came around the counter and stood in front of us. She gave me a questioning look. "Is everything all right, Roger?"

I smiled. "Yes, honey. A welcoming committee … from school." I didn't want her to be concerned. "Just here to let me know they are glad I made it home safely."

"Yes, your husband's safety is of our highest concern," Bull told her.

I could see the confusion on Gloria's face. She obviously knew they weren't from Texas Tech.

"Give us another minute, honey, will you?" I asked.

She studied my eyes, so I did my best to show that nothing was up. She finally shrugged, grabbed a bus bin, and went to clear some tables.

I watched Gloria walk away and asked, "Why didn't you do this at my house? I was there for over two hours. Wouldn't that have been easier and more private?"

Bull chuckled. "We like the coffee here. Besides," he nodded toward Gloria, "we wanted to meet your wife."

I fumed. "Leave her out of this."

"Sorry. It's a family affair. That's how important the recovery of that material is to our government." He leaned in closer. "Are you getting my drift?"

I didn't answer. I just glared at him with every ounce of hatred I could muster, and at this moment it was a ton of hate.

He leaned back. "Yeah, Simpson, I think you're getting the message. This isn't over. You have no idea how *not* over this is."

I shot him a smile I didn't feel. "Your high school English teacher must be very proud of how well you've mastered the English language." I gave him an inquisitive expression. "You *did* graduate, didn't you?"

Bull suddenly looked ready to explode. He leaned into me, and said with as much anger as he could put into a whisper, "There are lots of dangers out there, Simpson." His face went redder as he continued, "You think we are a threat to you and your family? Damn right we are. But if the Soviet Union gets word of this, you'll find out what real danger is like."

I sat back on my stool. I hadn't thought about the Russians. And then an idea hit me. I leaned toward Bull so no one could overhear me. "And exactly how would they find out about this? The fact that you believe I may have smuggled some alien material out of the crash site. Huh?"

A slight moment of uncertainty passed across Bull's face. "What are you getting at?"

"It wouldn't come from my Texas Tech people. You scared the crap out of them, so they won't say a word about this for the rest of their lives. The only way the Soviets could find out about what you *think* I have, is if it leaks out from you. I'm guessing CIA, right? Or maybe you're Air Force suits?" My vision drifted in and out as I said this. I needed to stay strong just a little while longer.

Bull stood and nodded to his partner to do the same. He reached into his pocket, took out a wad of bills, counted out three, and tossed them on the counter. "That should cover our coffee *and* your meal." He leaned down to grab his hat and said, "You best hope it's not your last."

Upside Down

Gloria

I walked behind the men talking to Roger, just back from clearing some tables. The smaller man leaned down to get his hat from the counter. I stopped when I overheard a threatening tone and caught something he said to Roger about how he hoped it wasn't his last. *His last what?*

He put on his hat and turned to see me holding a bin of dirty dishes. He glared at me. I went cold when the look in his eyes matched the threat of his voice. He pushed past me and walked out of the restaurant with the other man in tow, the door closing behind them.

Roger turned to see me standing there. His eyes went wide. "Gloria."

He jumped up and immediately cringed in pain. I watched in horror as he clutched at the counter and tried to catch himself. Roger's eyes rolled back, and he fell. His head hit the floor and he lay there face up, as white as a sheet.

I quickly dropped the bin, letting it clatter to the floor. "Sal!" I yelled, and leapt to Roger's side.

Kids jumped from their tables and stood over us.

Sal rushed from the kitchen and pushed his way through the kids. "Make some room. Give him room to breathe." He kneeled next to me. "What happened?"

"I don't know. I think those men threatened him. He didn't look good when he first came in, but I didn't think he was this bad. Something must have happened to him on the expedition." I leaned down and put my ear to his mouth. I could tell Roger was taking slow, shallow breaths. "Thank God, he's breathing."

"He must have passed out," Sal said.

I looked at Sal, "I need to get him home."

"Sure, Gloria." Sal stood up and motioned to a couple of boys in the crowd. "Tommy, Bobby. Help Mrs. Simpson get Roger into their truck."

I pulled up to the house and ran around to Roger's side of the truck. When I opened the door, I had to practically catch Roger before he fell out.

Mrs. Delbert rushed from the house. "Sal called and told me what happened." She got on his other side to help. "When he first got home, I told him he should stay here. He looked terrible and was in no condition to go to the Eat 'N Run. But he wanted to see you." She shook her head. "I knew I should have stopped him."

"That's okay, Mrs. Delbert. I doubt anything could stop Roger once he has his mind set on something."

Roger revived a little and mumbled, "You do know I can hear you."

"Good," I said. "Start listening to sound advice."

"Duly noted." He tried to walk, but couldn't do it on his own. We struggled to get him down the walkway to our basement apartment.

Once inside, we lowered him onto the couch.

"Thank you, Mrs. Delbert. I can take care of him now."

She stood there for a moment. "Are you sure, honey? Shouldn't I call a doctor?"

Roger waved his arm in the air. "No. No doctor."

I wondered if that might be the right thing to do, but decided against it. "No, I think he's just exhausted and needs some rest." I looked at her. "I'll let you know if I need any more help."

Whatever had happened to Roger, I wanted to know what it was without Mrs. Delbert here.

She nodded and went to the stairwell leading to the upper level. "You promise?"

I gave her a tentative smile. "I promise."

She walked up the stairs, through the door at the top, and shut it behind her.

I pulled Roger's legs up onto the couch and took his shoes off. He cringed and moaned as I did this. Why was he in such pain?

I put a pillow under his head and felt his forehead. It still felt cold and clammy, and his skin had a deathly pallor. I placed my hand on his chest and felt a slight tremble. Could he be going into shock?

"Roger, are you okay?"

He opened his eyes ever so slightly. "I'm okay. I just need to rest." The words came out in a whisper. Then he closed his eyes again.

I went to the kitchen and dampened a dishcloth, then went back to the couch. I kneeled down next to him, wiped his face, folded the dishcloth, and placed it on his forehead.

Worry tumbled through me. I stroked his hair, not only to try and calm him, but to steady myself as well. What could possibly have happened to cause this? And it scared me that those two awful men at the Eat 'N Run had something to do with it.

"Roger. What happened? Can you tell me what happened?"

He tried to say something but was too far gone. I couldn't understand him.

I let him rest on the couch for a while longer and then decided to put him to bed.

"Honey, let's get you to bed."

He nodded and did his best, but he was still very weak and could hardly walk. I had to help him. We made it to the bed. He sat on it while I pulled the sheets back. I took off his shirt and noticed red marks around his wrists, as if they had been bound. Why would someone do that to him? I laid him back and lifted his legs onto the bed. He moaned again. Every time I moved his legs, he moaned.

I undid his belt and removed his pants. When I finally got them off, I dropped onto the edge of the bed in shock. Both of his knees were swollen, covered in welts, and dark with bruises.

"Oh, Roger."

I pulled the blankets over him as tears flooded my eyes and rolled down my cheeks. I laid down next to him and held him in my arms. *What happened to you?*

Cacophony, Again

Lake Oswego, 1967

Frankie

Beanie closed the sliding-glass door behind him and walked over to my bedroom where I stood at my door, waiting. He held a sleeved 45 record in his hand and wore the glow of new-found freedom.

He said, "I'm free, free of my shackles. Do you have any idea what it was like to be grounded for so long?"

I closed the bedroom door and gave him a look. "We were both grounded that long."

He caught my drift, so decided to add, "With *my* mother?"

"Oh. Yeah. That does make a difference. I mean, I did have to put up with Suzie when she got bored with her usual methods of torture, like pulling wings off insects, and felt a special need to persecute me. But my mom is nowhere near what your mom is like. It must have been bad."

"Bad?" He gave me a twisted look. "Torturous. Do you have any idea how many implements there are in a kitchen that could provide a fairly adequate means of committing suicide?"

"That bad, huh?"

"Yes. Very that bad. But the torture is over." He walked to the record player, held up the 45 for a moment, and then pulled it from its sleeve, careful not to touch the vinyl surface. "This requires a special spin."

He set the 45 adapter onto the spindle, clicked the play speed to 45, placed the record on the turntable mat, and delicately positioned the needle to the first groove. After all, this was a Beanie record where total and ultimate care must be taken. That's why I *never* touch a Beanie record.

The song *Good Vibrations*, by the Beach Boys, filled the room. Beanie danced to the tune. His dancing was as bad as mine, so I retreated to the corner next to my desk and held a big drawing pad in front of me for protection against flying elbows.

He bopped around the room as he sang along.

I finally said, "Why this song?"

"Are you listening to the words?"

I tried to focus on them. "Okay, so it's a song about a girl, what she wears, and how the sunlight plays on her hair."

Beanie stopped for a moment and looked at me. "Ah, Kemosabe, you have found the truth within the song." He started to dance again as he said, "It also happens to be about good vibrations, which I am feeling right now at finally being free."

"Okay, got it."

He continued dancing for a while and then said, "But you, through your awesome insight, have uncovered the hidden meaning within." Then he made some sort of swirling motion and quickly stopped to face me. "How long have we been grounded?"

I thought about it. "It's not like I scratched marks into the wall to keep track. Maybe just over two weeks."

Beanie smiled and said, "Listen to the lyrics again."

I was never good at focusing on the lyrics. I'm more of a feel-the-beat kind of guy. So, I did my best. It was right after the chorus part where they sang about picking up good vibrations, and how a girl is giving them excitations.

Maybe I figured it out. "Are you talking about the part where when closing your eyes, she is somehow getting closer?"

"Correctomundo, my friend. We have been buried in this world of being grounded, while our girlfriends trek across Europe. But it has also been over two weeks since they left." He gave me a scheming little look and raised his eyebrows. "And they will soon be home. With heavy necking not far behind."

"You're right. I've kind of been focused on something else. But they'll be here in about a week."

The song ended. Beanie walked over, took the 45 off, and put it back in its sleeve. He thumbed through my stack of albums and picked out *Surrealistic Pillow* by Jefferson Airplane. He popped off the 45 adapter, pulled the LP from its cardboard cover, and placed it on the spindle. Beanie flipped the speed to 33-1/3 before placing the needle on the record. The solo drum intro to *She Has Funny Cars* filled the room.

"That should hold us for a while," Beanie said as he plopped onto my bed.

Now that he had stopped dancing, I placed the drawing tablet back on my desk and sat in the desk chair. "Our freedom also means we have a problem. Remember how I said I was focused on something else?"

Beanie stared at me from his position on my bed, very little concern showing on his face. "And what would that be my friend, at this moment of bliss?"

I sat forward in my chair, intent in my delivery. "We need to call Mr. Zimmerman so he can take us to Timberline Lodge. We have barely a week to find out what's in that compartment before the girls get back."

I knew Mom and Suzie had plans to go out later today. It was only a matter of when. Finally, after what seemed like a very long wait, they left. I grabbed Mr. Zimmerman's business card from my desk, and we raced upstairs to the phone on the kitchen counter. I picked up the receiver and dialed.

"Do you think he will keep his word?" Beanie asked.

I hadn't considered that. Now, I worried about the alternative. "Let's hope so, or it may be an issue getting to Timberline. We could go through a whole new phase of grounding if I get caught taking the Mustang out again."

The phone rang. It only took a moment for someone to pick up, but I couldn't hear what was being said. Clocks in the background sounded so loud, they washed out everything else.

I looked at the wall clock in the kitchen. It had just hit eleven o'clock. Great timing. And why always at eleven o'clock? It had been that same time when we first walked into his shop and heard this cacophony in person. I waited. Finally, the clocks stopped echoing through the receiver.

"Ahh, *das ist besser*. Zimmerman's Clocks, Locks, and Keys. How may I help you?"

"Mr. Zimmerman, this is Frankie Strickland. I was there a while back with my friend, Beanie. Do you remember us?"

"*Ja*. Of course, I do. You, with the special key."

"Yes, that's right." I nodded to Beanie that he remembered us. "You said you would drive us up to Timberline Lodge so we could check out the hidden compartment in the clock up there. Can you still do that?"

"*Natürlich*. I would be happy to. I need to perform some maintenance on the clock anyway."

Beanie grabbed my shoulder so I would look at him. "What's he saying? Will he take us?"

I swung my shoulder away to break contact and held my hand over the mouthpiece. "Give me a minute, will ya?"

Beanie shrugged. "I'm anxious. You wouldn't happen to have a 3 Musketeers bar lying around somewhere, would you? You know how I get when I'm anxious."

I glared at him, took my hand off the mouthpiece, and said, "When can you take us? We need to get up there as soon as possible."

"I also am excited for this adventure. I have a customer coming in later to pick up a timepiece, so today will not work. But I am free tomorrow. Say about nine o'clock?"

"Hold on, Mr. Zimmerman." I covered the receiver again and told Beanie.

"That's awfully early," Beanie said. "Teenagers don't get going that early. My mom will think something is up. How about ten o'clock? I think I can make that work."

I said into the mouthpiece, "Will ten o'clock work, Mr. Zimmerman? That would be better for us."

"*Zehn uhr* it is. Will you be coming to the shop?"

I hadn't thought of that. We can't ride our bikes there. It would take too long. "Uh, do you know where the Hunt Club is on Iron Mountain Boulevard? You know, where they ride horses?"

"I know of it."

I crossed my fingers. "Can you pick us up there? We'll wait for you at the entrance to the Hunt Club."

"*Ja*. That will work fine. I will see you there tomorrow at ten o'clock."

I nodded to Beanie and said to Mr. Zimmerman, "Thank you. We'll see you then."

Mr. Zimmerman hung up, and I put the receiver into the cradle.

I gave Beanie an excited look. "We're good to go."

Operation Paperclip

Frankie

We walked through the entrance of the Hunt Club. A few horses whinnied in the background, and the smell of straw and manure hit our noses as soon as we were inside. Some pretty crazy stuff had gone on here, and since we were a little early, we decided to check it out. The place seemed about as empty as it had always been. Someone rode their horse around the indoor arena, but other than that, we couldn't see anyone else. We walked past the arena, along the main hall to the far end, and stopped at the last row of stalls to our left.

"Remember how we loved to hang out at this place?" I said.

"Yeah, but that all changed once Mike held a knife to your throat," Beanie answered.

I nodded. "It's down this one, isn't it?"

"That would be correct, Kemosabe."

We walked past horse stalls on both sides until we came to one near the end on our right. The gate stood open. It didn't look like the stall had been used since the last time we were here over a year ago.

That had been a very scary time when Mike, the Russian agent, held us at knifepoint and directed us into this stall. Mel tried to bean him with a two-by-four, but he knocked her down instead with a swift karate kick to the head. Then he shoved her into the stall so hard she slammed against the far wall.

"I still can't believe Mike fooled us like he did. We all thought Tom was the Russian agent," I said. "I was so worried about Mel. He really beat her up."

"Well, thank God Tom showed up when he did and slammed that shovel against Mike's head. Otherwise, the Soviet Union would have ended up with the debris, and who knows what they would have been able to do with the alien technology."

Some of the rope Mike had planned to tie us up with still sat in a knot to the side of the stall. I kneeled and swept some straw out of the way to reveal a dark spot on the concrete floor.

I pointed to it and looked up at Beanie. "Does this look like dried blood to you?"

"Dried Russian blood, you mean. Tom hit Mike pretty hard."

I laughed. "How a shovel in a horse stall saved the world!"

I stood, looked around the stall, and thought about how close we had come to dying here. I felt it in a sudden chill. But maybe it was also because here we were, a year later, and danger still seemed to be lurking around every corner.

I shook off the thought. "We'd better get back outside. Mr. Zimmerman could be here by now."

We looked around the stall one more time, then walked to the building entrance.

We weren't there long before a Volvo station wagon turned into the driveway. It had blue paint with white trim around the windows, and a roof rack. Mr. Zimmerman's shock of Einstein-like hair gave away that he was at the wheel. He pulled up to us and rolled down his window.

"*Guten tag, Jungen,* are you ready for your great adventure?"

We sat in silence for a very long while. I was up front with Mr. Zimmerman, with Beanie in the back stretched out as if he were lounging on my bed back at home. It became apparent fairly quickly that Mr. Zimmerman was not one of the world's great conversationalists.

I watched the trees glide by as we made our way to the mountain. It would be almost a two-hour drive, and we were only halfway through it. I felt awkward sitting so close to someone I really didn't know. Especially an older adult.

I decided to fill the dead air with a question. "So, Mr. Zimmerman, how long have you lived here in the United States?"

He glanced over at me. "I came from Deutschland many years ago."

"Yeah. Didn't you say that's Germany?" I asked.

"*Ja.* My homeland."

Beanie sat up, suddenly interested in the conversation. "Isn't that the country we fought against in World War II, and was run by the Hitler guy who put millions of people to death?"

"The same. And, for such reasons, I came over to your country right after the war ended." He paused, as if wondering if he should go on, then added, "Have either of you *jungen* heard of Operation Paperclip?"

I looked to see Beanie shared the same blank expression I knew covered my face.

Beanie said, "No, not that I remember. Maybe it was covered in history when I wasn't paying attention, which would be most of the time."

Mr. Zimmerman laughed. "Well, you should pay attention. There is much to learn from the past. Although you seem to remember some things about history, such as what Adolf did."

"Yeah," Beanie answered. "I tend to perk up when there is a lot of war and death in the subject."

Mr. Zimmerman nodded. "Such is youth. However, this subject would not have been covered in your school courses. It was, after all, a secret program."

"Wow," I said. "A secret program! What did you call it? Operation Paperclip?"

Mr. Zimmerman seemed to sit up a little straighter, just as someone would do when telling an interesting story.

"During the war, Deutschland became quite advanced in rocketry. You may have heard of the V-2 rocket used against England in the war." He paused for a moment, then continued. "I was one of the scientists who developed the V-2 rocket system. My expertise, as you might have

204

surmised, had to do with the timing mechanisms for delivery and detonation."

"Wow," Beanie said. "You made rockets? Like the ones we have now, and aimed at the Soviet Union?"

"*Nein*. Not as advanced as that. But it was from our base of knowledge that your rocket system would be designed. So, as the war wound down, we were—"

A car honked at us. I looked in the rearview mirror on my side to see a trail of cars lined up behind us. Mr. Zimmerman was so focused on his story, he had slowed below the speed limit, and been driving like that for a while.

He shook his head and pulled off to the side of the road. "You Americans are always in such a hurry."

He rolled down his window, stuck his arm out, and waved the cars along. After the last car passed, he pulled onto the road again and continued with his story.

"Where was I?" he asked, as he rolled up his window. "Oh, *ja*. As the war wound down, it became obvious the army in our homeland would soon be overwhelmed. Many of our scientists hoped the American occupying forces would be our saviors. Most of us had been forced to work on these programs under the eyes of the SS. We felt like prisoners much of the time. I think your American Intelligence Service, the AIS, was concerned we might end up in Russia and work on such programs for them. Thus, Operation Paperclip was formed in order to get as many of our scientists to the United States as possible. They saved a number of us. I was originally sent to White Sands Proving Grounds in New Mexico, but I ended up at the Redstone Arsenal in

Huntsville, Alabama and worked with Wernher von Braun and others there."

The road now climbed toward Mount Hood. Mr. Zimmerman dug into his shirt pocket and took out a pack of Beech-Nut gum, removed one, unwrapped it, and popped it into his mouth.

"How did you end up with the clock shop?" I asked.

He chewed for a moment to get the gum working, before he answered. "After many years, most of us had served our purpose to your government. Eventually, we were allowed to stay in your country if we so wished. And some, such as Wernher, and Hermann Oberth, became big players in your NASA organization.

"I met a lady while at White Sands when I returned from Alabama. She was beautiful, intelligent, and from Oregon. And, she was interested in an older man who hadn't had time for family life yet. We married and moved here. While in Deutschland, when young, I worked as an apprentice for a clockmaker, eventually becoming quite good at it. This was well before the war started. So, to me, *es schien ein natürlicher Schritt zu sein*, a natural move to open a shop." He paused to study the road ahead. "Ah, this is Government Camp on our left. We will be to the lodge soon."

Beanie popped his head over the bench seat. "Why is it called Government Camp?"

Mr. Zimmerman laughed. "You think I have all the answers? I understand it acquired the name long ago when settlers first came to this area, though I don't recall the reason."

"Government Camp. It sounds kind of cool," Beanie said.

"And it is," Mr. Zimmerman assured him. "It is now quite popular with the skiers and tourists, being so close to the ski lifts and hiking trails on the mountain. The village is known for its hotels and restaurants. Even today, many who work at the lodge stay here, or come to eat when taking their meal breaks."

We turned left off Highway 26 and onto another road. Every once in a while, we would catch a glimpse of Mount Hood looming above us as we drove up the steep, twisting curves. I felt air pressure clogging my ears.

I turned to Beanie to see him moving his jaw around like he was trying to pop his ears.

"Beanie, remember at the airport? Mel told Katch that if you hold your nose and mouth closed and try to force air out, it puts pressure on the ears and they pop."

We tried it and it worked. It also made me feel a little lightheaded for a moment.

"Hey, that's a cool trick," Beanie said.

Mr. Zimmerman chuckled. "*Ein haufen amateure.* The easiest thing is to chew gum."

I remembered he had popped the stick of gum into his mouth earlier.

"Why didn't you let us know about this trick back when you ate a piece?" I asked.

He quickly glanced at me with a big grin, and then back to the winding road. "Such things need to be learned the hard way. Nothing should come easy. This, you should know from what I have just shared."

The car came to a point where the road split. We curved right, onto the one-way going up the mountain. I could see where the other road, coming down from the lodge, merged together with this one. There were a few maintenance buildings just up that road to the side. A snowplow sat in one of the buildings, along with a bunch of other equipment used during the winter. Maintenance trucks were parked at another building with a few workmen around them.

I lost sight of them as we continued up the mountain. The road wound a few more times, and then around a last turn. And there it was, Timberline Lodge.

"Wow, this place is far out," Beanie exclaimed, being someone who had never been up here before.

I had only been here once with my parents, but what I saw now reminded me of how awesome it had looked back then.

Gunther

Frankie

Mr. Zimmerman pulled into a parking spot near the entrance, and we got out. It was easy to park close since this didn't seem to be a busy time for Timberline Lodge. Hikers mostly used it in the summer, along with a few tourists who were here to check out the lodge. Nowhere near as busy as in winter when skiers came for the snow-covered slopes. I looked up to see only a patch of snow where a glacier battled the summer weather to keep its hold on the mountain.

Mr. Zimmerman followed my eyes. "Ah, the glacier." He put his arm around me as he led me to the back of the Volvo. "Did you know this is the only place in North America where the U.S. Olympic Ski Team can practice all-year-round? Perhaps, if you squint, you can see them up there now."

I tried to do just that, but it was too far away, and the glacier reflected the midday sun.

"Wow. That's pretty far out, Mr. Z," Beanie said. "How'd you find that out?"

"When you come up here as often as I have over the years, these little bits of information seem to find their way to you."

I diverted my eyes to the lodge. The whole lower level was made of huge boulders and stood at least twenty feet high. "Then you can probably tell us why the lodge has such a big rock wall."

"Ah yes. Actually, for two reasons. In winter this whole ground level is covered by deep snow. That is why the roof has such a steep pitch. To make sure the snow slides off so it doesn't collect on top. Also, since the lodge is built into the side of the mountain, this brings the front into level with the back of the lodge."

I could see Beanie's eyes brighten. "Oh, kind of like the daylight basement at your place, Frankie."

"Amazing craftsmanship," Mr. Zimmerman continued. "See how the expert stone masons have fit them together so very little grout was needed." He paused, as if in awe, even though he had probably seen this a million times. "It only hints of what is ahead." He nodded to us. "Shall we get our tools so we can continue this journey?"

Mr. Zimmerman opened the hatch to his Volvo, took out a toolbox and handed it to me. It was made of wood and open at the top, with a long, well-worn handle running the length of it. It looked really old.

He leaned in close and whispered, "We shall need these while I tune the longcase. After all, we must keep up our cover while on such a covert mission, correct?"

Beanie huddled in close, "Right you are, Mr. Z. We don't want anyone to know what we are really up to."

We headed toward the entrance. I looked to my left and noticed a part of the lodge where the roof slanted at the same steep pitch almost all the way to the ground. Two rows of windows—one on the first floor and another on the second—sat in the middle of this section, with their own little roofs. They split the sloped area in two, so that only the shingle roofing on either side of the windows dropped unobstructed all the way. Above them, on the highest level, sat two more windows gabled out from the roof, with a chimney nestled between them. These had to be the lodge's guest rooms.

We walked up some steps and into a massive stone entryway. It was more like a tunnel than an entrance.

"This stone entry keeps the snow from sliding down and landing on visitors," Mr. Zimmerman said. He turned to us just before we entered the lodge. "All right, *Jungen*, shall we reveal the long-held mystery of whatever is in that compartment?"

I shot a nervous glance toward Beanie, who gave me a firm nod.

I looked at Mr. Zimmerman. "Sure. Let's do this."

We walked through the first set of doors. They stood open. An Indian chief's face, feather headdress and all, had been carved into the wood of the door and painted in vibrant colors.

On seeing it, Beanie said, "How cool is that!"

"Yes, my young friend. Let us go inside and you will see just how *cool* it all is," Mr. Zimmerman added.

We continued to a second set of doors to the interior. I opened one side using a dark, wrought-iron handle. Some ironsmith must have made it on his forge back when this place was first built, but it looked like it had been made yesterday.

Mr. Zimmerman turned to us after we walked inside. "I can't recall if I asked. Have either of you been here before?"

"I have once, but Beanie never has," I answered.

He smiled. "Well then, let me give your friend the ten-cent tour."

"Far out, Mr. Z," Beanie said.

He laughed. "You *jugendlicher* and your language." He walked us to the right of a huge chimney in the middle of the room. "Everything you see was beautifully crafted by master artisans of their trades—from the handmade seating, all the way up to the intricate lighting overhead." He pointed to a light fixture above us.

I looked up to see a light fixture with what looked like hand-blown glass set in a wrought-iron frame. If these artists put this much effort into crafting such beautiful light fixtures and furniture, it made me wonder just how amazing the clock must be.

He continued his tour. "Note that at this level, the interior walls are also made of stone, but using a darker granite. See how they round up to archways at points all throughout the main level? This occurs where hallways and alcoves are located."

"What's with the big fireplaces, Mr. Z?" Beanie asked.

In the center of the room sat a grand six-sided stone structure of the same dark granite as the walls and archways.

"Ah. The centerpiece of the lodge and, other than the longcase, its most magnificent feature." He walked us around the chimney. "See how it has six sides, with three fireplaces? It is quite the magnificent structure, as it extends right through this ceiling and all the way to the roof of the lodge. Which, you will see when we reach the next level."

Beanie and I walked around it to see the three fireplaces. None had a fire going, what with this being summer and all. But it must be something to see when they did have a roaring fire.

Rocking chairs, uniquely designed with steel frames, sat in rows in front of the fireplaces. They had dark wooden slats for backs, and crosshatched white leather strips to make the seats.

Beanie did a full one-eighty and said, "Wow. This is amazing."

I laughed. "I know, right?"

Maybe I'd only been here once before, but this area sure stood out in my memory. How could it not, when it felt like you had just walked into a different world?

Mr. Zimmerman pulled us from our thoughts. "Over this way. We must inform them we are here."

He nodded to a hallway ahead, then walked under one of the stone arches and up to a counter built into an alcove area along the hallway. It looked like this was where people checked into their rooms.

"Ah, Gunther, what a pleasure to see you again," a man behind the counter said.

Beanie and I gave each other quick glances. He whispered to me, "Gunther?" We both tried to keep from chuckling. I think it was kind of like where in school when you learn your teacher has a first name. You really never think of them as being real humans, so it kind of throws you off.

"Hello, Carl. How are Nadine and the *kinder*?"

"Doing great. In fact, Nadine asked that the next time I see you, I am to thank you for the wonderful table clock you sent over for her birthday."

"It was my pleasure." Mr. Zimmerman motioned to me and Beanie. "I have brought two apprentices with me. They came by the shop a while ago, very interested in timepieces. Perhaps bored with their summer away from school, and with the hope to quench their thirst for knowledge."

Beanie and I tried to look as intelligent as we could. I'm not sure how well we pulled it off.

Mr. Zimmerman continued, "What better place to take them than here and your Timberline longcase. I will have them assist me while working on the clock. With your approval, of course."

"Perfectly fine with me." He looked at us. "You can learn a lot from Gunther. He is an expert in his field. We are lucky to have him keep our precious timepiece in order."

He took a key from a drawer and handed it to Mr. Zimmerman. It looked like the key we had, but bigger. Mr. Zimmerman thanked Carl and directed us to a stairway across from the counter. The steps, railings, and stairwell walls were made of beautifully crafted wood. We headed up the stairs. Large knobs on the post tops were carved into animals like beavers and pelicans. We went up, turning once on a small landing, until we came to another landing and a hallway.

The stairs continued up, but we stopped here. I stepped over and peeked through one of the small panel windows set into double doors on my right. It showed a long hallway lined with doors on either side. A couple walked toward me with luggage in tow. These must be the guest rooms on this level.

Mr. Zimmerman noticed I had stopped. He tapped me on the shoulder. "This way, *mein Freund*," he said, and nodded toward the main room.

We walked into it.

"Wow," Beanie said, on seeing the room.

The whole space was wide open and centered around the same six-sided stone chimney as below. Mr. Zimmerman had been right when he said it rose right through the floor and continued all the way to the ceiling. What he didn't say, however, was that the ceiling happened to be two stories above us.

Seating areas around the chimney divided the space into comfortable little sections, but nothing rose higher than waist height in order to keep the open feel.

Beanie wandered into one of the areas in front of a fireplace. "You know, if I ever did learn how to ski, this would be a great place to sit and read a book while my broken leg healed."

"That's about as true a statement as I have ever heard," I told him.

Mr. Zimmerman had been very patient to let us take it all in, but now motioned us to follow him. "This way, *Jungen*."

He led us along a perimeter walkway that ringed the entire room. Paintings of Northwest scenes covered every wall. Little alcoves appeared once in a while along our path, filled with a few comfortable chairs, a table, and a lamp. A mountain lion carved into a long panel of wood had been set into an area just above the main entry into the room.

Beanie kept spinning around as we walked, trying to take everything in. I found myself doing the same, even though I had been here once before. Above us, there was a third floor, but only around the perimeter, so the center remained open. A wooden railing ran around it. I could tell there were tables and chairs up there, and a bar to one end. Maybe that was where all the drinking took place. The clinking of glasses seemed to confirm it.

When we first came up, I saw a sign with an arrow pointing up, indicating a place called the Ram's Head Bar. That must be what was above us. I think there were guest rooms on that level also. From outside, I had seen two more rows of windows above this one.

We continued around the circular walkway and past the Cascade restaurant where I had eaten lunch with my parents. Once past the restaurant, the outer walls on this side of the lodge were lined with sets of paneled windows overlooking the mountain. We were now at ground level, just like Mr. Zimmerman had said, due to the lodge being built into the side of the mountain.

One big section of paneled windows showed a perfectly framed view of Mount Hood. Adirondack chairs, lined up in two rows, faced the mountain. A few older people sat in them enjoying the view.

The lodge was built right at the timberline, where trees couldn't live above this level on the mountain. Thus, the name Timberline Lodge. A few of these trees framed the mountain from this vantage point. I could see why the people were sitting there. The mountain, even bare as it was, filled me with chills. To have something so magnificent, so close—as if I could simply reach out and scoop a handful of volcanic soil from its side.

I looked over to see Mr. Zimmerman farther along the walkway, standing in front of a railing. I hurried to catch up, then slowed as I came nearer, stopping at Mr. Zimmerman's side.

I remembered the close-up picture of the longcase clock in the book. What it didn't show was the top and bottom of the clock, or where it stood.

Beanie said, "Are you seeing what I'm seeing?"

"Yes, and I can't believe it," I answered.

Moments ago, I had thought the view of Mount Hood to be amazing. And it was. But now that I could take in the entire clock from top to bottom, I was blown away. What stood before me fell under one, unbelievable observation. How had a tree grown into the side of Timberline Lodge and ended up as a clock?

Langley

CIA HQ, 1967

Bull

Bull Patton paced the strip of carpet between his desk and the fourth-floor view from the windows of his CIA office at Langley. He expected a call from Miller, and the arranged time had already passed.

Bull studied the Potomac River and the little island in the middle of it that he had come to appreciate like an old friend. He was glad he had stayed. Maybe this view was one of the reasons.

Those at the top had offered him a promotion and position of higher regard after he recovered the alien material taken by Roger Simpson from the Roswell crash. Thus, tying up the last loose end that could have exposed the cover-up and destroyed the government's reputation.

The promotion was what he had wanted all along and yet, when the offer came, he turned it down. He would lose hold of his little corner of the world, his black ops connections, and his sense of separation from the rest of the Central Intelligence Agency. Maybe even his purpose.

Besides, he liked his view. And new developments with the Simpson girl just confirmed he had made the right decision. This gadget called the Orb had put everything back into motion. He wanted that device and the technology it could deliver.

Depending on what it was and what it did, it could bring him the type of power even the topmost position at the CIA could never achieve.

The phone rang and broke his train of thought.

He picked up the receiver and answered as he continued to look out on his special little island. "Yes?"

"Sir, I have Agent Miller on the line."

"Put him through."

The line clicked. "Director Patton, Miller here. I've just checked into a hotel in Plouharnel, west of Carnac. I thought it best to stay in a different town. Carnac is small and I didn't want to run into Melanie Simpson unexpectedly."

"Are you sure she will make it there?"

"Yes. It didn't work out to give her and her friend a lift as we had offered. Her grandmother put a halt to that opportunity. Too bad. It would have been the perfect scenario to find out what they are up to. Now they are getting a ride from a young man named Eddy. Something her grandmother apparently arranged. Nadia found this out. She's still in England keeping tabs on the situation there. We needed to split up. She will track them as they travel to Carnac."

"Why did you need to split up? Wouldn't it have been better for both of you to follow them?"

"It was mostly a safety precaution. It's possible Melanie may have recognized me from the fiasco that happened at Pike Place Market a few weeks back. I was sure it had been too dark and too far away for her to get a good look at me. But during breakfast at Brightwood Manor, it appeared otherwise. I don't think she's put it together yet, or she would have immediately turned down our offer of a ride. I'm hoping she never will."

"Now, what?" Bull asked. He felt frustrated with the slow progress.

"Wait for her to arrive and keep tabs. If it works out, we might try to bump into them as tourists taking their advice. Maybe we can find out why she's coming here."

Bull walked over and dropped into his chair, sitting upright and rigid at his desk. He pulled on the phone cord, stretching the curls out of it until the cord was nearly straight. "Do you feel the Orb is hidden somewhere in town, or amongst the Stones?"

"No idea. But that's what this is all about, isn't it? To find out one way or another."

"Keep me informed. We need to keep this moving. I don't want any other interested parties to get wind of it."

"I understand."

"Look," Bull said, his frustration mounting. "Roberts is also working a lead. The two boys have some sort of key. It could be to a location where the Orb is hidden. Roberts will stay on top of things there. Between the two of you, we should be able to find this Orb. It's important we do this quickly and get it before someone else does. I want regular check-ins from you. Do you hear me?"

"Yes, Sir. We're doing everything we can."

"Not everything you can, or we would have the Orb!" Bull stretched the cord even tighter. "We need that device, *now*. Whatever it takes."

He slammed the receiver down in its cradle before Miller could reply. He didn't like how long this was taking.

The phone cord snapped back into place. A few curls jumbled around each other—out of sorts—just like the man who had slammed down the receiver.

Eddy

Isle of Wight, 1967

Mel

We watched out the living room window overlooking the driveway, waiting for Eddy to arrive. I sat on the edge of my chair because a deep sense of apprehension wouldn't allow me to do otherwise. I think Katch felt the same way, based on how she sat. We were about to go to France with a guy we had never even met. Hmmm…maybe apprehension was too light of a word. But if this was the only way to get to the Stones, then so be it.

Last night, Emilee had made us repack our things twice after seeing what we originally planned to bring. "As I had said, you will only be there for a few days. You shan't need all of that."

Finally, after a second shot at it, she told me to pack what I could fit in my backpack. That would be good enough. Katch didn't have a backpack, so Emilee dug up a rucksack to lend her.

Now the packs sat at our feet as the sound of gravel crunched outside.

Emilee stood. "That would be Eddy."

Katch and I stepped over to the window a bit faster than we meant to. We both wanted a look at him before we had to face him directly. A small four-door, slate-blue sedan with a white top pulled up to the front door and stopped.

We heard a chuckle from behind us. "Come on, ladies. He won't bite." She walked into the hall and out the front door.

We watched as Emilee approached the car and Eddy got out. Katch and I shot looks at each other.

He was tall and manly looking, and strikingly hand-some in that very British sort of way. Polished and proper. Dark sport coat, khaki pants, white shirt, and blue tie. Some sort of emblem on the jacket pocket.

Emilee walked over and gave him a hug. A wide smile took to his face. His hair feathered in a slight breeze—thick and rich and blond. He looked tanned, which was a hard thing to manage in England.

"Oh, my God," Katch said. "He's really good-looking."

"Yes, he is. But we have boyfriends. You remember, right? That corny guy you talked to a couple of days ago." She looked at me. "His name is Beanie. Remember him?"

She frowned. "Yes, I remember him. But it still doesn't keep me from thinking about how much of a hunk this Eddy is."

"A much older hunk. And one with a fiancée. The one Emilee told us about when we were packing."

"Yeah, yeah. I know."

Emilee pointed to our window. We both jumped back, all of a sudden feeling like Peeping Toms.

"We should go outside," I told her.

223

She nodded and giggled at the same time. "Okay."

I grabbed her. "Try not to stumble all over yourself. We don't want him to see us as foolish schoolgirls."

"But, Mel. Look at him. Can you believe we're going to spend the next few days right up close to him, breathing the same air?"

I tugged on her arm to get her to move. We both picked up our bags and headed for the door. I stopped just before going through it. "Don't forget. We have boyfriends."

We walked outside. He looked even better up close.

Emilee introduced me. "Eddy, this is my granddaughter, Melanie."

He took a few steps toward me. "Brilliant," he said, flashing a big smile. "A pleasure to meet you."

I shook his hand and couldn't help but feel a jolt of electricity race up my arm. I tried to ignore it.

Emilee turned to Katch, "And this is her good friend, Kachina."

He shook Katch's hand and I caught the corner of her eyebrow raise, no doubt feeling that same electricity I had.

He looked me up and down, and then said, "Interesting trainers you have there."

I looked down at my high-top Converse sneakers. Not exactly typical British footwear. I don't think either what Katch or I wore impressed him. In addition to my high-tops, I wore a sleeveless t-shirt and some jeans. Katch sported her usual hippy outfit, inclusive of leather sandals and a headband.

Eddy looked at Katch. "What have you got there?" He nodded to the pouch Katch wore on a strap over her shoulder. It might have looked like a normal purse, except that it was made in the traditional Hopi manner with brushed leather, beads, and feathers. It had silver and turquoise accents, and a carved bone clasp inlaid in silver.

"A medicine pouch. I'm a Native American medicine woman. I don't go anywhere without it."

"Brilliant," Eddy said. "Then I'll know who to go to if I get a scrape or cut."

Katch and I looked at each other, equally deciding to ignore his comment, which was obviously based on his ignorance of the Native American peoples.

I took my backpack off.

"Here, let me assist you," Eddy said, taking it from me. "I'll place your bags in the boot."

He grabbed our packs and went to the back of the car.

Emilee shot us both a glance while he was behind the raised lid of the trunk, quickly reading the expressions on our faces. She leaned toward us and said, "Well, you two indeed look gobsmacked." She muffled a laugh and added, "I suppose I failed to mention what a good-looking chap he is. Perhaps a shortcoming on my part, based on your faces?"

"Oh, I suppose he is," I whispered, mostly in defense of how we really felt.

She gave us a serious look. "I trust him. I wouldn't send you with him if I had worries. And, he is very attached to his lovely fiancée. Plus, he knows the area and will be able to help you out when you get to the Carnac Stones."

I gave Emilee a hug. "I'm sure he will be fine. Thank you for doing this."

Katch also hugged Emilee.

She put her arms around our waists and walked us to the passenger side of the car. "Well, you best get on your way. You have a bit of a trip ahead of you, from here to Portsmouth and then across the channel. I've given Eddy your itinerary and made arrangements along the way for you."

I gave her a kiss on the cheek, and we got into the car.

We were halfway to the Fishbourne ferry landing before anyone spoke. I didn't know what to say. Apparently, neither did Eddy.

He seemed very aloof, almost in a cold-shoulder kind of way. It was hard to tell what he expected of us, or thought of us. I couldn't get a read on him at all, other than seeing he didn't plan on doing whatever he could to make us feel comfortable.

Katch sat in the back behind me. I'm sure she picked that side to keep a keen gaze on our driver. I glanced back at her once to see her fixated on him. Yes, he was a hunk, but not *that* big of a hunk.

Eddy finally cut into the silence. "Your grandmother has amazing intuition, and twice as much influence as you might expect, whatever that expectation may have been. She can pull strings, whereas for anyone else, they would simply be non-existent threads."

"What do you mean?" I asked.

"She has everything all put together. Tied up in a nice bow."

"Huh?"

He glanced at me before he returned his eyes to the road. "This trip. All planned out. Staying at places that have probably been booked up for months." He turned to me and gave me a smile that could melt chocolate. "As I said, she has her ways."

Katch finally found her voice. "What do you mean, exactly? How is it all tied into a nice bow?"

"Oh. Well, we have special access to the ferries. They always have a VIP entry set aside for those of stature. Most others wait, sometimes for hours. We will get right on." He winked at me. "Which is a good thing, because the trip from Portsmouth to the ferry port at Ouistreham, in France, is over eight hours. We will be tired, so of course, our accommodations there are already arranged. See what I mean?"

"I guess so." I had no way to judge.

"Then, once we get to Carnac, she has you set up at the famous Hotel le Tumulus. It sits right at the base of the Saint-Michel Tumulus—the largest, most famous, and oldest funerary architecture ever found.

"The owner of the hotel is the daughter of Zacharie Le Rouzic, a great archaeologist. He first excavated the tumulus in 1900. Not long after, he founded the hotel so that he, his colleagues, and noted others could be close to the tumulus during the excavation." He glanced over. "Did you know this tumulus is older than the Great Pyramids of Egypt?"

"No. Not a clue," I answered. I mean, how could I? I didn't even know what a tumulus was. And I wasn't about to ask.

"And the hotel is only about a kilometer from the Carnac Stones," he added.

"How do you know so much about all of this?" Katch asked. "Is that why you came here last summer?"

Eddy threw us a big grin. "I'm studying at Oxford for a Bachelor's Degree in Ancient Studies."

"Is that like archeology?" I asked.

He frowned and shot me a totally unexpected look. Like I was a dumb girl. No, more like I was the dumb girl he expected me to be.

"Don't be daft. Ancient Studies is a classic liberal arts degree. Very prestigious. It incorporates the study of ancient civilizations, religion, language, and literature." He gave me a quick glance and raised his eyebrows to show I should be impressed, then turned his eyes back to the road. "In addition, we study philosophy, art history, military history, architectural history, religious texts, and law as it relates to the Studies. And ... yes, archeology."

Silence drifted through the car, smothering us with his pretentiousness.

I glanced over at him, trying not to catch an indignant eye.

He kept his focus on the road as he spat out, "Ancient Studies is so much more than *just* archeology."

I could feel Katch tighten in the back seat, even though I couldn't see her. Just as I felt myself tighten up. I think Eddy's other side, the one I worried about, had just exposed itself.

Hotel le Tumulus

Carnac, France, Mid-August, 1967

Mel

The English Channel decided to be pretty rough, so the ferry trip across was grueling and the longest eight hours I had ever spent. It also made me realize I didn't exactly have sea legs, or maybe I should say sea stomach. I wasn't about to hurl over the railing like I'd seen people do in the movies, so had to race to the bathroom a couple of times. It was the same for Katch. But we suffered through it.

Eddy just laughed at us. At least he did until he got bored, and then disappeared for the remainder of the ferry ride.

Our stomachs finally settled down enough so we could make it to the front of the ferry. We studied the coastline of France as the ferry came closer to shore. Someone speaking in English said that this whole area of coastline was where D-Day took place. It made me think that if this had been the weather on D-Day, they would have called it off and we might all be speaking German right now.

It was very late by the time we reached the Ouistreham Ferry Port and finished going through customs. The ferry ride had drained us. All we could manage to do was crash on our beds as soon as we got to our hotel room.

We slept late the next day, got a quick bite to eat, and then had another five-hour trip with Eddy to Carnac. Neither his mood nor his attitude had changed. Eddy turned out to be all we had hoped he wouldn't be—a logo-encrusted sports coat stuffed full of arrogance, and about as enchanting as a massive zit on the tip of your nose.

I was thinking this drive with Eddy had become almost as grueling as the ferry ride, when suddenly off to my left I saw lines of stones.

"Katch, look!" I pointed out the window.

"Wow. Are those the Carnac Stones?" Katch asked.

Eddy nodded, indifference in his tone as he said, "The few stones on your right are the tail end of *Le Menec* East. The ones on your left are called the *Alignement de Toulchignan*."

They reminded me of oversize gravestones lined up in a cemetery. "I thought they would be bigger," I said.

Eddy didn't answer right away. I wondered if what I said had offended him. Then I realized that anything I said seemed to offend him.

His manner turned a bit defensive. "The Stones tend to get smaller toward the end of the alignment, such as here. Much smaller than in *Le Menec* West. We'll see them tomorrow."

Before I could even take it in, we had passed the stones and they were gone. But I had seen enough to know I finally made it here—to the Stones of Carnac.

A little while later Eddy turned onto a small country road and took a left at a sign for the hotel. He drove up a sloping hill. Ancient rock walls ran along both sides of the road, which was now gravel.

Hotel le Tumulus appeared up ahead, with its steepled tower rising into the air. To the right of the steeple, three gables with windows overlooked the valley below. The white paint of the hotel stood out in the rich hues of the lowering sun. The hotel looked magnificent, and displayed every bit of charm that could possibly be found in a classy French country resort. I didn't expect this at all.

Eddy pulled up to the side entrance. The car had hardly stopped before he jumped out, raced around it, and opened our doors. For about two seconds I was impressed by his gallantry, and then he spoke. "Out with you two birds."

I glanced over my shoulder to Katch in the back seat, making eye contact. She gave me a shrug. Neither one of us could quite figure out what was happening. We got out. Eddy ran to the back, grabbed our bags from the trunk, and dropped them on the driveway at our feet.

He pointed toward some steps leading up to a door. "There you go. That's the lobby entrance to Hotel le Tumulus. Just as promised." He jumped back into his car.

I leaned down to his open window. "Where are you going?"

"Emilee only arranged accommodations for the two of you. She knew I planned to stay with a chum. I'm headed there now so we can hit a pub and take in a few long-awaited pints. Cheerio."

With that, he drove off, obviously happy to dump us. I jumped out of the way to keep from being hit by flying gravel.

We walked through the hotel doors, up to the front desk, and smack-dab into our first experience with a foreign language. Although, when I think about it, our American-ized English was the foreign language here in France.

I found communicating with the staff to be a little tough going. If they knew any English at all, they didn't let on to it.

We eventually made our intentions known, mostly through pantomime, which I am sure looked ridiculous. We got more than a few curious looks from the staff, who seemed to have come out of the woodwork to gather around and watch these two American girls gesticulate all over the place while trying to make themselves understood. There seemed to be a lot of conversation between the staff during this whole process, with a few snickers mixed in as well. All in French, of course, so I couldn't understand a word of it.

It wasn't until I mentioned my grandmother that they let on they understood. "Ah, *oui, Mademoiselle* Harris."

The woman behind the desk had me sign a guest book. All the while, she gave Katch and me odd looks as if she were trying to figure out who we were. Especially when she read my last name as Simpson, so wouldn't have a clue that Emilee was my grandmother.

A young boy, who had been lurking in a corner, was summoned over and given instructions. He led us up a flight of stairs to our room on the top floor. He opened the door and handed me the key.

I looked at Katch. "I don't have any francs to tip him."

"Just give him a dollar. I'm sure that will do."

I dug into my bag and pulled out some bills. I took a dollar and handed it to him.

He stared at it for a moment, turning it in his hands to look at both sides. I don't think he had ever seen one before.

He said, "*Merci*, very cool!" then turned and walked down the hall, still staring at the dollar bill.

I looked at Katch. "I thought none of them could speak English."

She laughed.

We turned our attention to the room. It wasn't just a room though, it was a suite, with three gabled windows very much like the ones we had seen while coming to the hotel. But these were on the other side and facing the Saint Michel Tumulus.

I looked out the nearest window. Saint Michel's Church sat above us on top of the tumulus, cast in the golden hues of the sunset. It was as if the sun had lingered on the horizon just long enough so we could appreciate this beauty. In that light the church looked so close I felt like I could reach out and touch it.

I pointed it out to Katch. "Now we know what a tumulus looks like."

She glanced out the window, apparently not as impressed. "What? A big hill with a church on top?"

"I guess. But it is kind of cool looking, don't you think?"

She shrugged and threw her bag onto the bed. I think she was still upset about how Eddy had treated us.

I turned to take in the room again and had no doubt this must be the best suite in the place. I now understood the looks we got from the staff. At least Eddy was right about one thing, Emilee *had* pulled some magic to get this suite for us on such short notice. It was right in the busiest part of the summer, when a place like this should have been booked for months.

The staff must have thought some sort of huge celebrity was coming. Then we showed up. A girl in a sleeveless tee shirt and high-top Converse sneakers. And a friend wearing hip-hugger bell-bottom pants, a leather pouch strung over her shoulder, feather earrings, and a Hopi headband. No wonder it took a while for them to figure us out. I'm sure we were a big disappointment.

The suite was huge, with a giant, king-size bed, a fluffy, white comforter, and six very plush-looking pillows. At the far end of the suite, a recessed area led to what looked like a private bath. I was glad to see it because the hotel in Ouistreham didn't have one, so we had to use a common bathroom. Not a fun thing.

A couple of overstuffed chairs and a small, round table were grouped under the center window. A cellophane-wrapped basket sat on the table with a card attached. It drew me over.

"Hey, Katch, check this out."

She came and stood by me. "A gift basket? Who would send us a gift basket?"

I laughed. "I'm sure it's from Eddy. He is such the perfect gentleman, just as Emilee said he would be."

Katch chuckled, then went serious. "Maybe we should figure out how to get a hold of his fiancée. You know, warn her?"

I thought about it. "Naw. She probably deserves him."

"I still feel sorry for her, though."

I looked at Katch and shrugged. "Too bad." I refocused on the basket. "It looks like it's stuffed with food."

"Good, because I'm starving. I wondered how we would get some food. We never thought to exchange our dollars for francs when we arrived at the port."

"Even if we did have francs, and went down to the restaurant, we wouldn't be able to read the menu or know what to order," I added.

We were both absolutely ravenous. Eddy had refused to stop along the way to eat, or even buy some snacks. We did stop once at a petrol station for gas and a bathroom break, but they didn't have any food. I think Eddy was dead set on getting rid of us, though we didn't know it at the time.

We each sat in a chair and stared at the basket.

My stomach figured out what was in front of us and rumbled.

Katch heard it. "Well, read the card. See what it says."

I took the card, opened it, and read to Katch:

> *"Melanie and Kachina,*
> *I thought you might be famished from your adventures.*
> *With my compliments,*
> *Emilee"*

"That is so Emilee," Katch said.

We unwrapped the basket as delicately as two starving teenage girls could manage, which meant we pretty much ripped it apart. It looked like Emilee had bought out an entire store. We found a treasure trove of French food arranged in artful layers on a bed of straw: Lu Tuc crackers; a small baguette; Maille mustard; cheeses like Brie, Emmental, Roquefort, and Port Salut; foie gras spread; pork pate; Saucisson sec salami; smoked salmon; Tapenade spread; apples and pears; small little drinks of some kind; and a bounty of treats like La Maison du Chocolat, mini-madeleines, butter cookies, truffles, fruit-flavored hard candies, and an Eiffel Tower tin filled with milk chocolate pralines.

We were so in heaven.

I woke up to morning light as it filtered into our room. I got up and walked over to the window, noticing along the way the carnage the gift basket had become. We really did a number on it last night.

I looked out the window at the Tumulus Saint Michel. There was an entrance at the base of the hillside I hadn't noticed before. A walkway became lined by stone walls as it went deeper into the hillside. It ended at a door right where it would go underground. I tried to remember what Eddy told us about the tumulus. Something about it being older than the Egyptian Pyramids. And about funerals.

Did they bury people there a long time ago? I wasn't sure how I felt about sleeping next to a bunch of bones.

The sky was clear, with only a few puffy clouds in the distance. A perfect day for our tour of the Stones. Eddy told us to be ready to leave around ten this morning. That was before he left us the way he did. I wondered if he would keep his word, but I also knew it wouldn't stop us from exploring on our own if he didn't.

I looked at Katch, still buried under the down comforter. She had pillows tucked around her head to block the morning light. A few strands of her hair peeked out from between the pillows to lay over one like thin wisps of shiny darkness.

A knock came at the door. *"Petit déjeuner en une demiheure."*

I opened it a crack to see a woman walking away.

"Excuse me," I called.

She turned. *"Petit-déjeuner,"* then smiled and said in a heavy French accent, "Breakfast…in one-half hour."

That's when I figured out most of the staff could probably speak English pretty well, but maybe just refused to use it. I suppose they thought we should speak their language since we're in their country. I get that. But they sure seemed to be set on making it hard for those of us who didn't speak French.

"Katch, breakfast is in a half-hour. We miss it and who knows when we'll be able to eat again."

Katch threw the pillows from her head and sat up. "What?" She looked like the waking dead. "You're kidding, right? How am I supposed to get ready in half an hour?"

I laughed. "Use some of that Hopi medicine magic of yours."

She fell back onto the bed and moaned. "I may need to."

• • •

Eddy was already ten minutes late.

"Think he will come?" Katch asked.

"Doesn't matter. We're still going to the Stones one way or another."

We waited on the hotel porch in front of the restaurant in a couple of lounge chairs. Our perch overlooked the valley and the driveway. Breakfast had been every bit as good as the gourmet items we enjoyed the night before. It was worth getting ready so quickly. The French really did know how to make food an art form, in both look and taste.

I couldn't believe we were finally here in Carnac. So close to the Stones. I exchanged some dollars for francs at the front desk. Then I bought a tourist map of the Carnac Stones they had in the lobby.

We spent our time waiting for Eddy by studying the map and trying to interpret the French descriptions. We did our best to convert meters and kilometers to feet and miles. We finally gave up. But I remembered Eddy said the Stones were only about a kilometer from the hotel. Katch and I tried to remember from school whether that was more or less than a mile. We finally gave up, but knew the Stones were close. We could walk there easily enough if we had to.

We also could see the map had a fair number of dolmens marked on it. That made me wonder which one my dad was at in the film we saw of him holding the Orb. I had no idea there were so many. I was pretty sure I would know it when I saw it. Or, at least I hoped I would.

A car turned onto the gravel driveway. I sat up to take a better look and recognized it immediately.

"A 1966 Ford Cortina," I told Katch.

She looked down the driveway and laughed. "An MK-1."

"Slate-blue—"

"With a porcelain-white top," she finished.

"In excellent condition, and barely worked in," I added.

"Practically new. Only twelve-thousand kilometers on the odometer."

We both laughed. We had heard this a dozen times on the trip.

Eddy had arrived.

Bad Dreams

Lubbock, 1947

Gloria

Roger slept the rest of the evening and all through the night.

And through the phone calls.

They started in the late evening just after I had gone to bed. The first time I answered, the caller, a man, said, "Your husband took something of ours. Tell him to turn it over to us, or he will die." And then hung up. The call racked me with terror. Not just the words, but the deep-set threat in the voice that said them. What did he mean? What could Roger have of theirs? I hoped with all my heart it was a prank call.

But the next one came a half hour later, and they continued every half hour after that. I think the calls were planned to come just as I fell back asleep. Someone seemed to know how to do this as a way to intimidate and terrorize. And in each call, the voice became more ominous and the threats more alarming.

I prayed the calls would stop, but they didn't. I wanted to disconnect the cord from the wall, but it was wired in.

And then I thought, what if I need to use the phone to call out? What if someone tries to break in? I would need the phone to call the police.

I took the phone off the hook and laid it on the table. At first, just a dial tone sounded through the receiver. But soon it switched to a loud, pulsating, high-pitched noise. The phone sat on a nightstand next to the bed and I didn't want it to wake Roger. I didn't want him to know what was happening. It would upset him, and he needed his rest.

The wall cord had enough length that I was able to move the phone over to a small table along the bedroom wall with a reading chair next to it. I tried taking the receiver off there, hoping it would be far enough away that it wouldn't bother him. It only took a few minutes of that high-pitched noise to know it wouldn't work.

I decided to sit in the reading chair, wait for the calls, and answer as soon as it rang so it wouldn't wake Roger. The threats worsened. I couldn't stand it any longer. I tried to hang up as soon as I picked up the receiver, but the phone would ring again only moments after I placed it back in the cradle. So, I had to answer, if for no other reason than to get a short breather between the calls.

That is how it went all night. The caller said terrible things, and threatened us. I thought back to the restaurant when I had compared the kids to Pavlov's Dog. Now I was the one anticipating the ring of the phone, with a deep-set terror hitting me each time it did.

Then, a few hours before dawn the calls changed. There was one more call where the man spoke. "If you don't care about your husband, then maybe you should worry about your baby."

I dropped the receiver and it tumbled to the floor as I ran to the living room and threw myself onto the couch. I put my arms around my swollen belly, feeling the baby inside. Feeling the threat inside with it. A dull ache built within me as I cried in deep, winded sobs. I buried my face in a pillow to stifle the sound.

But the phone started its high-pitched, pulsating noise again. I ran to the bedroom and hung it up so it wouldn't wake Roger. I wiped the tears from my face and took up my watch on the phone again. I had to.

That was the last thing the man said to me. After that, every time the phone rang, the line would be silent. I could tell the man was there, breathing heavily. A scary, ominous kind of breathing. Like in some sort of horror movie.

Between calls, I constantly peeked through the drapes to make sure no one was standing outside the window. I had to check, each time worried I would see the silhouette of a man, or a glint of moonlight reflecting the sharp edge of a knife blade.

One time I shouted into the phone, "Stop this. Please stop this!" But Roger woke to my voice. I raced over to him and said it was all right. Everything was okay. I stroked his head until he fell back asleep. My eyes drooped from exhaustion, but I kept my vigil in the reading chair, hoping the calls would stop.

And they finally did. Just as a hint of sunrise showed on the horizon. I fell into a fitful sleep and a crazy dream where small beings stood over me as I lay on a table. They seemed inquisitive with their large, dark eyes. Maybe they were trying to calm me. I got the distinct feeling they were worried about the baby.

Then a tall, beautiful woman with platinum hair and stunning blue eyes stood among them. She smiled at me and reached out to touch my bare abdomen. A sensation of warmth flowed through my body, and a sudden sense of calm overtook me.

I awoke when a sunbeam filtered through the window and landed on my face. I shifted a little to get the light out of my eyes and tried to remember my dream. But, like so many before, it remained elusive. Only the sense of it still lingered.

And then I remembered last night and the terrible phone calls. I sat up quickly and looked around the room, half expecting someone to be standing there, watching us. The horror of what happened filled me again. I jumped from the chair and checked all the windows to make sure they were latched. I ran to the front door to make sure the deadbolt was set and the doorknob locked. I wanted to put a chair against the doorknob, but worried that if Roger saw it, he would ask me why it was there. I didn't want him to know about the phone calls. Not right now, when he needed to get healthy again.

I leaned against the door. My stomach started to hurt, so I wrapped my arms around it and the baby inside, as if to protect it from whatever might be out there. Then my abdomen cramped up and I doubled over in pain.

The baby! Please don't let something be wrong with the baby. I made my way to the couch and fell onto it. The terror of those calls, that voice, and the threats consumed me all over again. I couldn't let that happen. I needed to calm myself, so I tried taking in slow, deep breaths. Eventually, the cramping stopped and I fell asleep. I don't know for how long.

I got up and went to check on Roger. He seemed to be sleeping peacefully, but his knees were still red and swollen. One of them was worse than the other. I pressed against the top of the kneecap and my finger sank into it, where normally it should hit solid bone. Liquid of some form filled the whole area. I let Roger sleep some more, not wanting to wake him. I laid cold, damp cloths across his knees, and refreshed them every ten minutes or so.

I called Sal to let him know I wouldn't be coming in to work for a few days. He understood and said not to worry about it. God bless him.

Roger finally woke in the late morning. His color had come back. He wanted to get out of bed, but couldn't do it on his own. I grabbed a cane Mrs. Delbert had brought down for him to use. She had it from spraining her knee some time ago.

With the cane's help, I was able to get Roger to the living room where he sat on the couch. I took some ice from the freezer and wrapped it in a couple of towels. Then I grabbed two Ace bandages from his first aid kit and used them to wrap the ice around his knees.

He put his hand on mine as I finished wrapping his second knee. "Thanks. That feels much better."

I patted his hand and said in a firm tone. "You need to eat. I doubt you had two bites of your burger yesterday, and who knows when you ate before that." I stood. "I'm going to make you breakfast so you can build up your strength." I put my hands on my hips to show my intent. "And then you are going to tell me everything."

He nodded, looking up at me from the couch. "How long have I been out? What happened to me?"

"You passed out at the Eat 'N Run yesterday. You've pretty much been out of it since then."

"What time is it?" he asked.

"Just after ten in the morning."

He looked like he suddenly realized something. He started to get up. "This is Tuesday? I'm supposed to be at work."

I shoved him back down. "Not to worry. I called Ken this morning and let him know you were injured on the expedition, and wouldn't be able to come in for a while. He said he was sorry to hear you are hurt and offers his prayers for a speedy recovery. He wants you to call when you are ready to go back."

"I guess I should have expected that of you."

"It's what I do." I leaned down and kissed him. The kiss produced a smile, which meant everything to me.

It didn't take long to whip up some eggs, bacon, and toast. I sat next to him on the couch while he ate. I didn't fix anything for myself. My stomach was too tied up in knots from what happened last night.

I had a thousand questions, but didn't want to interrupt him. He needed to eat. When he finished, I took the plate to the kitchen and then settled on the couch next to him again.

He told me about how something had got caught up in the storm, maybe struck by lightning, and then crashed into the desert not far from their camp.

"It was the strangest thing," he said. "Almost like I was drawn to the crash site. Like I had to be the first one there. Something inside me told me so. I still don't know why I felt that pull."

He shared how he had come across the crashed spaceship, alien bodies, and what happened when the military showed up. He told me how he had been treated, tortured, and humiliated.

I grabbed him and held him tightly while he told me this. I placed my head on his shoulder so he couldn't see the tears welling up in my eyes.

"But why would they do this to you? Did they torture everyone?"

Roger didn't answer right away. Maybe he needed to think about his answer. "Everyone was questioned. But they paid special attention to me because I organized the expedition, and had been the first one to the crash site."

Then a feeling of shock hit me when I remembered I had been the one to pick the site. I looked over to the kitchen table. I had sat right there when he was trying to figure out where to go, and pointed to an exact spot on his map showing him where to take his expedition. A spot not more than a mile from where the spaceship crashed.

Roger could feel my body stiffen. "Gloria, what's wrong?

I couldn't answer. I just shook my head. I mean, what could I tell him? That this was all my fault?

I tried to recall what made me do that. What would drive me to give him such advice? I remembered telling him that maybe I had learned it in school, or from someone at the Eat 'N Run. But those were just guesses. And now, with the spaceship crash, I had to wonder. Could this have something to do with the bad dreams I've had all my life?

Or with what my mother told me? Right here in this very room when I was seventeen years old? I always thought I had run away from her. That she was crazy, and I wanted no part of her. But a different thought rocketed through me now. What *had* I really been running from?

The answer hit me just as hard. It wasn't my mother I had run from, but what she told me—that we have been visited all our lives by beings from another world. And with that, came the realization, their visits hadn't stopped for me.

I sat back on the couch and shuddered with the thought I had hidden these feelings all my life. Blocked them out as soon as they tried to work their way forward. But now they had finally surfaced and taken solid form for the first time.

What Mother told me about the visitations must be tied to why I sent Roger there, and to why he was the first at the crash site. And the cause of his pain and suffering. I grabbed a pillow and held it against myself. If all this could be true, then it was my fault for what the military put him through—and for what we are facing now.

More Calls

Roger

By late afternoon my knees had improved, thanks to having a Florence Nightingale in the house. Now I could walk on my own with the help of the cane.

But over the hours that Gloria tended to me, I could see something building in her; a sort of tension that increasingly grabbed at her. Her usually relaxed smile grew tighter as the day progressed, pulling at her mouth, making her lips barely visible.

All I could think was something must have scared her. I didn't get it right away. She covered it pretty well early on, but she couldn't keep it up. It must have happened last night while I was so out of it.

She could see I knew something was wrong, so puttered around the kitchen doing busy work in order to avoid me. I finally called her over and motioned for her to sit by me on the couch.

I took her hand. "Gloria, did something happen last night? I can see it in your face. Something is scaring you to death. And I know it's more than what happened to me."

She just looked at me, shook her head, and wouldn't say a thing. Tears formed in her eyes. I took her into my arms and stroked her back, running my hand across it in a slow and reassuring motion. It was apparent she didn't want to tell me; maybe to protect me from what had happened.

I took my time. Baby steps. My persistence finally paid off.

She lay against my shoulder, her arms around my waist. She told me about the calls. "They were terrible. Threatening. To you, and to our baby."

"And to you, also." I pulled her in tighter, hoping it would help her feel a little safer. "I'm sorry I wasn't able to help."

She sat up. "I'm glad you slept through them. You needed to. You had gone through enough as it was." She took my wrist and pulled my sleeve up. "I saw the marks on your wrists, and what your knees look like. They tortured you!"

I took her hands and put on a formidable face. "That's over. I don't want you to worry about it."

She settled back against my shoulder and we sat there quietly for a moment, focused on the warmth of each other's bodies. I was glad we hadn't received any more calls today. Then, I had to wonder if they would start up again tonight. I hoped they wouldn't.

But they did, just after the sun went down. I told Gloria I would take care of it and not to answer the phone. The calls came more often than what Gloria said had happened last night. Sometimes only minutes apart. I answered them all, and every time a man said the same thing to me, "Turn over the material, Mr. Simpson, or your family will disappear." And my reply was always the same, "I don't know what you're talking about, so stop bothering us."

Gloria became visibly tense every time the phone rang. She couldn't stand it any longer. "Roger, why do they think we have something they want?"

I couldn't tell her about either the material or the device. It would be better for her own safety if she never knew such things existed. I hadn't even told her one of the aliens was alive, and we had communicated with each other. All I had told her was I came across a crashed spaceship and dead alien bodies.

"I don't know, honey. There's nothing here they want."

"How can I believe you? They tortured you. What, just for the fun of it? I don't think so. Are you hiding something from me?"

I needed to protect her. "Honey, please trust me on this. There is nothing here they would want."

Which was true, since right now I didn't have either the spaceship material or the device. Though, that fact would change on Saturday when I was due to meet with Tom. And then, with all of this happening, I wondered about going to Roswell for our rendezvous. How could I leave Gloria, even for a day? But I had to get the device back. If I didn't meet Tom at noon on Saturday, there would be no way to track him down. We only used first names, and I hadn't a clue as to where he lived.

Gloria said, "Roger, I'm so sorry. This is all my fault."

I looked at her in astonishment. "What? How can you take the blame for what has happened? You weren't even there."

She broke into tears. "But I'm the one who told you where to go. I pointed right to that spot on the map and convinced you to go there."

I hadn't thought of that. I still wondered why she had been so adamant about it. But there was no way she would know what would happen. It didn't make any sense, and I didn't want her to feel any guilt. This was my burden for what it's doing to our family.

"Gloria. That's the craziest thing I've heard. How could you have known what would happen? It was just a coincidence."

She opened her mouth to say something, but stopped. She settled back against me, trying to stay her sobs. I could only hope I had convinced her that she had nothing to do with this.

She finally said, "Roger, I'm scared."

"I know, honey. I know. We'll get through this."

The phone rang again. I picked it up. Same routine— they said something, and I said something. I wasn't going to let it get to me, but each time the phone rang I could tell it terrorized Gloria. She had been the one up all last night dealing with these calls.

I reached over to pull the phone cord from the wall, but Gloria stopped me. She said we might need it in case of an emergency. I wanted to do anything to make her feel safer right now, so I didn't yank the cord out. Still, I needed to make the calls stop.

I went to the bathroom, brought out a couple of thick towels, and wrapped the receiver in them. The pulsating tone became muffled enough that I could just barely hear it when in the bedroom, and not at all from the living room. Now, there would be no more phone calls.

The evening went on. We had dinner and tried to relax on the couch, listening to Les Brown and Doris Day on the radio. Neither of us could really settle down. Gloria kept getting up to check the windows and door, worried someone might be out there. My thoughts were on the calls. I was sure they were just threats, all in an attempt to get me to turn over the satchel. I couldn't imagine they would do more than threaten us. They certainly weren't going to make us disappear. But I worried about how this affected Gloria and the baby. She became even more tense as the evening wore on. The tendons in her neck now looked to be strung as tight as piano wire.

I reran the idea of turning over the material, but came up with the same answer every time. Even if I did, they would think I had held some of it back. They would never stop pursuing us. And there was no way I would give them the device. The alien had implanted a quest within me, through whatever process such advanced races were capable of. No matter how hard I might try, I wouldn't be able to go against the quest—even if it endangered my family. That thought burned right through me.

An advertisement came on for Chesterfield cigarettes. Gloria got up to check the windows once again. I jumped when she suddenly screamed and fell back from the window.

"Roger!"

I grabbed my cane and quickly hobbled over to her.

She trembled with fear and threw herself into my arms. "Someone's out there. He was right at the window, staring at me when I opened the curtain. The look in his eyes…" She sobbed into my chest and pulled me tighter. The bulge of the baby pressed between us.

Men in Black

Roger

I pulled the curtain back slightly and looked outside. Two men in dark suits stood at the door. I recognized them.

I held Gloria tighter, and tried to still her shaking.

"It's the two men from the Eat 'N Run," I said. "Everything will be all right. I'm sure they're from the government. They won't do anything to us. They can't. We're citizens and have rights. And they certainly won't do anything while Mrs. Delbert is upstairs."

One of them pounded at the door. "Mr. Simpson, let us in. We'd like to chat with you."

"Go away," I shouted through the door.

"Do you want us to break it down? Flint here would love that."

Gloria's eyes grew wide with fear.

"Go sit in the kitchen. I'll see what they want."

She grabbed me even tighter. "Roger. Please don't let them in."

"Honey, we don't have a choice." I knew it wasn't just a threat. They would break the door down if I didn't let them in.

I waited until she sat down at the kitchen table, and then opened the door to see the guy named Bull and his buddy standing there.

"Hello, gentlemen," I said. "It's a bit late for a social call. What can I do for you?"

The look on Bull's face showed he didn't take to my witticism. "Like I said, we need to chat." He pushed his way past me.

I tried to block him but he was too stocky and strong. Now I knew where he got his nickname. He barged through me like a bulldog. The other man followed, all six-foot-three of him. He tipped his hat to me as he stepped inside. "Thanks for the invite," he said, a curt little smile on his face.

Bull looked over to Gloria at the kitchen table. "Good evening, Mrs. Simpson. It is a pleasure to see you again."

Gloria stayed silent, which was good. I didn't want their attention directed at her.

"What do you want?" I asked.

Bull smiled. "Let's get the family together first and settle ourselves in."

He nodded to his man, who walked over to Gloria and motioned her toward the living room. "Mrs. Simpson, why don't you join Bull and your husband?"

She turned to me and I nodded. She got up, came over, and sat on the couch. Bull looked at me and pointed to a spot next to Gloria. I sat down.

"Now that the two of you are comfortable, let's get to the business at hand."

He walked over to the kitchen where his man had taken station in a chair at the kitchen table. Bull dragged over one of the chairs, and pushed the coffee table out of the way with his foot so he could set the chair in front of us. He turned it so the back faced us, and then straddled it.

He tossed his hat onto the couch next to me, then took off his jacket in a way to indicate this could be a long night and laid it over the back of the chair as if it were a hanger. A gun rested in a shoulder holster under his left arm. He brushed at the neckline of the jacket with the back of his hand as if to clean something from it, and then leaned his forearms across the top.

"This can go easy, or it can go hard. Your choice. You see, you have put your government in a terrible situation. We don't want the public to know about the crashed space-ship, or the aliens found with it. Just not a good idea. Panic could set in. Our national security would be put at risk. There could be rioting in the streets." He looked at Gloria. "I'm sure you wouldn't want such things to happen, would you, Mrs. Simpson?"

Gloria gave a slight shake of her head. I wondered if she was going into shock. Her trembling had stopped, and her look seemed blank and distant.

"Good. I'm glad you agree." He turned to me. "You don't want to disappoint your wife, now do you, Mr. Simpson? It might upset her, which wouldn't be good, considering her condition."

I jumped up from the couch. "Don't you even think that way. Get out of my house or I'll call the police."

He chuckled in response. "Go ahead."

I grabbed my cane, limped to the phone in the bedroom, and pulled it from the towels. The bedroom doorway gave me a view of Gloria and Bull. I hung up the receiver for a moment to reset it, and then put it to my ear, throwing Bull a defiant look. My finger sat poised to dial the first number, but I stopped. There wasn't a dial tone. I tapped on the cradle to reset it. Nothing.

Bull yawned and said, "See? That game can be played in two ways. You take the phone off the hook so we can't call in. Now, we disconnected the line so you can't call out. Tit for tat."

I hung up the phone and walked over to the stairwell. I went halfway up and called through the door at the top, "Mrs. Delbert, we need you to call Sheriff Wilks." No answer. "Mrs. Delbert?" She still didn't answer.

I struggled up the remaining steps to where I could shout right through the door. "Mrs. Delbert! Are you there?"

Her living room was right on the other side. It's where she spent most of her time. But still, no answer. I thought about looking for her, but I didn't want to leave Gloria with those two monsters.

Bull called to me from below. "She's not up there."

I limped back down the stairs.

Bull gave me a self-righteous look. "You see, Mrs. Delbert left about twenty minutes ago. Your Sheriff Wilks called her. Apparently, someone broke into her business and burglarized it. They did a very good job of vandalizing the place as well. It will take some time to board up the windows and clean up the mess. I doubt she will be back anytime soon. I'm sure she is wondering why someone would do such a thing. It's an insurance agency, after all. Not much cash, and certainly no valuables."

He motioned me toward the couch again. I sat next to Gloria, not sure what to do.

He nodded to his man. "Flint, let the Simpsons know we mean business."

Flint stood and flipped the kitchen table over, sending a centerpiece and a couple of plates crashing across the kitchen floor.

Gloria screamed.

Flint smiled at her, then picked up the chair he had been sitting in. He threw it against a row of cabinets where it smashed into pieces and knocked a cabinet door off its hinges. "That what you mean, boss?"

Bull nodded. "For starters." He turned to me; an impertinent look set on his face. "How bad will you let this get? Do you *really* think there is a limit to how far we will go to recover that satchel and the alien material?"

He looked at Flint again, who nodded and went to the bedroom. I heard things being tossed around and breaking.

I jumped up. "What are you doing?" I started for the bedroom.

Bull moved so fast I barely noticed. He jumped up and punched me hard in the stomach, right where I had been injured during the war. I dropped to my knees. The pain from landing on them rocketed through me. I couldn't catch my breath. The combination caused me to nearly pass out. I fell onto my side on the floor, wrapped my arms around myself, and moaned uncontrollably.

Gloria dropped down next to me. "Stop it. Stop it!" She leaned over me, holding me in her arms, coaxing me to breathe. I finally caught some air. Gloria helped me onto the couch. She brushed my hair from my face and held onto me as if our lives depended on it. And now I understood that maybe they did.

Bull grabbed the chair he had knocked over and set it upright. He turned it so he could sit in it the normal way. He plopped onto it, leaned against the back, and crossed his legs.

"We don't know whether you have the satchel here or not," he said. "My guess is probably not. But all the same, we're still going to tear your house apart stick by stick to search for it." He smiled. "And, if nothing else, it will be good therapy for Flint." He uncrossed his legs, leaned toward us, and whispered, "You see, Flint has aggression issues and needs to vent them every once in a while. Believe me, it's a good thing it's your furniture and not you." He sat back again.

Flint came out and grunted his approval. He walked to the kitchen again, where he threw open cabinets and tossed out their contents. Stemware splintered against the floor and canned goods flew across the room. He ripped open every box we had in the cabinets and shook out the contents everywhere.

Gloria jumped up and ran to the kitchen. She pulled at Flint and screamed at him to stop. He turned and backhanded her across the face. Gloria fell to the floor, crying out in pain.

I struggled to get up from the couch, but my knees wouldn't let me.

Bull shoved me back down. "Don't bother." He looked at me with a strange combination of sympathy and disgust. He walked over, helped Gloria to the couch, and dropped her next to me.

Flint continued through the house, overturning and destroying everything he touched.

Bull leaned down to me so close, I could feel his hot breath on my face. "This isn't going to stop, Simpson. Not until you turn over that material."

The Longcase

Timberline Lodge, 1967

Frankie

I couldn't believe it. A tree. An actual, freakin' tree!

"It is a beautiful thing, is it not?" Mr. Zimmerman said.

Beanie, who stood on his other side, said, "It's, like, the craziest thing I've ever seen, Mr. Z."

I turned to Mr. Zimmerman. My eyes must have been bulging.

He looked at me and laughed. "I thought you would be impressed."

We stood at the center of a low railing, which overlooked an alcove two and a half feet below our level. Two big posts marked the end of the railing with steps on either side to get access to the alcove.

I walked down the steps on the left. A table with seating sat tucked into a recessed area. I put the toolbox on the table and walked over to the clock. On the other side of the alcove, a door led outside to the area with the Adirondack chairs. The whole alcove had to be about eight feet deep and twenty-four feet wide, with about a fourteen-foot-high ceiling.

It had two big sets of paneled windows with views of the mountain. But between them stood the tree.

It looked as if it had grown right into the side of the lodge. It had to be nearly four feet wide and stuck out at least two feet from the wall. Four stubby, twisted branches splayed out at the top, reaching up so they seemed to penetrate the wooden ceiling above. The roots did the same at the base of the tree, where three thick toes clawed into the ground, grasping it like clamps, digging deep into the wood-paneled floor.

I walked over and stood in front of the tree, but it wasn't just a tree. It was also the longcase clock. The one from the book. The one with the hidden compartment.

A large, intricate clock face sat embedded just below the branches. Under it, a cabinet had been carved into the trunk, ending just above the thick roots. A beveled glass door enclosed the cabinet. Delicate gold leaf swirled from the four corners of the glass to frame the opening. Inside, a brass pendulum swung slowly back and forth.

Beanie came down the steps, followed by Mr. Zimmerman.

"But, how?" was all I could say.

Mr. Zimmerman said, "When the engineering team for the Timberline Lodge project decided this was the perfect place for the lodge, they found this twisted, dead tree standing on the site. As they laid out the foundation, they discovered the tree would be right where this portion of the exterior wall had been designed to go."

"Why didn't they just cut it down?" Beanie asked.

Mr. Zimmerman seemed to consider his answer. "The whole idea of the lodge was to have it fit in with the environment. You have seen this firsthand throughout the design of the lodge and its contents. For example, the use of natural and native materials." He walked over to the tree and patted its side. "This is a Western White Pine, common to the Cascades, but rarely found this far up a mountainside. Estimates put it at well over 300 years old when it died. And who knows how long it sat here after that. Certainly, long enough to have lost all of its outer bark, leaving the inner wood to weather and bleach in the sun."

He caressed the trunk with his hand. "They couldn't just destroy it. Not when it represented the very intent of the lodge, which was to blend in with its environment. So, they decided to incorporate it into their design instead."

"Why is it so short?" Beanie asked. "I mean, for a tree and all."

"An astute question," Mr. Zimmerman said. "Had it been taller, there may have been a different outcome. And it should have been taller, even in this harsh setting. By all appearances, the top looked to have been struck by lightning when the tree was still rather young. The lightning fractured its top and stunted its growth. So, it was never able to get taller, though the tree continued to grow in girth. See how the trunk and branches are twisted? We believe heavy snows and winds shaped it to be as we now see it. Note how the roots grab at the ground. It dug its toes deep into the loose volcanic soil to keep its hold through centuries of torment."

I studied the tree with wonder.

Mr. Zimmerman added, "They knew they could not cut it down. But then, as they looked closer, faint carvings could be seen on the trunk. These only truly came out while they delicately sanded and treated the wood."

I stepped closer. The whole tree wore a smooth, golden luster of polish, from the twisted branches above to the dug-in toes below. And sure enough, there were faint patterns of lines and dots on the trunk. Some lines were thicker than others, and the dots were of varying sizes.

"Once they saw these, they knew they must build the wall around the tree."

Beanie came over and stood next to me. He traced his finger along one of the lines that led to a dot, then continued to where it disappeared at the wall. I wondered if it continued on the outside.

"Who do they think made these carvings?" Beanie asked.

Mr. Zimmerman shook his head. "A specialist was brought in. At first, it was thought American Indians made them. But after much study, the carvings didn't appear to match any known carvings typical to the Indians of the area. So, we really have no idea."

Something about these lines and dots seemed familiar. "How did they end up making the tree into a clock?" I asked.

"Ah, another good question. That is where Otto Kieninger, the clockmaker, stepped in. He had been making smaller clocks for various locations throughout the lodge. But here he recognized a masterpiece in the waiting. It didn't take long to convince the architects he could work with the woodcarvers to hollow out the tree, and then turn it into a longcase clock as never seen before."

I stepped back as Mr. Zimmerman moved to the front of the clock. He turned to us, and took something out of his pocket. The key he had received from Carl at the front desk. "Shall we?" He turned to the clock, unlocked the glass case, and opened it.

The Hidden Compartment

Frankie

I stepped over next to him and peered inside. I tried to see where the hidden compartment could be, but nothing stood out. No little latches, or knobs, or even any seams. Just the solid insides of a tree, smoothly hollowed out … but with a bunch of clock parts, weights, and gears inside.

Mr. Zimmerman waited for a moment and then said, "Well-hidden, wouldn't you agree? I believe I had serviced this clock over two dozen times before I noticed one little flaw in the wood; a hole the size of a small pin. It took a strong light and a magnifying lens to see that it looked manmade." He took out a penlight and pointed to a spot. "See. Just here. By pushing a pin or the end of a paperclip into the hole, a small patch of wood flips up to divulge where a key is to be inserted. I, of course, lacked such a key, so have never opened the compartment."

He turned off the penlight, put it back in his pocket and said, "Otto was truly a genius."

I reached into my pocket and fingered the key. I didn't want Mr. Zimmerman to see what might be hidden in the compartment. How should I do this?

Mr. Zimmerman pulled over a stout wooden chair from a corner of the alcove. He smiled at me. "Easier than hauling a stepladder up here. One needs to stand on this to be able to reach the compartment."

He held onto the side of the trunk to steady himself as he stepped onto the chair, then turned to me. "Hand me the key and I will retrieve whatever is in the compartment for you."

I shook my head. "No deal, Mr. Zimmerman. I'm opening that compartment myself." I pulled the key out of my pocket and held it up. "You want this key like we agreed? You're only going to get it after I find out what's inside." I paused for effect. "If anything is even in there." I decided to put that sense of doubt in the air, just in case.

Mr. Zimmerman stood there for a moment, as if wondering what to do. Why was he so worried about me opening the compartment?

"Well, Mr. Zimmerman? Are you going to get down and let me up there?"

He slowly nodded, as if accepting defeat. "Then help this old man down, *Junge*."

I took his arm and helped him down.

"I'll need to borrow your penlight, Mr. Zimmerman."

He reluctantly took it from his pocket and handed it to me.

I jumped up on the chair and studied the clock from this closer angle. Above the cabinet, behind beautifully beveled glass, sat the clock face. It had what looked like a moon phase dial above the hour marks. There were details I could see this close up that were lost from farther away. Gold leaf, in intricate little patterns, swirled across the face and around the Roman numerals, which stood out in relief to indicate the hours.

About ten inches of polished wood sat between the bottom of the clock face and the top of the pendulum cabinet. I almost missed the carvings there; they were so light. It looked like three stars had been carved into the wood at an angle, the one on the right closest to the top, with the one on the left at the bottom, and the other star between them. They reminded me of something, but I couldn't remember what. Did they have something to do with the lines and dots carved across the trunk?

Beanie stepped closer. "What's going on?"

I looked down at him. "Oh, nothing, just some carvings up here I noticed. Something about them is familiar."

Beanie shook his head. "Now, don't go all Ferdinand on me and start smelling the flowers like Mel did back at Pike Place Market. Get on with it."

I glared at him. "Shove it, Beanie."

"Sorry," he said, "But you are, like, right there, and I really want to know what's in that compartment."

I flipped on the penlight and searched the inside wall of the cabinet. Even with the light I had a hard time finding the pinhole. It was only then I realized I didn't have anything I could use to open it.

"Mr. Zimmerman, did you happen to bring a paperclip or a pin with you? You know, since we would need one?"

Mr. Zimmerman slapped at his pockets. An expression of surprise showed on his face. "Oh, I didn't think to get one from the shop before I left." He gave an apologetic look.

"Perhaps there is something in the toolbox you can use. I am sorry. After I discovered the pinhole, I soon forgot about it since I didn't have a key to open the compartment. I only remembered when you brought the key into my shop."

I thought about what I might have on me that could work, but nothing came to mind. This could be a problem. Then Beanie's hand appeared in front of my face holding a safety pin.

I took it and looked down at him. "How did you happen to have one of these on you?"

He kind of shuffled his feet for a moment, then said, "Mom pins my name into everything. This one is from my jacket. I have others."

I didn't want to think where some of those might be located. "We all know your mom is a freak, but right now, I'm glad she has her quirks."

I found the hole again, then slowly inserted the tip of the safety pin. I took it slow, not wanting to push too hard and screw it up. A latch clicked and a small piece of wood flew up against the cabinet wall. Inside, the penlight showed the hole for my key. I took it out of my pocket and inserted it into the opening.

I turned it to the left but nothing happened. I worried it wouldn't work. But when I tried it to the right, a small compartment popped out below the key. It only came out about an inch. It was about eight inches wide and five inches high. The front curved to the shape of the cabinet wall. I had probably looked right at this spot a bunch of times while I studied the inside of the clock. There were no seams to show where the compartment had been located.

I looked down at Beanie and smiled. His eyes were wide with anticipation. I pulled the compartment out a little farther. Then I thought about Mr. Zimmerman. I glanced at him to see he had moved into position to get a better view. I quickly shifted my body to block him as I reached into the compartment. My hand hit a hard surface, but it wasn't the bottom of the compartment. Something was in there.

I slid my fingers around it to take it out. It felt like a cardboard box. Maybe like the type of hard-sided box a nice gift from a fancy store would come in. It felt square, but was probably less than an inch high. I immediately knew it couldn't be the Orb. The box was too flat. I took it out and quickly shoved it into my jacket pocket so Mr. Zimmerman wouldn't see it.

"Nothing in there," I said, trying to put a sad tone to my voice. I pushed the compartment closed.

"What do you mean?" Beanie cried out. "Like in zero? Nada? Nothing? You've got to be kidding me."

I tried not to laugh at how excited he had become. "No. Empty. Nothing." I took out the key, closed the latch, and jumped down from the chair.

I said, "I'm sorry there wasn't more excitement, Mr. Zimmerman."

"I am fine either way" he answered. "It was not of my concern to begin with." He held out his hand. "The key is all I care about."

"Oh, yeah." I thought for a second. Was there any reason I shouldn't give it to him?

Beanie decided for me. "Frankie, it was our deal. Whether we found something or not."

I nodded and then laid the key in Mr. Zimmerman's hand, along with the penlight.

"*Danke, Junge.*" He smiled, placed them in his pocket, and then quickly took a few steps backward and turned to his left. "Mr. Roberts, I have done as you asked."

I quickly spun around.

"Hello, Frankie."

I turned to see a man at the railing of the alcove. I had no idea who he was, but knew this couldn't be good. "Am I supposed to know you?"

He moved over to the steps I had come down. A strategic move to block us from going that way. "You probably don't recognize me. You were too busy getting mad at your girlfriend." He laughed. "You really shouldn't treat her so poorly. She's been going through some rough times."

I didn't know what he meant at first, then a thought hit me. "The professor from NICAP. The trap at her house. That was you?"

He smiled. "That was me, less the glasses, bow tie, and sports coat." He put out his hand. "Now, give me whatever you took from the compartment."

"I didn't take anything. The compartment was empty," I told him.

Then it hit me. I took a step toward Mr. Zimmerman. "You set us up, didn't you? How could you do that?"

He gave me a guilty look. "I am very sorry, Frankie, *mein Freund*. I really do like you boys, but Mr. Roberts from your government came into my shop right after you left that day. He knew I was not an American citizen and had worked for the Nazis in Deutschland during the war. He said you were after something that belonged to the government, and it may be in the Timberline clock. He threatened to have me deported if I didn't help him." He moved over by the far steps to create more distance between us. Maybe even to block our escape in that direction. "There was little else I could do?"

I stepped closer to Beanie and shot him a quick glance to let him know we may need to bolt. His look showed he understood my intent.

"Frankie. Hand it over," Roberts said. He made a bring-it-here gesture. "You did a good job blocking Mr. Zimmerman, but you didn't know I was up here with a perfect view of the compartment. I saw you take something out and put it in your pocket."

I couldn't let this Roberts guy have the box. Mel's dad had put it in the compartment for her to find. Whatever was in it belonged to Mel.

I grabbed Beanie's jacket and pulled him with me. "Run."

Sliding on Shingles

Frankie

I took off for the door going outside. There was no way Mr. Zimmerman would try to stop us. But just as I reached it, a man stepped through, his hand on the grip of a gun in his jacket pocket.

I yanked Beanie toward the steps. "This way!" I pushed past Mr. Zimmerman and ran up them. Roberts tried to cut us off, so we angled through a seating area by the chimney. Beanie was right behind me, but Roberts' man lunged and grabbed his ankle. Beanie tripped and fell.

"Get off me!" Beanie yelled. He kicked at the man's head until he let go.

I grabbed Beanie and pulled him to his feet. We quickly skirted some lounge chairs and ran for the hallway to the guest rooms I had seen earlier. It was all I could think of to get away from these guys. I only hoped there weren't more of them.

I shoved my way through the doors. A cleaning cart sat just on the other side. I quickly pushed it in front of the doors.

Beanie helped me, a wild look in his eyes. "I hope you have some sort of big plan here."

"Yeah. To get away."

We raced down the corridor. I checked doors along the way but they were all locked. Then I heard a huge crash behind us as the men smashed through the hallway doors, sending the cleaning cart toppling over. We darted through a door at the end of the hallway. It opened to a stairwell. We had the choice of up or down.

Beanie looked at me. "Well, Sherlock, I think down. Up probably won't get us to the parking lot."

I nodded. "Excellent deduction, Watson."

We shot down the stairs. Then a man turned the corner of the midway landing coming up toward us, his hand in his jacket pocket, and a 'got you' look on his face. We were trapped.

"Up, maybe?" Beanie said.

"Concur."

We shot back up the stairs to the landing on the first-floor just as Roberts opened the door. Beanie threw his shoulder into it, and drove him back. We headed up the stairs to the second floor.

Beanie started to open the door. I stopped him when I saw a man through one of the windows running toward us.

I looked up the stairwell. "Might as well go for broke."

I pulled Beanie with me and ran up the stairs to the third floor. It was as high as we could go.

We raced through the door. The men were catching up and right behind us now. Another cleaning cart sat near a linen closet on our left. A worker was taking dirty sheets out of a hamper. I grabbed them out of her hands and threw them at the men. Beanie pulled the cart across their path.

The sheets billowed open like miniature parachutes, enveloping the men. They tripped over the sheets and crashed into the cart. We kept running, but I knew it wouldn't be long before they caught us.

An older couple came out of a guest room just ahead, dragging their luggage. Before they could close the door, I grabbed Beanie and shoved him into the room.

"Hey!" the man shouted.

I slammed the door shut and bolted the lock.

I could hear Roberts giving orders. The doorknob jiggled.

"Open up, Frankie. It's over."

I didn't answer.

Beanie looked at me. "I think that's about it, Kemosabe. Nowhere to go."

The whole door bulged visibly as they slammed their shoulders into it. The doorjamb creaked and cracked. I thanked the craftsmanship of whoever made the door.

I ran to the window, pulled the drapes aside, and looked out. I couldn't believe it. We were in a room over one of the cantilevered roofs I had seen when we first got here. But we also happened to be four floors above the ground. It looked like a long way down. I unlatched the window, pulled it up as far as it would go, and then stuck my head out.

I felt Beanie over my shoulder. "You have got to be freakin' kidding me. We're not really going to do this, are we?"

"It's our only chance."

Beanie shrugged. "I sure hope Mel appreciates the fact we committed suicide for her."

I looked to my left, remembering the long section of shingled roofing I had seen when we first got here. It looked steep then, but really steep now. I tentatively stepped out of the window and onto the roof. I tested it to make sure it would hold.

Just then the room door crashed open. The sound of splintering wood and shouting men filled the room.

Beanie pushed me out so fast, I almost slid off the end. He jumped out after me and we quickly worked our way over to the shingles.

Roberts poked his head out the window, then shouted to his men. "Get them."

We knew it was now or never.

Roberts' man stepped onto the roof and made a grab for Beanie, but missed him.

I looked at Beanie. "Think of it like skateboarding."

I stepped onto the shingles and stood like I would on a skateboard going down a steep hill — knees bent, with a low center of mass. I immediately started to slide. It was hard to keep my balance as my feet skipped over each layer of shingles. I slid so fast I had no way to stop myself, and shot off the end at the bottom. I landed in a bunch of branches on a small tree before I dropped to the ground in a heap.

Beanie wasn't far behind, screaming at the top of his lungs. I looked up to see he had fallen backward and now slid on his back. He hit the tree and tumbled down the branches to land on me.

Beanie groaned. "Wow, and they didn't even charge us for the ride."

I pushed him off. We needed to get out of sight. I stood and pulled Beanie over to the wall below the shingle slide to where we couldn't be seen.

I checked to make sure I was okay. "Nothing broken, just bruised," I said. "How about you?"

"You mean other than my jacket and shirt riding up my back and leaving half of my skin on those shingles? Yeah, other than that, I'm fine."

I looked at his back. He did have a couple of bad scrapes. "I think you'll live."

I snuck a peek at the window above, just as Roberts stuck his head out. He argued with his man still out there about sliding down after us. His guy appeared to be smarter than he looked, because he refused to do it and crawled back inside. Then Roberts stuck his head out the window again, trying to see where we went.

"Let's stay here for a minute so they don't spot us."

"I need to catch my breath anyway," Beanie said.

"So, how much do you weigh?" I asked. "I was fine with dropping four floors and smashing into a tree, but nearly died when you landed on me."

He shrugged. "I stopped weighing myself a long time ago. Just one of the many things I do to avoid self-inflicted negative input."

"Well, let's avoid some more negative input, and get out of here before they find us. They might be on their way down."

I took another quick peek. "I don't see anyone at the window now. Let's go."

I ran across the parking lot to the far side where the pavement ended, shot over the edge, and fell down a steep embankment. I slid to a stop, and Beanie landed on top of me.

I pushed him off. "What, again? Is this a thing with you now?"

"I can't help what gravity does to me," he responded.

I scrambled up to the edge of the pavement to see if anyone might have spotted us from the window. No one was there.

Beanie climbed up next to me. "So, what's your next big plan? I don't think we can expect a ride home from Mr. Z."

"Ten-four to that," I said.

Then we saw Roberts and his goons come out of the main entrance and split up to search for us.

I grabbed Beanie, ran down the embankment, and hid behind some nearby trees.

"I'm pretty sure they didn't see us," I said, "so won't have any idea where we are."

"And…?" Beanie said, then gave me a look like he expected more. Like maybe how we get out of this mess.

I wasn't sure what to do, but then something came to me.

"This way," I told him, and pulled him with me. "If we keep heading down the mountain and to our left, I think we'll come out near the maintenance buildings."

"I'm all about that," he said. "Good idea."

We raced across a small meadow, skirted around a couple of boulders, and stopped behind another bunch of trees. We were completely out of view of the lodge now.

Beanie slapped me on the back. "Hey, this is a good plan. Maybe we can get a ride home from someone there."

"That's what I'm thinking."

We worked our way down the side of the mountain, trying to keep to the left as best we could. We made our way through patches of pine trees, around boulders, and over deadfalls.

Just as I wondered if we had missed it, we came through an opening in the trees, and there they were, the maintenance buildings.

We scrambled down the embankment and between two buildings to a parking area. Three men stood near a work truck, about to get in.

I grabbed Beanie's arm. "Hurry, I think they're leaving."

We raced over to the men just as they opened the doors. They quickly looked up at us, startled by our sudden appearance.

One of the men said, "Where'd you two come from?"

Beanie was about to say something, but I jabbed him with my elbow to get him to stop. Who knows what would have come out of his mouth?

I gave a big sigh, like we were in a quandary. "My brother and his friend ditched us and took off. He's a real jerk. Talked us into coming up here like it was some cool, big brother thing to do, but did it just so he could strand us. They chased us into the woods. We worked our way down here." I gave him a hopeful look. "You wouldn't be headed to Portland, would you?"

He studied me and then Beanie. He could see we were a little beat up, and had pieces of bark and pine needles stuck to our clothes and in our hair. I think it helped convince him.

"No, but we're headed to Government Camp for lunch. Maybe you can catch a ride to Portland from there."

Beanie and I beamed at each other.

Beanie said, "That would be great. Thanks."

"No problem. Hop in the back." We jumped into the bed of the truck as the men got into the cab. The engine started and soon we were headed down the mountain.

We scooted lower in the truck bed so we wouldn't be seen, just in case Roberts and his men were in their cars searching for us.

Beanie gave me a quizzical look. "So did you, or did you not, get anything out of the compartment?"

I smiled, then took the box out of my jacket pocket and showed it to him. It was about seven inches square and half an inch high, with a piece of paper tape wound around it to bind it shut. Handwriting on the tape said, 'Mel Belle.'

"What is it?" Beanie asked.

I looked at him. "I have no idea. But we'll find out once Mel gets back."

"Which leads us to that other unanswered question," Beanie said. "We still don't know how he put the box in the clock to begin with?"

We had wondered about this back at Mr. Zimmerman's clock shop. Just how did Mel's dad do this all in such an open area? And, how did he get into the longcase compart-ment to begin with, when it seems the only cabinet key was kept at the lodge?

I shook my head. "Not a clue."

"And what about that guy Roberts and his men? Why were they after us?" Beanie asked. "Do they think we still have some of the alien debris from the Roswell crash?"

But a greater worry hit me. "I hope it's not because they found out about the Orb."

Switch

Lubbock, 1947

Roger

Gloria stood in the center of our apartment, studying me. There wasn't a whole lot of trust in her eyes. I had filled her in on the plan Roy, Billy, and I came up with last night. But she really didn't want to hear it because she didn't think we could pull it off.

"Won't it just get us into more trouble?" she asked.

I tried to reassure her. "Don't worry, honey. We'll be okay."

She nodded, but her reserved look remained. Too much had happened over the last few days. She had become withdrawn and anxious.

I leaned in and kissed her on the cheek. "I'll be right back."

I opened the front door and carried two travel bags filled with our belongings out to the truck. It was Friday morning, and all I knew was we couldn't stay here any longer.

Gloria had been like this ever since Tuesday night when we were attacked by Bull and his stooge, Flint. Then, when she went to get groceries the next day, she was accosted by Flint again. He pushed her cart into a corner where no one could see them. She tried to get by him but he blocked her in, and then pressed against her so hard she felt him against her swollen stomach and the baby. He made it clear they weren't done. She managed to push him away and race out of the store.

When she told me about feeling his hot breath against her ear while whispering his threats, the look in her eyes crushed me. Whatever he said really frightened her; more than anything had so far. A new level of threat. I wouldn't let her out of my sight after that. Throughout the rest of the day she would double over every once in a while and cringe in pain. I worried for her, and for the baby. I called our doctor and arranged for her to see him the next day at ten o'clock.

I picked up the Thursday edition of the *Lubbock Morning Avalanche* from the side table in Doctor Greeley's waiting room and tried to read. But it didn't take. I couldn't get my mind off how it was going in there. He'd been with Gloria for the last twenty minutes.

The door to his examination area opened and he came out. Gloria wasn't with him.
I stood and he motioned for me to join him in a corner where we could talk privately.

"Roger, what's going on?"
"What do you mean, Doc?"

"What I mean is, *something* is going on to cause such extreme stress. It's written all over Gloria's face. She's as tense as anyone can get, and her blood pressure is sky high. I don't think she's been truthful with me as to why she would be like this. I've been a doctor long enough to know when a patient isn't being honest. You need to understand, she's having some real problems. If things don't change, and I mean quickly, she may lose the baby. The indications are already there."

"We are both under a lot of stress," I told him. "I went on the expedition and was gone for almost a week. Not only that, but I was in charge. My first time. So, I'm sure my stress in all of that washed onto her." These were lame reasons, but I had to keep going. I didn't want to give him time to think. "Maybe I shouldn't have gone while she's pregnant. And then, when I got hurt at the site, she—"

"Yes. I heard about that. Your coworker at Farmers Supply, Dale, was in yesterday for his checkup. He told me you had been hurt and missed work. I'm still upset you didn't come in to see me."

Why did Dale have to mention it? Probably, just to cause me problems. Like now. There was no way I could have seen Doctor Greeley. He would have asked how I got welts around my wrists, and no doubt have a good idea of what it would take to make my knees look the way they did. He might have figured things out. I was glad the welts on my wrists had healed enough to where they were hardly visible anymore.

"Sorry, Doc. It wasn't bad enough to come in. Gloria turned out to be quite a Florence Nightingale. But still, she worried about me. And then some other things happened that added to her stress."

"All excuses." He poked the end of his pen hard into my chest and held my eyes with the seriousness of his own. "I'm going to tell you right now, you better change things and fast, or she may lose the baby."

All the way home from the doctor's office I thought about what we could do. Gloria sat quietly in the passenger seat, but I could feel her tension flow from every pore. I had no idea what Doctor Greeley told her, but it had to be something similar to what he said to me.

Then an idea hit me, but it would take Roy and Billy's help to pull it off. I was glad the phone line had been repaired. I would need it now. When we got home, I called them, but kept the calls short and cryptic, in case the phone was tapped. Just long enough to set up a meeting so we could go over my plan.

I had Gloria stay upstairs with Mrs. Delbert while I was gone. I met with Roy and Billy at the Tartan Lounge that evening. I filled them in on what had happened to Gloria and me ever since I got back from Roswell. When I shared my plan with them, they were on board immediately.

All I knew was I had to take Gloria away to somewhere we couldn't be found. She needed to get some rest. And I needed to meet Tom in Roswell at noon on Saturday. I had originally planned to go by myself, but that wouldn't work any longer. I couldn't leave Gloria alone. This plan, if everything went right, would take care of both problems. It was just a matter of pulling it off.

Now, it's Friday morning and we're ready to put the plan into play. I came back from dropping the luggage in the bed of the truck. Gloria still stood by the door, holding her purse in a way that betrayed her trepidation.

"We can do this," I said, making sure confidence flowed through my words. I raised her chin so she could see into my eyes. "*You* can do this. Okay?"

She nodded, then looked down at the ground, not wanting to maintain eye contact.

I took her hand. "Everything will be fine."

I walked her to the truck and helped her in, then got into the driver's side.

As I rolled my window down, she said, "You know they'll follow us."

I studied the tension in her face. "Yes, they probably will. That's why we have this plan in place." I turned to face her better and took her hands. "Look, we can't stay here any longer. Who knows what they will do next. And like I told you, I need to meet someone in Roswell tomorrow."

I started the truck. We took off and headed for Texas Tech. This plan had to work. There wasn't a plan B. I drove toward the entrance on College Avenue. It was the farthest one from where I planned to end up on campus, and would make it easier to spot if someone followed us. Especially since it was summer, and there wouldn't be much activity at the school.

Sure enough, a car seemed to be making the same turns we did through the campus streets. I kept a steady pace. I didn't want to draw attention in any way to the fact I knew they were back there. I worked my way toward the agricultural part of the campus.

"Is someone behind us?" Gloria asked.

I hoped she hadn't noticed, but she had. "Yes, but we can lose them."

I looked down to see her hand gripping the front edge of the seat, her fingers digging into the cushion. I put my hand on hers to reassure her.

The college's agricultural barn was just up ahead. I drove through the large, open barn door. Billy pulled it closed as soon as we were inside. The smell of farm animals and musty straw filled the truck cab.

The barn had a long drive-through area for tractors and livestock trailers to come in, unload, and continue out the other side. The sound of whinnying horses and grunting pigs came from somewhere in the barn. I stopped the truck next to a car parked halfway through the building.

Roy ran over and looked through my window. "Hello, Gloria. Good to see you again." He nodded to me and then went to the back of the truck and pulled our luggage out.

I walked over to Gloria's door and opened it for her, helping her out. "I need you to get into the passenger side of Roy's car."

She slid out from the bench seat and said, "I still don't know if this will work."

I tried to reassure her. "Honey, it will."

She looked at me with doubt in her eyes. "I sure hope so."

I opened the car door and helped her into Roy's car.

Billy ran past us toward the far end of the barn. "Hey, Gloria. Have a good trip."

I closed the passenger door and walked to the back of the car.

Roy tossed the last bag into the trunk and closed the lid. He looked at me. "Here are my keys."

I gave him mine.

"You understand the directions to the cabin?" Roy asked.

"Yeah, we should be able to find it."

"Okay. Well, good luck." He shook my hand and then got into the driver side of my truck.

I got into the driver side of his car. Gloria and I watched Billy open the barn door at the far end, then race back to get in the truck with Roy. He put on a blonde wig and sidled up to Roy like they were on a date. I laughed.

"What are you laughing about?" Gloria asked.

I nodded toward Roy and Billy. "Check out the couple in our truck."

She looked over at it. "Oh, God. I hope I don't look that bad."

"I don't know. I think Billy looks pretty good."

Gloria hit me in the shoulder. "You want to switch girls with Roy?"

I laughed. "Hell, no."

"I didn't think so."

Roy started up the truck and headed out of the barn. While they drove away, I backed Roy's car into an empty stall to get out of sight. Just in case anyone should check. I turned off the ignition.

"What are we doing?" Gloria asked.

I gave her a quick kiss. "What's needed to make sure we're safe. We'll wait here for a few minutes, just in case."

I put on the fedora and sunglasses Roy had left for me on the seat.

"What? A disguise?"

"I can't have them recognize me if they are still out there. And, when we leave, I'll need you to lay down on the seat so you won't be seen. At least until we are clear of the area. Okay?"

She looked at me as if I was crazy. "Whatever you say, Mr. Secret Agent Man. This is your plan."

I waited another minute, then started the car and drove out of the barn.

Gloria laid down, placed her head in my lap, and looked up at me. "The things I do for you."

I chuckled. It was good to see she still had a sense of humor.

Once out of the barn, I followed a road through some agricultural fields, then worked my way onto U.S. Highway 62 where it would connect with the road to Roswell. All the while, I checked my rearview mirror.

My plan had worked. No one followed us.

Katy's Cafe

Roswell, 1947

Roger

I pulled over to the curb on West Second Street in Roswell, just at the corner of Main. I looked at my watch to see it was about five minutes past noon, the designated time to meet Tom at Katy's Cafe.

We had just checked out of a hotel after an uneventful night. The first in a long time. I looked in my rearview mirror to make sure there wasn't a car coming and got out. I closed the door as Gloria slid across the bench seat to the driver's side and rolled down the window.

I leaned in to talk to her. "I shouldn't be more than half an hour. Meet me back here. Park if I'm not back yet, okay?"

She looked at me with a bit of concern. "I don't like being separated."

"I know, honey. But we agreed in the hotel room that this was the best plan. That way, you can get the groceries we'll need up at the cabin, while I take care of this business."

She shrugged. "Okay."

"You have the list and enough money?"

She took a sheet of paper from her purse and held it up. "Yes."

"Don't forget the ice for Roy's cooler in the trunk."

"I won't."

I leaned in and gave her a kiss. "I'll see you in half an hour."

A car came, so I jumped over to the sidewalk. Gloria waved to me, pulled out behind the car, and headed toward the A&P Market we had seen on our way into town.

I turned the corner onto Main Street, and Katy's Cafe was right there. I walked in the front door and gave my eyes a little time to focus. It was a long, narrow cafe, mostly filled by a lengthy counter on my right. A few men sitting at it looked up when I came in, then turned back to their plates of food. Tom wasn't one of them.

The far end of the cafe had two booths, back-to-back. Both were taken. The first one by a couple, but the last one by a single man facing me. It had to be him.

I walked over and breathed a sigh of relief when I recognized Tom. I slid into the seat facing him. A carafe of coffee and two cups sat on the table. I worried when I didn't see the satchel.

He grabbed a cup and poured some coffee for me. "I was beginning to wonder if you'd make it." He refilled his. "I let the guy at the counter know we were only having coffee, so we wouldn't be disturbed." He lifted his cup and took a sip. "Unless you want to get something else?"

I leaned forward and kept my voice low, since there was someone in the booth right behind me. "No, I'm fine.

Thanks." I had to know. "Do you have the satchel with you?"

He pulled it from under the table and placed it on top. He also leaned across the table and spoke in a low voice. "Here," he said as he pushed it across to me. "That's some strange stuff you've got in there. Way more advanced than us lowly earthlings could come up with."

I grabbed the satchel, pulled it across the table, and safely into my arms. A sense of relief filled me, now that I had it back in my possession.

"I didn't really have a chance to check this stuff out when I put it in here," I told him. "There wasn't time, and I was too overwhelmed by seeing the spaceship and alien bodies to give it a lot of thought. It was a bit of a shock to find out we are not alone in the universe."

"I get it." He paused for a moment, then chuckled. "It definitely was an otherworldly experience."

I fingered the buckle, wanting to unlatch it and look inside, but knew I couldn't. "The device?"

"Yes. It's in there. Funny though. I tried to figure out how to open it, but couldn't." He leaned even closer, inquisitive in his posture. "What is it? Some sort of weapon?"

"No. Not a weapon. Something more important. I really have no idea. I mean, the alien's message to me. It all seems so cryptic."

Tom thought for a moment. "I remember what the alien told me. It felt so odd, because what he said was in my head. Not through spoken words. Maybe for that reason it seemed all the more important. He told me I needed to help you get the device out of there. He didn't want the military to get it." Tom shuddered a little. "I can still hear him in my head as if he were telling me this right now while sitting here drinking our coffee."

"I think he implanted thoughts in our heads that we have no control over," I told him. "All I know is that I am the guardian of the device now, and I must protect it with my life, if that's what it takes."

Tom studied me for a moment. I think he could read the stress on my face from the last few days. "Speaking of which, what happened when the military arrived?"

I told him how we were all taken to the Roswell Army Air Field and interrogated. I gave him the gritty details on what they did to me, and then to us at home. He needed to know how much danger we were in, including himself. I told him they knew I had given him the satchel at the crash site, but not who he was.

He sat back in his seat and stiffened at this news. "What if they followed you here?"

"No, they didn't. I came up with a good way to lose them. I know it worked."

His face took on a sense of relief. "Good. But it looks like we're both in a bit of hot water."

"I don't know where you live or what you do," I said, "and it's best to keep it that way. But I want to stay in touch."

He nodded. "Same here. You don't go through something like we did without feeling a kinship over what took place. Just the fact we both communicated telepathically with an alien puts us in a group of two. And somehow, I think the alien wants this." He thought for a moment. "So, how do we do this without their getting wind of it?"

I looked at my watch. It was time to meet Gloria. I thought for a moment. "I need to get going. How about we do this? When I get back to Lubbock, I'll get a post office box. You do the same here."

"No, not here," Tom said. "It's time to move. I'll do that when I get somewhere new."

I pulled a pen and notepad from a pocket on the outside of the satchel where I knew it would be. "In the meantime, I'm going to give my address to you." I wrote it on the page, tore it from the pad, and handed it to Tom. "As soon as you get a PO box, mail me a letter with the address. We live with Mrs. Delbert. I wrote her name down. Send the letter to her, not me, just in case anyone is watching the mail. Include a note to let her know this letter is for me. And use a bogus return address. Once we get the PO boxes set up, we can work on other ways to communicate from there."

Tom took the slip of paper and put it in his pocket. "Will do."

The Stones

Carnac, 1967

Mel

Eddy brought his friend with him. They came up to where we sat. Both were dressed in expedition-like gear: khaki pants, vests with multiple pockets, those flashlights with the ninety-degree bend in them clipped to their vests, and lace-up boots.

Eddy introduced us to Henri, who made sure we understood his name was spelled with an 'i', not the Americanized version with a 'y'. And he pronounced it more like 'awe-rey' than Henry. But he did speak English, thank goodness, though it wore a heavy French accent. I don't think either Katch or I minded because it was also a very sexy accent. And Henri wasn't too bad to look at either. We weren't going to do anything, but we didn't have a problem with the view.

Maybe this would all go okay. Even Eddy seemed to be in a better mood. Probably a combination of the pints last night and now having his friend with him.

We hopped into the car. They sat in front, with Katch and me in the back.

We drove a short distance and then onto a small road between some very old stone buildings. We pulled into a little dirt parking area right at the Stones.

I lit up as soon as I saw them. There they were, right in front of me. Finally! Huge stones of granite lined up in rows, hundreds of them running off into the distance. Much bigger than the ones we saw on the drive yesterday. I looked over to Katch to see the same look of excitement in her eyes.

I got out of the car and Katch scooted out after me.

Eddy said, "This is the far western end of the *Alignments de Carnac* known as *Le Menec* West. From here, the Stones extend northeast for about four kilometers through *Le Menec* East, the *Kermario* section, and finally *Kercescan* to the *Le Petit Menec*. Experts believe the Carnac Stones were placed here over two thousand years before Stonehenge. That means these stones have been here for over six thousand years. It is a number that takes a while to sink in." He paused as he looked out at the Stones, maybe to give us time to absorb this. A moment later he said, "Well, let's crack on."

Eddy walked away from the Stones and disappeared around the side of a nearby farm building with Henri. Katch and I looked at each other and shrugged. It was opposite to the way I wanted to go, but we followed anyway. We rounded the corner to find them standing in the middle of a grassy area.

"Now, this is the proper place to start," Eddy said. He held out his arm and made a full turn with his body. "We are standing in the middle of a cromlech."

Henri added, with a very French smile, "*Le cromlech est un cercle de pierres*." He stopped for a moment, embarrassed, then said, "*Pardon*. In English, a circle of stones."

I could see some stones on the other side of the grassy area that looked like they were lined up more in a curved pattern, rather than a straight line. That must be what they were talking about.

Eddy went on. "We focused on this cromlech in our studies because it's not actually a circle as most of them are, but in the shape of an egg, which is rather unusual."

His mention of the shape struck me. I quickly took out my map and looked at this end of it. The map had close-up views of various points of interest throughout the Stones, like locations of dolmens and menhirs. I hadn't noticed this before because it was in the bottom left corner of the map. It had a small aerial picture of this particular cromlech with a thin, white line drawn to outline the ring of stones. I grabbed Katch's arm as the recognition of the shape hit me. She turned to see the shock on my face.

The boys had walked farther on, but I whispered anyway. "Katch, look at this drawing of the cromlech."

She studied it, then turned to me. "Yeah, what about it?"

"This isn't just an egg shape. It's in the shape of the Orb. Remember in the film when my dad held up the Orb? At one point, there was a close-up of it. The Orb has this very same shape."

Then something else hit me. "And my locket, too. It has the same shape." I pulled it out from under my shirt to show her and held it next to the cromlech on the map. "See? It's the same. Maybe this is an energy point and one of the reasons my dad came here."

Katch's eyes showed she was taking this in. "Now that's just friggin crazy."

I laughed, nervously. "I know. Isn't it? This is really spacing me out. Why would this cromlech be in the same shape as the Orb and my locket, when we were just told most of them are circles?"

I suddenly had the urge to touch one of the stones. I walked across the field to the biggest one in the row. It was a mottled gray color, as weathered granite tends to be, with patches of white and brownish lichen all over it. I placed my palm against the surface. I'm sure it was me more than the stone, but my body tingled all over. I was touching a stone placed here over six thousand years ago—one of the many stones laid out in the very shape of the Orb we seek.

Somehow, I knew my dad must have figured this out as well. Maybe he even stood right here and touched this very stone. I looked over to see Katch touch a stone next to me, her eyes closed. She seemed very focused, saying something under her breath. I could just make out a Hopi chant, similar to the one she and her grandmother used the night they pointed to the constellation Orion, and called them my Sky People.

I had to think. What was the message Katch's grandmother gave Mrs. Gallo at the airport? It was right when we were ready to fly out. Something about tuning into the earth and hearing the song of the universe. Maybe that's what we were doing right now.

Katch looked over to me, her eyes wide with the keenness of a new understanding. "There's definitely an energy here. I can feel it."

Eddy and Henri walked up to us before I could respond.

"Why don't you two quit faffing around, and let's get on with it?"

But he said this in a fun, joking sort of way. Not condescending, which was his norm. He turned and led us out of the field.

Henri walked with Katch and me. He said, "Last summer we invited a group from Eddy's university to study the *Alignments de Carnac*. That is how we got to know each other and became friends."

Eddy stopped so he could add, "We had an expert on the Stones with us. Professor Hemling. He ran our field study. We focused on this cromlech because of its unusual shape. The professor has been studying the formation in relation to geometric calculations. Without getting into the minutia of it all, he believes this shape, and the alignments themselves, are relational to set geometric patterns— such as circles, triangles, squares, and rectangles. But he is still early in his studies."

We walked over to the stones of *Le Menec* West. I went up to a stone, which stood tall above me. I couldn't get the smile off my face. I don't know what it was exactly that put it there, but I couldn't have had a wider grin than the one on my face right now.

Katch looked over at me and laughed. "Well, aren't you in your element!"

The boys had odd looks on their faces like they didn't have a clue what was going on. Emilee must not have told Eddy about my father being here. No doubt, she left that up to me.

We wandered through the Stones for a while. I tried to spot the ones my dad and Professor Lofton stood next to in the film, but it was impossible. And with over 3,000 stones here, it could be any of them.

We went back to the car, and Eddy gave us a driving tour of the alignments. We stopped once in a while to get out and walk through the Stones while Eddy and Henri shared some points of interest. We were near the beginning of what Eddy called the *Kermario* alignment when I saw a dolmen.

"Stop. Stop, Eddy," I shouted. "I want to look at that dolmen."

Apology

Mel

He pulled the car over. I jumped out and ran to the dolmen. It sat right at the elbow of a curve in the road.

Katch wasn't far behind. "Is this the one?"

I shook my head. I knew right off it wasn't. "No. It's too small. But it is a dolmen."

I would have needed to crawl to get inside. We walked around it instead. At the back, it looked like one of the capstones had fallen off the top. The room was open to the sky at that point. Definitely not the one my dad had been at.

Eddy walked over. He looked at Katch. "I'd fancy a moment with Melanie, if you don't mind?"

Katch checked with me. I nodded. She walked over to where Henri studied a cluster of stones not far away.

I turned to Eddy and wondered what this could be about. "What's up?"

He shifted uneasily and shuffled his feet. He looked like he was trying to figure out what to say, or maybe how to say it.

"Look, Melanie. I've been an absolute wanker to you. And I'm sorry. I needed to tell you that."

I looked up at him, expecting to see arrogance. Instead, there seemed to be some honesty tucked into his eyes, backing up what he just said.

"A wanker, huh? In American English, isn't that like an asshole?"

"Truly right. An asshole."

I leaned against a stone of the dolmen, crossed my arms, and gave him one of my patented 'You're kidding me' looks I usually reserve for Beanie. "And your apology is supposed to set everything right? You've treated Katch and me like crap ever since we left Brightwood."

He didn't answer. Instead, he turned his eyes to the ground, probably to avoid my scowl, and kicked at a tuft of grass.

"Was there a reason?" I asked. "Or do you just like to intimidate fifteen-year-old girls? Then again, maybe you just think we are too young and immature to be worthy of your time."

"Hah." He looked up and laughed. "I've been the mental one, what with throwing a huge wobbly and all. Bloody right, that! You and Katch have been the mature ones. You haven't complained one bit, for all the ways I have treated you badly. It's just that—"

I held up my hand. "Stop. If you're going to grovel like this, Katch should be here to hear it."

Eddy nodded. "I know. I'll apologize to her soon enough. Believe in that. But not now. I owe you this directly, and alone, because of your grandmother. She and my mum are very close, and not long ago she helped our family out of a bad situation financially. We owe her."

"But, why do you think you owe this to me?"

He looked off into the distance as if remembering something, then turned to me. "You would need to have been there when Emilee suddenly found out she had a granddaughter. That bit of news changed everything for her. Mum and I went over to the manor as soon as we heard. She was so excited. It was as if new life had been breathed into her. I think it was because she felt so alone before, not knowing where her daughter, your mother, could be, or if she was even still alive. Then the call came that she had died. But with it, the miracle of Melanie happened. You created a family for her again. That's why you deserve a straight-up explanation."

He paused, leaned against the stone next to mine, and looked out toward Katch and Henri in the distance. I followed his eyes to see Katch glance back at me. "Henri is filling in Katch as we speak. He offered to do it so I could talk with you." He studied me before he continued. "It wasn't until I complained to Henri at the pub about having to babysit you two, as I called it, that he pointed out how daft I had been in the way I treated you both. I was too bloody busy sulking to even notice."

I thought about this. "What were you sulking about?"

"I was all set to go to Egypt with some lads from Oxford. Another summer learning expedition. We were to study the pyramids, and only a few days from leaving. I was excited to go. And then Emilee called. She has done so much for our family; it was impossible for us to refuse her request."

"Because you owed her?"

"Yes. And because she wanted to make you happy. She knew coming to the Carnac Stones would accomplish that. She was aware of my planned trip to Egypt and I could tell she felt bad to be asking. She even offered to pay for a trip there later with some chums, if I would do this for her. My mum told me Mrs. Bea had already laid a firm hand down, letting your grandmother know she must attend to matters at Brightwood Manor. She had been gone nearly a month overseas to be with you. Mrs. Bea could do only so much without her there. Things couldn't wait any longer. But Emilee would have dropped everything in the moment, and brought you here herself, if I had told her no."

I slumped against the stone. I didn't realize I could cause such a commotion. "Thanks for telling me. And for bringing me."

"Well, all the same, even though I knew it was the right thing to do, I was in a bit of a strop."

"What?"

"Oh. It means throwing a temper tantrum."

I turned to him. "Yep. That would be a good description. I can see how missing the trip would piss you off, though. But I'm not sure treating us the way you did was the way to deal with it."

"Nor I," Eddy said. "Besides, I don't think the pyramids of Giza are going anywhere for a while. I'll make it there someday."

I studied him. "I hope you do."

He smiled. "Thus, the tail-between-the-legs apology."

Should I trust him now? I thought back to a few times when I had thrown tantrums of my own, and how I had always been embarrassed about them later, when I could think straight. They were not particularly proud moments.

"I'll think on it—accepting your apology, that is. Let's see how it plays out from here. If you're just goofing with me, it will come out eventually."

He smiled. "Fine with that. A load off, which I've been feeling the weight of ever since pints with Henri last night."

I smiled. Maybe he would be different now. What a relief that would be.

He stepped over so he could face me. "Why are you here anyway, Melanie? What is the big interest in the Carnac Alignments? And don't give me a cock-and-bull story about studying them in school, which is what Emilee told me."

I didn't see any harm in sharing at least a part of the reason. I had been leaning against the stone. I pushed myself off so I could stand to face him. "It's about my dad. I wanted to see them because he was here, at the Carnac Stones. It was one of the last things he did before he died a few years ago. He and a professor were studying them in relation to Earth's energy. Something to do with ley lines."

"Really?" Eddy replied. He looked curious. "That's interesting. In the past, there has been research of a similar nature throughout Europe."

"I think my dad and the professor thought there was an energy point here at the Stones." Then I remembered something. "Your pyramids in Egypt—"

"Yes. What about them?" Eddy asked, now a bit intrigued.

"They believed the pyramids were also an energy point. And there were other locations throughout the world."

Eddy was quiet for a moment. "Then that would possibly explain what this bloke, Tony Wedd, proposed in 1961. He put forward a theory that leys were established by prehistoric communities to guide alien spacecraft."

That shocked me. I fell back against the stone again, suddenly weak with the thought that my dad and the professor could have been pursuing the same theory.

It must have shown on my face. Eddy said, "Oh, so you think that's what your dad was doing here?"

I hadn't been thinking that at all, until right this minute, when he brought it up. But it made so much sense. I didn't want to share that with him. He hadn't gained my trust yet, if he ever would. And I certainly wasn't going to tell him about the Orb.

I said, "I'm not sure. It could have been something like that."

He brightened. "Well then, if that is the case, I certainly understand why you are here, as far-fetched as the reasoning may be."

Katch and Henri walked up. Katch nodded to me, sharing a look that told me Henri had filled her in.

"Well then, would you like to continue our tour?" Eddy asked.

"Actually, there's something you might be able to help us with," I told him.

He looked curious. "Fair enough. What would that be?"

"We want to find a particular dolmen my dad was at."

Eddy and Henri smiled at each other. Henri said, "We know all the dolmens at the *Alignments de Carnac*. I am sure we can find it. Do you know what it is named?"

I tried to remember. The name was odd and had sounded French. I looked over at Katch. "What did Professor Loften call the dolmen when we watched the film of them here?"

She thought for a while. "I think it had the word 'main' or something like that in the name."

"Yeah, that sounds right. Something like 'Main Carinon'. I remember now, because it reminded me of the word 'carrion', which is something dead."

"That's kind of morbid," Katch said.

"Oh, I don't know," Eddy tossed in. "After all, the general theory is that these dolmens are burial tombs."

We all laughed, then Henri's look turned to one of puzzlement.

"What's wrong, Henri?" I asked.

"I can't think of any dolmen in the *Alignments de Carnac* with a similar name."

Eddy nudged Henri. "Hold on. What about the *Dolmens de Mané Kerionned*?"

I brightened. "Yes, that's it. That's the name the professor told us."

Henri said, "But that isn't in the Alignments."

"What do you mean?" I asked.

Eddy said, "It's like two and a half kilometers from here. What made you think the dolmen was in the Carnac Alignments?"

I shook my head. "I just assumed, I guess. Maybe because it was on the same film that showed him here at the Stones."

Katch put her arm around my shoulder and smiled. "Well, it's a good thing we figured it out. Let's go there."

The Hidden Dolmen

Mel

We went to Eddy's car and drove to the *Dolmens de Mané Kerionned*. It only took ten minutes, but this dolmen definitely wasn't in or near the Carnac Stones.

We came to an intersection and Eddy turned right. The road sign said it was called La Glacière. Like in a glacier, I guess. Kind of a weird name for a road.

Not long after we turned, Henri pointed out the window to our left. "There it is."

Eddy slowed the car.

I looked out to see a group of stones sitting right next to the road. "Those are them?"

Henri nodded. "*Oui. Le Dolmens de Mané Kerionned.*"

I thought of how unimpressive they looked and wondered if this could be right. I guess I expected something on a grander scale, more along the lines of Stonehenge.

Eddy said, "There's a parking area up ahead."

We took a left onto another road just past the stones and parked. Everyone got out. A trail led through the woods toward the dolmens.

Katch grabbed my hand as we walked. "Are you excited?"

I glanced over at her. This was the first place I knew for sure my dad had been. "More like apprehensive."

Scrub brush and some sort of pine trees lined the trail. The trees were thin and spindly, and the brush unruly and ugly. Not like back home with lush, green undergrowth below perfectly straight pine trees. Nothing about the area looked impressive. In fact, it almost looked depressing.

The trail opened up to a clearing and the dolmens.

"Here it is," Henri said proudly. *"Dolmens de Mané Kerionned*, just as you requested."

This couldn't be right. They both appeared to be too small.

Katch looked at me, and I could see in her eyes she thought the same thing.

There were two dolmens and a few freestanding stones, known as menhirs, around the area. The first dolmen we came to was small, and partially buried in the ground. Too small to be the one my dad stood in front of. You couldn't even get inside it, unless you stooped really low.

Another dolmen stood on the far side of the clearing. That one had more potential. Katch and I walked over to it. I looked back to see Eddy and Henri still at the first one, discussing something about it.

This dolmen was bigger. We could easily walk under the capstone and inside.

Katch said, "I remember in the film; your father stood at the front entrance to a dolmen just like this." She looked so hopeful. "This could be it."

I tried to think back to when we watched the film. I was so excited to see my father again, much of the footage was emblazoned in my mind. "Yeah, maybe you're right."

We looked around inside. I couldn't believe we were standing right where my father had been. Then I remembered something from the film, too. This couldn't be the dolmen my father stood in, when he felt the focused energy from the Orb.

I turned to Katch. "This isn't right. It might be the dolmen he stood in front of, but it isn't the one that showed him inside. This dolmen has huge gaps between the stones where you can see out. The walls of that dolmen were filled in. It had large, standing stones for the sides and top like here, but smaller rocks filled the area around them, so you couldn't see out. Remember how it looked really dark inside? The only light had come from the camera. This can't be the one the professor said my dad was in when he felt the focused energy."

I couldn't be more disappointed. We had come so far and thought this would be it. But it wasn't. There had to be a different dolmen. One that was completely surrounded in stone. We walked back out to where Eddy and Henri waited.

"This isn't it," I told them. "At least not the one my dad stood inside of. That has to be a different dolmen."

Henri smiled. "Ah, *mon très cher ami*, but you have not seen the buried dolmen yet."

I turned to him. "What buried dolmen?"

Big smiles covered both their faces.

"We saved the best for last," Eddy said. "Perhaps this will be the one you fancy." He unclipped the flashlight from his vest. "This way."

They led us toward the road where we had first seen the dolmens as we drove by. We were nearly to it when I noticed a hole in the ground in front of us. Then steps going into the hole. They angled down to a walkway that disappeared underground. A buried dolmen, just as the boys had said.

"This way," Henri directed.

I walked down the steps and was below ground level by the time I reached the bottom. All three sides of the walkway were lined by perfectly straight stone walls. Green moss and light gray lichen covered them. This open part of the dolmen was only maybe seven feet long. Then the walkway went under a capstone and disappeared into darkness.

Henri took his own flashlight from his vest, turned it on, and shined the beam toward the far end.

We walked inside. It got wider the farther back it went. The whole thing was huge. It had to be at least seven feet at the widest point, and maybe thirty feet deep. Eddy, the tallest of us, could stand straight up in it with room to spare.

Right away something told me this was it. I turned to Henri, "Can I use your flashlight?"

"*Certainement.*" He handed it to me.

"Thank you." I gave him an appreciative smile. "Hey, uh, do you guys mind if Katch and I check this out on our own? It's that, well, my dad was here. I guess I want it to be just the two of us right now."

"Oh. Right so," Eddy agreed, though grudgingly. "We'll be off."

Henri added, "We'll wait for you up above. It will give us a chance for additional study of those dolmens and menhirs."

I gave them my nicest smile. "Thank you."

They walked back to the steps and went up them.

I turned to Katch, grabbed her arm, pulled her a little farther inside and said, "This is it. I'm positive."

She whispered back, "I remember seeing this in the film. I think you're right."

"The professor said Dad felt the Orb gain more strength down here. A more focused energy. Why would that be?"

"It must have something to do with Earth's energy fields," Katch said. "Those ley lines. Maybe this is a point of energy he found using the Orb?"

I thought about what the professor had said. Katch was right about the relationship to the ley lines. And I remembered what Eddy said about the man who thought these ley lines and energy points could be used by aliens. But most of all, I remembered what my dad said about dolmens being possible portals.

And that last thought triggered a memory. I practically froze in place.

Katch asked, "Are you okay?"

I looked over at her. "I had a dream about this place."

"You what?"

"A dream. I forgot all about it until just now. Being down here must have triggered the memory."

"That's crazy."

"Let's get to the end. I need to find out if something I saw in my dream is there."

We walked toward the back of the dolmen. I shined the flashlight beam from side to side as we went.

Katch stopped me. "Hey. Hold it. Shine the light on that stone again." She pointed to a big stone on the right-hand wall. I focused the beam where she told me. "Look," she said. "There are carvings on it."

We both got closer. Sure enough, someone had carved designs into the stone. Probably way back when they built this place. We moved to other stones along the wall and saw the same thing.

"Let's get a look at the back wall," I said.

When we got to the back, I shined the light on it. Two big stones covered most of the back wall. The one centered in the middle had a bunch of carvings on it. They were all interconnected. In one place, there were three circles on a diagonal, but they had lots of other lines running to or around them.

Katch saw the circles. "That looks kind of like Orion's Belt."

I said, "In my dream, I saw the three stars of Orion's Belt right here in this end stone. But they were bigger than these, more intricate, and weren't carved into the stone. Instead, they stood out in relief, as if the stone around them had been carved away."

Katch looked like she was thinking about something. "You called it a dream."

"Yeah. Why?"

"Often, what people think of as dreams are really visions." She took my hand and we walked back toward the entrance. "Grandma taught me to know the difference." She looked at me. "I never told you, because it's not our way, but Grandma said I had completed my training. I'm a full-fledged medicine woman now. And this medicine woman is sure it wasn't a dream, but instead, a vision."

My eyes went wide at her insight. "You really think it was a vision?"

"We're here, aren't we? How could it not be?" Then she added, "Maybe you just haven't fulfilled the vision yet."

"If that's the case, I guess the big question is, when *will* I fulfill it?"

Katch said, "Sorry, but visions have their own timetables. There's no way to tell."

A disappointing answer. I shrugged it off. "Remember when the professor said Dad believed this could be a portal of some kind?"

"I do. He also told the professor the Orb wouldn't reveal anything more to him."

A chill ran through me when I remembered what the professor said next. "Professor Lofton told us my dad had a vision in this dolmen."

"And you had a vision of being here," she added, making the connection. "Maybe that *was* his vision; of you being here."

I shook my head in disbelief. Could what she just said be true? I tried to absorb all of this as we continued toward the entrance.

Katch suddenly grabbed my arm to stop me. She took the flashlight from my hand. Her eyes went wide. She said, "And part of your father's vision in this dolmen revealed that the Orb was meant for you, right?"

"Yes," I answered.

She pointed the flashlight at a stone in the wall. It was on the opposite side of the ones we had already checked. Three prominent circles had been carved into the stone. There were no other carvings. Just the three circles. They were on the same diagonal and in the same placement as the three stars in Orion's Belt; carved thousands of years ago into a stone on the side of this dolmen. As if intended for me to see today.

I shuddered with the thought of how far I had come in discovering my father's path, and now to be making it my own.

I said to Katch, "When the professor told me my dad said the Orb was meant for me, I didn't believe it." I wrapped my arm around hers, holding it tight. "But I'm telling you, Katch, this is really freaking me out."

"What? Just you? I'm as freaked out as you are." She held my arm as tightly as I held hers.

I turned to her. "We have to study this dolmen some more. I need to figure out how to complete the vision. But we can't do it now, and we can't do it with the boys here."

"What are you getting at?"

"We're coming back later tonight, without them."

Alto Lake

Sierra Blanca Mountains, 1947

Gloria

I couldn't remember the last time I cooked trout, and never over a wood-burning stove. For that matter, I couldn't remember the last time I had even gone fishing, which was exactly what Roger and I did today at Alto Lake. What a relaxing time. The sun above us, the weather warm, and the fish hungry. I fought with Roger over baiting my own hook. There are limits.

I told him, "It's a man's job." When he fought me on this, I added, "Well, if I have to bait my own hook, then you have to cook your own fish."

That settled it.

Roy not only helped us escape those men, but he also let us use his cabin. I didn't mind at all that it was a bit rustic, had no electricity, and required the use of an outhouse. But it did have an old-fashioned pitcher pump in the kitchen, which truly was a godsend. I would have drawn the line at hauling buckets of water.

What we got in exchange for the rustic setting, was a sense of freedom from the danger we had lived under for the last few days. We came straight here after Roger's meeting in Roswell. This whole area is fairly isolated and although there are other cabins, none of them are anywhere near ours. After a few days up here, I was finally able to relax.

Roger came in the front door carrying a load of wood. "Wow. That smells great."

I smiled at him. "Wait until you taste it."

He put the logs into a bin next to the fireplace. The cabin sat high in the Sierra Blanca Mountains. It must have reached the low forties last night. A fire later would be welcome, and romantic.

I pulled the cast-iron frying pan from the stove and set it on a hot pad on the counter. Everything was ready: fresh trout cooked with lemon and dill, green beans with pearl onions and bacon, and potatoes fried in the bacon grease.

"Sit down, honey," I told Roger.

I had already set the table and lit a couple of candles to give the room a romantic feel. The renewed peace of mind changed everything for me. I could see it in Roger, too.

He came over and gave me a big hug and a kiss. I melted into his arms. It felt good to finally be able to do so.

After dinner, I made a pot of coffee in a stovetop coffee pot and left it to perk while we washed the dishes. The coffee finished perking, so I removed the basket of grounds and set it in the sink to deal with later. Roger took two coffee mugs from the cupboard and I filled them.

He grabbed the blanket from the couch and held the door open for me. A couple of rocking chairs sat on the porch, bookends to a small table between them. I placed the coffee mugs down, and we settled into the chairs to watch the show.

New Mexico sunsets can be special, and this one looked to be just that, with wispy clouds taking on the colors of the setting sun. Roy's cabin was perched on a hill facing west, with the sun perfectly framed by the ponderosa pine trees. I think they put the cabin in this spot for that very reason. An absolutely perfect place to watch the sun dip to the horizon, the clouds now ablaze with color.

"Isn't it beautiful?" I said.

Roger reached over and took my hand, leaning over to kiss the back of it. "Tonight, I am surrounded by beauty."

"Well, aren't you the romantic."

We stayed outside until the sun went down and the sky darkened. Up here, the stars came out quickly, and were so bright I could practically reach up and touch them. But now colder air had settled in. This high up in the mountains, it was as if the cold waited in the shadows for the sun to disappear, and then reached out to grab you. I shivered.

Roger noticed. "Let's go inside where it's warmer."

He stood and helped me from my rocker. Once inside, I realized how cold I had become.

Roger built a fire and tended it until it had a nice blaze going. I refilled our cups from the pot on the stove, and handed one to him.

It steamed as he sipped at it. "Thank you. Still nice and hot."

We settled onto the overstuffed couch in front of the fireplace. Roger propped up some pillows and leaned against the end. I sat beside him, laid my head on his chest, and tucked my legs under myself as best I could, considering my growing condition.

Roger draped the blanket over my legs, then put one arm around me and reached over with the other to feel my belly. "Any kicks yet?"

I smiled. "Well, something happens down there once in a while. I think I can feel it rolling around, or maybe it could be a little kick. But the baby is still pretty small, so it's hardly noticeable."

He kept his hand on my stomach, a look of concentration on his face, maybe hoping he could feel it also.

I gave him a peck on the cheek. "Don't worry. It won't be long before the baby kicks up a storm. Maybe another month or so." I moved out from his arms and stood. "But what the baby has become really good at is pressing against my bladder. I'll be right back."

Roger started to get up. "I'll grab the flashlight and come with you."

I pushed him back down. "What, so you can watch me pee? Not a chance. I'm a big girl."

I headed out the back door. It took a moment in the dark to get my bearings. The outhouse sat a respectable distance from the house. A worn path led to it. I listened to the absolute silence of the wilderness, so different than the noise of the city. It enveloped me in its arms. I looked up to see a vastness that reminded me our little world was just that, little.

The stars above shone even brighter than earlier, and a sliver of moon showed on the horizon. I had grabbed the flashlight on my way out, but decided not to use it. I didn't want to destroy this feeling with an artificial ray of light. The moonlight and stars gave just enough light to find my way to the outhouse.

I finished my business and made my way back to the cabin. I had used the flashlight inside, but now turned it off so I could watch the stars again on my way back.

A shape appeared in front of the cabin door as I got closer. A man's shape.

"Roger, is that you?" But I knew immediately it couldn't be. The man was too tall and wore a hat. A lighter flicked.

Flint stood there, only a few feet away, a wicked smile on his face as he lit a cigarette.

I screamed.

He took a puff from the cigarette and calmly exhaled smoke into the air. Then he closed the lighter, and darkness enveloped us again. I flicked on my flashlight and pointed it at him. The stark image of his face in that light scared me. I ran down the path toward the outhouse.

"Nowhere to go, Gloria," he shouted. "You best come back. I'm sure your husband would prefer you didn't run into the wild and get lost, or eaten. You know: bears, cougars, creatures of that nature. And there isn't another soul for miles."

The door flung open and Roger shouted my name, having heard my scream. "Gloria? Gloria!" Then he saw Flint. "What?"

I stopped running when I heard Roger call my name.

Flint turned to Roger and raised a gun. "Get back inside," then waved the gun at me. "Both of you."

I ran to the cabin and fell into Roger's arms.

"Inside. Now!" He nudged the gun into my back.

Roger pulled me into the cabin.

Flint followed us in. He closed the back door and herded us over to the couch.

"It was a good try, getting away and all. And you actually did a pretty decent job of evading us."

He took his hat off, laid it on the dining table, and then walked over to the fireplace. He kept the gun pointed at us the whole time.

I hid behind Roger.

"But it didn't take long to convince your friend, Roy, to tell us where you were. You see, there is always a way to get the information we need."

Flint took a puff from his cigarette and then flicked it into the fire.

"And what I need right now, from the two of you, is information."

Flint

Roger

I pulled Gloria to me and put my arms around her. She buried her face in my chest. Big, deep, emotional breaths racked her body. All of her tension came rolling back as I felt her tighten in my arms.

"What did you do to Roy?" I shouted.

"Nothing he won't recover from," Flint answered.

I helped Gloria onto the couch. She wouldn't let me go. She had a vice-like grip on my arm. "Gloria, please. I need you to let go."

Something inside of me raged. I couldn't let Flint do this to us again. I wasn't worried about the device, or the satchel of alien material. They were well hidden, and he would never get it out of me as to where. But there was no way I would let him touch Gloria this time. Somehow, I needed to figure out a way to overpower him.

"Please, Gloria." She wouldn't let go. I made eye contact with her. She stared at me with the same look of shock on her face I had seen just a few days ago. She finally released my arm.

I turned to Flint. "What do you want?"

He laughed. "What? You think what we want has changed?"

He stood by the fireplace, holding the gun on me. I looked around the room for some sort of weapon. I thought to grab the fire poker, but he was right there. How could I do it without getting shot? The axe was outside, but I couldn't leave Gloria. There had to be some way to overpower him.

"Roger," Flint said. "This is a case of simple math. One, you give me what we want. And two, we let you go. One, two. It can't get any easier than that."

I had to stall. "Where is Bull? I want to talk to him."

Flint moved to the middle of the cabin. "What, you think Bull would spend his valuable time to come up here? He has better things to do." Flint holstered the gun and took a large, wicked-looking Bowie knife from a sheath on his belt. "He knows I can handle this, and sometimes Bull prefers not to have to deal with the gory details." Flint ran the tip of the knife blade along the back of his wrist. A line of blood blossomed along the cut. He grinned at me. "Sharp, huh?"

Flint was absolutely nuts. I needed to do something, and quickly. At least he put the gun away, so he couldn't shoot me if I tried something. I looked around the room again. The poker still didn't make sense as an option. He wasn't by the fireplace anymore, but if I tried for it, he would be on top of me before I got close.

He took a step toward Gloria and brandished the knife at her.

What could I do? My eyes settled on the coffee pot still on the stove. A small amount of steam emanated from the spout.

He turned to me, and held up the knife so the blade reflected the flames from the fire. "Perhaps I can persuade you with the help of your wife."

I stepped between them. "Don't touch her."

Flint thrust at me with the knife. I dodged, but it stabbed into my side.

Gloria jumped up and screamed. "Stop it. Stop it. Don't hurt him." She jumped on Flint and pounded on his back. "Stop it. Stop it!"

He threw an elbow into her and she flew across the room.

I took a thick pillow from the couch and pushed it against Flint, driving him back, using it to protect myself. He speared the pillow with the blade and yanked it from my grasp. He pulled it off the knife and tossed it across the room, then came after me again.

I stepped back and worked my way toward the stove. Flint followed, coming closer, ready to stab me again. I reached down to where the blade had pierced my side. My fingers came away sticky and covered in crimson. Flint saw this and his eyes turned demonic; like a frenzied shark having just smelled the fresh scent of blood.

I shuffled closer to the stove. He lunged at me with the knife. I quickly sidestepped and knocked his arm away. I reached for the coffee pot and threw the hot coffee at him. He dropped the knife and screamed as he reached for his face.

I took the cast iron frying pan from the counter and smashed it against his head. He fell to the ground, but quickly recovered and dove for the knife. I smashed it against his head again. And then again. He wasn't going to hurt Gloria anymore. I stopped when blood trickled from his head and formed a small pool on the wooden floor-boards. He lay still, possibly dead.

A groan came from across the room. Gloria. I raced to her side. She lay on the ground clutching her stomach. Her pants were wet, with a small pool of liquid on the floor under her waist.

I got on my knees, turned her toward me, and lifted her head in my hands. "Gloria, are you okay? Gloria?"

She slowly opened her eyes. They fluttered as she said, "The baby. My water broke. I think he hurt the baby."

I flashed back to when Flint struck out at Gloria. He had elbowed her in the stomach.

She moaned and clutched her middle again.

A small patch of blood had also appeared between her legs. "Oh, God."

I wrapped her in the blanket from the couch and threw on my jacket.

"Roger, the baby." She tried to focus on me, but couldn't. Her eyes rolled back.

I picked her up and carried her to the car where I jock-eyed the passenger door open and laid her on the bench seat. Then I ran around to the driver's side, got in, and carefully placed her head in my lap. I started the engine. My foot hit the accelerator and the tires spun. I raced down the mountainside as quickly as I could. I needed to find a doctor, and fast.

Ruidoso and Beyond

Roger

I drove along the gravel road as it curved down the hillside. I hurried as best I could, being careful not to jostle Gloria too much. Tall pine trees hemmed us in on both sides. Everything seemed heavy with the night.

State Route 48 shouldn't be too far ahead. It was black-top, and I knew I would be able to make better time. Once I reached it, I raced toward Ruidoso, only a few miles away. I prayed I would be able to find a doctor there. But even then, it had to be almost ten o'clock, and I worried that no one would be around who could help us.

Gloria moaned, wrapped her arms around her midsection, and doubled up into a ball on the seat.

"Honey, we're going to get you to a doctor, okay?"

She opened her eyes, and said with a shallow voice, "Roger. The baby. The baby." She closed her eyes and moaned softly.

I drove as fast as I could and finally reached the Ruidoso valley. A smattering of lights appeared below. I drove down the hill. A few minutes later we entered the town. State Route 48 ran right through it, but the street looked abandoned this late at night. I rolled my window down and slowed the car to a crawl. I crept along, listening for any human-made sound, hoping for a sign of life. The only sound came from the crunch of my tires on the pavement.

I had about given up hope when I heard music in the distance. Around a curve, a place called Billy's Bar and Grill appeared. The door opened and light spilled onto the street as a man walked out. He stood for a second, seeming to get his bearings, and then walked over to a nearby truck. He opened the door and got in.

I quickly pulled up next to the truck and stopped. The man started the engine and then lit a cigarette. I leapt out, ran over before he could leave, and banged on his window.

He jumped at the sudden pounding, and looked over at me. "What the hell?"

"I need a doctor," I pleaded. "Is there a doctor in town?"

He rolled the window down and studied me. Then he looked down at my side. "Mister, you've got blood all over yourself. Are you bleeding?"

I was so worried about Gloria, I had forgotten Flint stabbed me. My shirt and pants on my left side were covered in blood. I shook my head. "No, it's not for me. It's for my wife. Our baby."

He got out and looked at Gloria as she lay lifeless on the bench seat of the car.

"Jesus. What happened to you two?"

I grabbed his arm. "Please, just tell me. Does the town have a doctor?"

He pulled his arm away and looked at me as if I was a little crazy. Perhaps he thought I had done something to her, and now was worried about his own safety.

Finally, he answered. "Yes, Mister. There's Doc Holbert over in Hollywood. But he went to Alamogordo this weekend for supplies. He won't be back until tomorrow."

I couldn't believe it. "No! There must be another doctor up here somewhere."

He shook his head. "Doc Holbert is it. Other than that, you need to go to the hospital in either Alamogordo or Roswell." He glanced at Gloria on the bench seat again. "Your best bet is Roswell. A better hospital if your wife is hurt bad." He pointed down the road. "Once you get to Hollywood just up yonder, stay on the Billy the Kid Trail to where it becomes State Route 70. It's a little farther, but the road don't wind as much, so it'd be easier on your wife."

I shook his hand. "Thanks."

He nodded. "Good luck."

I jumped into the car and headed toward Hollywood and Route 70. I knew the road since we had come this way a few days ago. I also knew it would take well over an hour to get to the hospital. It scared me to wonder if Gloria and the baby could make it.

Gloria lay on her side with her head in my lap. She hadn't moved for the last half an hour. I could tell she was breathing, thank goodness, but other than that, I wasn't sure how she or the baby were doing.

A wave of nausea overtook me and my vision blurred. I nearly drove off the road. I pulled the car over and sat with my head against the steering wheel for a moment, trying to collect myself. How much blood had I lost? A quick check showed my shirt and pants soaked with it. I pulled my shirt up to see blood still seeping from the knife wound below the ribcage on my left side. There was no way to tell how deep the knife had penetrated, but the cut was wide and made by a long blade. I had to stop the blood flow or I wouldn't make it to Roswell.

There was a rag in the glove compartment. I had seen it there earlier. Gloria moaned as I reached over to get it. She must have felt me move as I leaned over her.

"Gloria?"

She didn't answer.

I put the rag under my shirt and pressed it against the wound. I held it there with my left hand, and used my right to pull back onto the road. The steering wheel felt sticky with blood.

I tried to figure out how far Roswell was from here. We had passed a little place called Glencoe about ten minutes ago. If I was right, we were almost halfway there. The road had straightened, now that we were in the foothills, and I could make better time.

I used my sleeve to wipe beads of sweat from my forehead. A sign I was weakening. I pushed the rag against the wound again to keep it in place. It was soaked with blood.

I soon waned in and out of consciousness and couldn't keep my focus. The car glanced off a guardrail. It wouldn't do to lose control and end up in a ditch, or worse. There hadn't been another vehicle on the road since we left Hollywood. Maybe a good thing, since I was swerving all over the place.

Everything seemed wrapped up in darkness, only appearing when caught in my headlights. All I had was the sliver of moon and the stars above to keep me company. I rolled the window down. I needed fresh air to help me stay alert. That's when I noticed a large star on my side of the car. Much larger than any other stars in the sky. It sat on the horizon. Perhaps that's why it seemed so big. Like when the sun goes down and appears to get bigger.

But I still thought it odd that I hadn't noticed it before. North was to our left. It must be the North Star. How had I managed to miss it? Maybe the hills had blocked the star from view.

I nearly ran off the road again. I slowed down. My thoughts felt jumbled and I couldn't focus anymore. My vision faded in and out. I had lost too much blood. I couldn't keep the car from swerving over the lines.

Gloria stirred on the bench seat and mumbled something.

I reached down and rubbed her arm. "It's okay, honey. We'll be there soon."

I looked out my window to see the star had moved. Now it sat a little farther to the front of us. Had the road curved in a way to cause that?

I tried to concentrate, doing everything I could to stay on the road. But my attention returned to the star. Something about it made me look at it again. Now it was in a different spot. And much bigger. I must be seeing things. It worried me. But I couldn't concern myself with a star. I needed to focus on the road.

Gloria stirred again. She said something, but she was so weak I couldn't make it out. I pulled over to the side of the road and looked down at her. She lay on her side, her head still in my lap, and her eyes closed.

"Honey, what did you say? I couldn't hear you."

She squeezed her eyes and furrowed her brow as she wrapped an arm around my leg and held on tight. "They're here."

I had no idea what she meant. "Who's here?"

She mumbled something again, but it was so low I couldn't grasp what she said. She lay there, her eyes tightly closed, a firm hold on my leg. She had to be in even worse shape than I was; way beyond making any sense.

I pulled onto the road again. The star had somehow shifted to be in front of us now. And it was much bigger; as big as a full moon. I knew we were headed east, so how could the North Star be in that spot? My mind must be playing tricks on me. It sat on the horizon, and seemed to hover there.

Then I had the sudden urge to pull off the road. I tried to fight the feeling because I needed to get Gloria to Roswell. But I couldn't fight it. I felt like I wasn't in control of myself any longer.

I slowed as a side road appeared in my headlights. I turned onto it and drove until I came to a clearing in the trees.

I put the car in park, leaned against the steering wheel, and closed my eyes. My strength had sapped right out of me along with my blood. Maybe some rest; just a few minutes of rest might help. Then I could keep going.

The car suddenly shut down. Everything. The engine stopped running. The headlights flickered, and then went out. And the dashboard went dark. I sat there for a moment. How did the car lose power? I worried we were stuck. I needed to look under the hood and figure out what caused it.

"Gloria, I need to check the engine. I won't be long."

She held my leg as if she didn't want me to go. I pulled her arm away.

"It's okay, honey. I'll be right back."

I opened my door, got out, and leaned against the door frame to try and get my balance. When I felt stable enough, I took a tentative step toward the front of the car.

I immediately fell to the ground, too weak to even walk. I tried to get up, but couldn't. Just a moment of rest, and then I would try again. I finally managed to get onto my hands and knees. I crawled toward the side of the car, hoping to use it to help me up.

Before I got there, the ground below me filled with light, as if a full moon had just come out from behind a cloud. But the light was too bright. I looked up to see some sort of craft hover over the clearing in front of me. It couldn't be an airplane or a helicopter. Planes and helicopters make noise.

It sat there, hovering, not a sound coming from it. Light emanated from the shell of the craft and illuminated the whole area in frosty, white light. A row of colored lights rotated around its base. Whatever this was, it seemed as big as a house. No, even bigger. Like a great big, palatial ranch-style home, wide and flat, but with rounded sides.

It wobbled a little, and then tilted toward me. A row of windows appeared on the craft. There were figures inside. I could see them. But they weren't men. They were aliens, just like the ones I had seen at the crashed spaceship near Roswell.

One of them, I think the leader, caught my eyes. *Don't be afraid. We are here to help you.*

The ship glowed a deep orange as it descended to hover only a few feet above the ground. A ramp lowered. Four beings followed the leader down the ramp. The leader and two of the others came toward me. Two more went to the car.

I tried to get up. I didn't know what they planned to do. Then I floated into the air, an alien on either side of me.

I looked into the leader's eyes and heard his voice in my head. *It was necessary that we come, or you would have died. You are safe now.*

Then a thought hit me. Are they here because I'm the guardian of the device? That's it; they needed to help me. To save me. And then I felt a sense of relief as another thought came to me. They would also help Gloria and the baby.

I looked over to see the other two aliens remove Gloria from the car. She floated horizontally between them as they walked her toward the ship. They moved up the ramp and into the spaceship. We followed. A deep sleep enfolded me.

Shutdown

Plouharnel, France, 1967

Agent Miller stepped into the telephone booth on *Rue de Carnac* in Plouharnel.

He and Nadia, who had followed the kids to Carnac, had returned earlier from a long day of tailing Melanie Simpson all over the *Alignments de Carnac* area. They took dinner at a local restaurant, and then went to the hotel.

When they entered, he was given a note by the front desk clerk. A coded message from Bull notifying him he needed to call, and it was urgent.

He found an outside payphone at a nearby establishment. He passed three up to find one where it wasn't likely he would be overheard. The sun, just now setting between some buildings, reflected off the century-old cobblestones of the town's roadway. He picked up the receiver and dialed '0' for the operator. When she came on the line, he asked for overseas long distance, and then gave that operator a direct phone number for Bull Patton's office in Langley, Virginia.

A few moments later, Bull answered the line. "I'm glad you got my message. Do you have good news for me?"

That was the last thing Miller wanted to hear, but exactly what he expected. "I'm afraid not. This is a big dead end."

"And why would that be?"

Miller heard the disappointment in Bull's voice. He ignored it. "I think what these kids said back at Brightwood Manor is exactly what they're doing here, going on a big sightseeing trip. Nadia and I have been tracking them all day, and it hasn't been easy to keep from being spotted since they know our faces. All they've done is go on a long tour of the Carnac Stones and a few dolmens."

"A few what?"

"Dolmens. Burial tombs," Miller answered, trying to keep the frustration out of his voice. "Like I said, they've been sightseeing. Nothing about this whole trip hints of a search for the Orb. And there are two kids with them. I don't think they would share the secret of the Orb with these boys."

"What boys?" Bull asked.

"That Eddy kid, who brought them here, and a French boy. They're both dressed up like tour guides, and acting like it, too. There isn't any rhyme or reason to where they are going or to what they are doing. If they were looking for the Orb, I doubt they would be traipsing around like they are."

"Are you sure the Orb isn't there somewhere?"

"At one point, when the girls went into some sort of buried tomb, we thought we had something. But when they came out, they gave no indication of finding anything. Just to be sure, Nadia and I went into the tomb ourselves after they left. Nothing there. And no signs they had dug around looking for the Orb. A dead end for sure."

The other end of the line stayed silent for a while, then Bull said, "I trust your take on this. So, that's it?"

"Yes. I'm sure the Orb isn't here." Miller changed the subject. "What about Roberts and his lead on the boys with the key?"

"That idiot. He found out the key fit a hidden compartment in a clock. It was up at some lodge on a mountain outside of Portland. He had a good plan in place until, as usual, he screwed it up."

Miller felt sorry for Roberts. He would probably be reassigned after this. "What happened?"

"They got away. He lost them. How he did that up at a mountain lodge with only one road in and out, is beyond me. The only good from it all is that Roberts got a look at what the Frankie kid took out of the hidden compartment. He said it wasn't the Orb."

Miller leaned against the wall of the phone booth at that information. "Do you know what it was?"

"A thin box of some sort. Definitely not orb-shaped. Roberts tried to get the box from the boys, just in case it had something to do with the Orb. But, like I said, he lost them."

"What's next?"

Bull huffed. "That's why I left the message to call my direct line. We need to shut the operation down."

"What? But why?"

"Someone higher up the food chain caught a whiff of what we're doing and is snooping around. It's a good thing I have a fly on the wall and found out. They haven't latched onto any specifics yet, thank God. They wouldn't like that I'm running an unapproved black operation down here. But I can't have them prying into this. They'd take it away from me."

"I understand," Miller said.

"I've managed to put together a good cover story for what you and Nadia are doing over there, but it's best you get back." He paused. "I don't want to shut this down. Who knows what that Orb could do for us ... for me. But we need to. We'll have to wait this out, and it may take a while."

"I don't know, Bull," Miller said, thinking of other concerns. "We'll do whatever you say, but Major Burnham is still out there, and he isn't under the thumb of our government. We may lose this device to him."

"You needn't worry about Major Burnham for now."

"What do you mean?" Miller asked. "We lost him in that maze under Pike Place Market. I knew he was shot up pretty bad. I figured we'd find his body once we'd cordoned off the market and could conduct a proper search, but we never did find him."

"When you couldn't confirm he was dead, I was worried about the same thing," Bull said. "I put out feelers and tracked Burnham down. He's convalescing. That industrialist, Brighton Ingram, found a doctor who fixed him up. We're good for now. But we'd be fools to think they are finished going after the Simpson girl and the Orb."

"How about I set up a team to watch them when I get back," Miller offered. "If we can't do anything with the Simpson girl and her little gang right now, at least we can make sure Burnham doesn't get a step up on us."

"Good idea. It's important we find that device. Who knows what secrets it might hold that could make us rich and powerful, let alone the technology we would glean from it? When the Simpson girl gets back, set something up to keep a watch on her as well. Just because we're on hold, doesn't mean we can't have a plan in place. We need you back here. All is not lost."

"You've got it, Bull. I'll leave as soon as I can."

Ceremony

Carnac, 1967

Mel

We stood outside the lobby door on the driveway of Hotel le Tumulus. It was eight-thirty in the evening and the sun had gone down a while ago. Some puffy clouds in the distance still showed remnants of purple hues left by the setting sun.

The moon had just worked its way up from the horizon and was so big, it nearly took up the whole sky now.

"Check out that moon," I said to Katch. "I think it's full."

"It sure looks like it," she answered.

"Could that mean something?" I asked. "That we are doing this during a full moon?"

She focused on the moon as she thought about her answer. "A full moon has significance with the First People. The sun comes every day, but the full moon only once a month. For that reason, to many it represents the cycle of life and rebirth." She looked at me. "I guess we'll find out, won't we. I really have no idea at this point."

I thought it interesting that of all the days in a month, we would do this during a full moon. Maybe it did mean something.

The headlights of a car turned onto the driveway and bounced along it toward us. I looked over at Katch. "Do you have everything you need?"

She wore her Hopi headband and a beaded ceremonial tunic. An eagle feather hung from a braid in her hair. Her Hopi medicine pouch lay against her hip, its leather strap across her shoulder. She patted the pouch. "I'm good."

A taxi pulled past us and turned around in the driveway so it was pointed back down the hill. The driver got out and opened the back door so we could get in.

I nodded to Katch. "Okay then, let's do this." I got into the taxi and slid over for Katch.

"So," Katch asked, once she was settled, "have you figured out how we're getting back?"

I looked at her a bit sheepishly. "No, not really."

She gave a little laugh. "I didn't think so."

The taxi driver got in, turned so he could see us in the back, and said, "*Où aller?*"

I didn't know what he meant. I turned to Katch. "Was that a question?"

"I think he wants to know where to take us."

"Oh." I felt a little embarrassed. Of course. "Uh, *pardon. Le Dolmens de Mané Kerionned. Sur Rue La Glacière.*"

The driver gave us a puzzled look, harumphed, then turned back around and drove down the driveway.

Katch nudged me. "Not bad. You almost sounded French."

"I doubt the driver would agree."

We sat in silence for the few minutes it took to get there. When we arrived at the dolmen, I directed the driver to pull over. I paid him the francs he indicated, and added another two as a tip. I hoped it was enough.

He took the money, mumbled something, and then said as he drove off, "*Au revoir, vous les filles folles.*"

Katch turned to me. "Did he just call us crazy girls?"

I laughed. "I think so. It's probably because of that eagle feather in your hair."

"Yeah, I'm sure that must be it. Couldn't be your sleeveless t-shirt and high-top Converse tennis shoes, or the fact that we are two American teenage girls who wanted to be dropped off at a dolmen out in the middle of nowhere in the dark of night."

"I suppose those things might have something to do with it."

I laughed and grabbed her hand. We headed for the path to the dolmens. The full moon had risen higher now and could almost light our path without help, but I turned on the flashlight anyway because I would need it. This was the flashlight I had borrowed from Henri, but somehow forgot to return.

We made our way along the path. I handed Katch the flashlight so I could pick up little twigs and kindling-size branches. I planned to make a small fire once inside the dolmen. Nothing huge. Just big enough so we could see without using the flashlight. I made sure to get the driest kindling possible because I didn't want there to be much smoke.

343

We walked down the steps of the dolmen. At the bottom, Katch held her arm out to stop me. She said, "We need to perform the smudging ceremony here before we go in. To purify ourselves first."

I nodded and set the kindling on the ground. We hadn't been able to smudge since we left Brightwood Manor, so I agreed this was a good idea.

She handed me the flashlight, then opened her medicine pouch and took out her smudge kit. It consisted of a small abalone shell bowl, some dried sage, and wooden matches. She handed me the bowl and placed a small bundle of sage in it. She struck a match and lit the sage. A pungent, earthy aroma filled the air as smoke emanated from the bowl.

Katch went through the ritual of cleansing. She spoke in her Hopi language, but I knew what she said with each motion. I held the bowl out while she first washed her hands in the smoke to cleanse them. Then she followed the same pattern. First, she asked the Creator for only good thoughts. Then she used her hands to pull the smoke to each part of her body as she said, "For my eyes to see good things, for my mouth to speak good things, for my ears to hear good things, and for my heart to feel good things."

The last movement was to pull the smoke over her head, and thank the Creator. Once done, she took the eagle feather from her hair and cleansed it over the smoke. I handed her the flashlight and Katch clipped it to her belt. She took the bowl from me and held it so I could perform the same ritual on myself. She extended the feather into the air so her ancestors could see my spirit being cleansed.

I finished the same ritual. Katch pulled the bowl away, but I reached out to stop her. She gave me a questioning look.

I pulled the locket from under my shirt. "I want to cleanse this as well." I held the locket out to show the front to her. "These are the Carnac Stones. They inspired me to come here. How could the Stones be on the locket? And how is it I received the locket right after seeing my father here in Professor Lofton's film?"

She nodded. "And the half token inside. Don't forget about that." Her eyebrows raised in amazement. "Maybe we'll find out now."

I shared her look, and then said, "You're right. It must be dharma."

"Yes, I think so. As told by the stars."

I held the locket over the smoke and thought about my dad—how he stood in this very dolmen. And about who might hold the other half of the token. I finished and tucked the locket back under my shirt.

She handed me the flashlight and took the bowl, the sage still smoking. We walked toward the dolmen entrance. "Now I will cleanse this sacred site, and speak to the spirits here."

We entered the dolmen, and Katch used the feather to push the smoke into the entrance and against its surfaces. She said, "Grandmother envisioned for us to tune to the earth and hear the song of the universe. We ask for that permission now from the spirits of this dolmen."

I followed Katch as she moved deeper into the underground space. It seemed eerie, being so late at night, where both the dolmen inside and the world outside resided in similar darkness.

She waved the eagle feather like a fan over the bowl and said, "In the name of the Creator, please bless this dolmen and the spirits that reside within. Take away the negative and bad energy. Bring to it only positive and good thoughts. And, please protect those of us who enter this room. Thank you, Great Creator, for allowing this medicine woman to cleanse such a sacred space."

Katch then spoke in her native language, maybe some of the same kind of things. She worked her way along the wall to the end of the dolmen, and then along the opposite wall back to the entrance. There, she used the feather to push the last of the smoke out of the space, as if washing all the negative energy from the room. The dried sage expended itself as she completed the motion, and the smoke died out.

Katch finished with a Hopi chant and then cocked her head, as if listening for something. "Do you hear that?"

I stood perfectly still and listened intently. I heard a faint sound emanating from a distance. Almost like the vibration of a tuning fork resonating through the walls.

Katch smiled. "The dolmen. It's ready. I think it wants to finish your vision."

Solaria

Space, 1947

Gloria

"Gloria, do you remember me?"

I opened my eyes, feeling groggy, as if coming out of a stupor. A woman stood over me. Tall and slim, with stark, platinum-white hair, vibrant blue eyes, cream-colored skin, and beautiful Nordic features. "Solaria?"

"Yes, that's right." She placed her hand on my fore-head.

I felt a sudden sense of relaxation. An alien being stood at the end of the table, preparing some equipment. I was on a table. Like a metal or stainless-steel table. Hard, but not cold. It actually felt warm. I knew this because I lay here naked, but it didn't bother me. I had lain on this table before with Solaria at my side. It never bothered me at the time. Only later, when it snuck into my dreams.

Solaria leaned over me. "I can sense you are scared."

"Yes," I told her. "I'm worried I will lose my baby."

"That is why we came. To prevent such a thing from happening. You know we can save it, yes?"

"Yes. I trust you to save my baby." I looked around. "But where is Roger? He's hurt. You need to help him, too."

"He is being attended to in another room. A sharp object penetrated his body, and he has lost much of the fluid you call blood. We are in the process of replacing it through synthetic regeneration. His wound will also be repaired."

I felt a sense of relief. "Thank you, Solaria."

The room had a soft, white glow all around, but I couldn't distinguish any walls. It seemed both large and small at the same time. A light overhead had been focused onto my midsection. It looked like more equipment was stationed around the light, as if it hung from a ceiling I couldn't see. None of it looked like anything I had seen in a doctor's office or operating room. Not that I had ever been in an operating room, but I had seen them in movies at the theater.

A mechanical arm lowered from the ceiling and hovered above my face. It had something that looked like a showerhead attached to it.

Solaria leaned down so I could see her. "You will sleep now. We must start, so the baby can be saved."

She leaned back and placed her hand on my forehead. I closed my eyes. A flush of air brushed against my face, and I fell into a deep sleep.

I woke to find myself fully dressed, sitting on the edge of the table. I noticed my pants were clean. They had been drenched in fluid and blood, but not a trace of it showed any longer.

I looked at Solaria. "How did my clothes get clean?"

She laughed. "We are an advanced technological organization with the knowledge of many species. There are few limits to what we can do here on our spacecraft. Neither you, nor Roger, will bear any signs of bodily damage. Though you will feel tenderness for a while within your reproductive organs."

"I don't understand," I said. "What about the baby? Did I lose it?"

"No," she said, "but you must make a choice." She came over, sat on the table next to me, and reached out to hold my hand in hers. "We saved the baby. But he *was* hurt. We also delivered him prematurely by nearly four months. Do you know what that means?"

I shook my head.

"He will need many months of specialized care in order to survive and develop into a healthy child."

I nodded, wondering how I would be able to do that. Then I realized something. I looked at her. "You said 'he'?"

She smiled. "Yes, you had a baby boy."

I brightened. "Can I see him?"

She stood. "Come with me. I'll introduce you."

We walked to the wall. Solaria waved her hand and a doorway appeared. She led me down a hallway bathed in soft light. We passed a smallish alien who walked with a Nordic-looking male. Neither of them gave me a second look, as if humans walked amongst them all the time.

Solaria stopped at a point in the hallway and turned to me. "Your child is very small, and in a fluidic incubator that replicates your womb. He has a broken leg, so you will see a gel cast on it."

I let her know I understood, but wasn't sure if I could handle the sight of my baby like this.

She waved her hand and a doorway opened. Inside, the room was similar to the one I had been in. But in this one, a glass-like box sat on a table in the center of the room. It must be the incubator Solaria mentioned.

We walked in.

Two females, similar to Solaria, worked at the incubator. One of them monitored a wall of light suspended in midair. It appeared to have graphs and indicators on it. They nodded to Solaria. One of them waved her hand and the wall of light disappeared. They stepped out of the room, maybe to give us some privacy.

I walked up to the table to see my baby suspended within the box, floating in a fluid of some sort. He was so tiny and wrinkled. Small enough to fit in one hand. And very fragile. "Oh, my God. He's so little."

"Yes, and as you can see, he needs very intensive care to survive."

Where could I get such advanced care? Did it even exist at our hospitals? The kind of care that could save such a small baby? Certainly not in Roswell or anywhere close. I would need to go to a large city. Could I even get him there before he died? I put my face in my hands and cried. How could I take care of him?

Solaria pulled me to her chest. "You and I have known each other all your life, from when you were a small child. Just as we have known your family for generations. Your lineage is special. We recognized it long ago as we sought the biological entity we call the Intrepid One."

She lifted my head so she could see my eyes, then wiped away my tears. "Many of our council believe the

Intrepid One will come from your line. This baby is special and needs to be saved. He could very well be that which we seek. However, he is your child. You may leave with him if you wish. It is your decision to make."

But if I wanted my baby to live, there was only one option. I knew it was best for him to stay with Solaria. I couldn't even begin to know how to keep him alive. And in her care, he would become a strong young man.

I put my hand on the glass of the incubator. "Solaria, will you take good care of him?"

"Yes, Gloria. He will grow big and strong, and learn to use his mind to an extent far greater than your smartest humans."

She put her arm around me, and held me while I looked at my baby boy. "Your husband is fine now. The two of you will drive back to the cabin at the lake. There, everything will be as it was when you first arrived. No signs of a struggle, no blood, no body." She slowly turned me toward her. "You will both believe you have returned from Roswell, where you had a miscarriage at the hospital. You will believe the doctors tried to save the baby, but lost it due to the great amount of stress you have gone through. You will spend time at the cabin to recover." She hugged me. "I am sorry, but it is best if you don't remember any of this. It would only trouble you."

I cried. "But why can't I remember my baby? He's part of me. And part of Roger."

Solaria led me over to a recliner-like chair and helped me onto it. She kneeled next to me and wiped the tears from my eyes again.

"You will have other memories."

She took something from her pocket and showed it to me. A locket on a chain.

"What is this?" I asked.

"A memory," she said. "Lean forward." She hooked the chain around my neck.

I lifted the locket and looked at it. It had an oval shape and glistened with the color of silver. There were scenes of some sort engraved on the outside.

"Why are you giving this to me?"

She wrapped her hands around mine so we held the locket between them. "Keep this locket always," she said. "You will hand it down to your daughter."

Before I could say anything, she placed a hand on my forehead and the other, with the locket, against my heart.

My eyes closed and a warm feeling filled me. Then a vision of a young girl with long, shiny blonde hair, about eight-years-old, came to me. She was playing catch with Roger in a park.

Solaria's voice resonated in my mind. *In a few years you will have another child. A girl. Who will be extraordinary. She will become your whole world.*

I fell into a deep sleep with wonderful dreams about her.

Portal
Carnac, 1967

Mel

I picked up the twigs and kindling, and we walked farther into the dolmen to about ten feet from the back wall. We sat on the ground cross-legged, and I laid the kindling next to me. Katch handed me the box of matches from her pouch. I took a few twigs that still had pine needles attached and placed them on the ground between us. Then I put some more twigs on top of them. I struck a match and lit the pine needles. A flame erupted, and I quickly placed some larger twigs on the fire.

Once I had a little fire going, I raised my eyebrows in question and asked, "What do we do now?"

Katch placed her hands out to the sides of the flame, palms toward the fire, and closed her eyes. She performed a chant and said something in her native language. Then she opened her eyes.

I waited for a moment, and finally asked, "Should we expect something to happen?"

She shrugged. "I have no idea. This is new ground for me. I asked the life-force within the dolmen to come and guide us. I guess we will see if it heard me."

We waited, but nothing happened. I added kindling to the fire.

Katch looked over at me and said, "Tell me more about your vision."

I thought about it while I stared at the fire. I remembered that a flame had appeared, pretty much right here in this same spot, but it was blue. Then it twirled and grew, and the circles on the wall glowed yellow.

I said, "In my dream there was a blue flame. I was hoping this flame would turn blue."

Katch smiled and took a pouch from her bag. She tossed some small grains of something onto the fire, and the flames actually turned blue. A rich, metallic smell filled the air.

"Is that what you mean?" she asked.

I freaked out. "Wow! How did you do that? Hopi magic?"

Katch laughed. "No. Its mineral name is Tolbachite; found in Arizona. Grandmother likes to use it sometimes in ceremonies when a fire is involved. The mineral represents the earth. The wood, the spirit of life, and the air, the invisible force of nature. She believes the mineral pulls energy into the fire, to combine these elements and make them one."

I quickly glanced over to the stone at the end of the dolmen, but didn't see the yellow stars I hoped would be there. I looked down at the flame as it slowly turned back to a flickering yellow.

"The flame I saw in my vision stayed blue and swirled," I told her. "It grew in size and caused circles to appear on the stone. They glowed yellow, and then turned to an amazing golden hue."

I stopped, because something else from my vision came to me. I reached around the flame and grabbed Katch's hand. "There was a man in my dream."

Katch smiled. "Oh, really. Well, isn't that interesting?"

I shook my head fervently. "No, not like that. He was … he was …"

A voice came from the entrance of the dolmen, "Like family?"

A man stood there, just inside the opening. His outline visible against the cool, pastel light of the moon, which now filled the area by the steps.

We both jumped up.

"Stay away," Katch challenged. "I have a knife, and I know how to use it."

But I didn't feel threatened like Katch did. I knew him. "Trap?"

Where did that come from? And how did I know his name?

He took a few steps closer to where I could just make out his features in the light from our fire. He was young, maybe four or five years older than me. Medium build and tall, with a mop of wispy hair.

"Hello, Melanie … and Kachina." He smiled at her. "You have no need for a knife."

The flame of the small fire turned from yellow to blue. Katch and I both looked down to see this.

"Melanie, how do you know him?" Katch asked, her face knotted in confusion. "You just called him by name."

355

A very bewildering point. "Don't ask me how, but I do."

Trap took a few more steps into the dolmen. I think he moved slowly for Katch's benefit. With each step, the blue flame grew in size, and then it slowly swirled. It sat a few inches above the ground now, the kindling below it consumed and gone.

I glanced toward the back of the dolmen. The three stars of my vision had appeared, laid out in a diagonal line on the center stone, glowing a dull yellow.

He said, "You remember me, don't you, Melanie?"

A memory came flooding back of him standing over me. "You were there, when I was shot."

Katch shrieked, "What? What are you talking about? Someone shot you?"

I put my hand on my stomach where the bullet had entered. I remembered the blood. "At Pike Place Market. I nearly died. Trap saved me."

"You almost saved yourself," Trap said. "You stopped all of the bullets except one." He smiled. "We'll need to work on that."

I could see Katch thinking of something. "At the Virginia Inn. When we came to pick you up. You looked like you had been in a trance. Then you couldn't remember what happened while you were at Pike Place Market. I saw you glance down and touch your stomach with a look of shock on your face. I always wondered why you did that."

I wanted to get a better look at Trap. "Come closer."

He took a few more steps and then stopped.

I turned on the flashlight and shined it at him. It reflected off his green eyes before he put his hand up to block the beam. "Really, Melanie. Do we need that?"

But I didn't anymore. I shut off the light. I remembered those eyes from when he leaned over me after I had been shot. They were like beacons in the dark of night. "You laid me down and put your hand on my wound. Your touch felt warm, a healing warmth. You told me you were my brother."

"And I am."

Katch took a protective step forward. "And exactly how could that be? She doesn't have a brother." She set her feet firmly between Trap and me, before rolling into her next point. "And what? Now, you just show up out of the blue? And here of all places?"

I found it kind of funny she said 'out of the blue,' since when he did appear, the flame turned blue.

I looked at Katch. "I did almost have a brother once, or maybe a sister. But Mom lost the baby."

Trap smiled. "But she didn't lose it."

I shook my head. "What do you mean?"

He continued, "I have always been in your life, Melanie. You only knew our time together as distant dreams, but they were real."

I suddenly thought of dreams I had repressed for years. From when I was small, right up until a few weeks ago. Dreams of the two of us together. Of one dream when I was only four years old and my hand had been fixed after I burned it, and another as we played with a ball of energy.

And the most recent one of us here, now, from my vision. What he said was true.

"I remember."

I looked at the back wall to see the stars had turned from pale yellow to a stronger hue, verging on gold. I pointed to the wall. "Katch, look."

Her face washed over in shock when she saw the stars. She turned toward Trap again, her eyes still full of questions. She wasn't completely sold on this idea yet. How could she be?

"Can you prove it?" she asked. "That you're her brother."

"I can." He looked at me. "Take out your locket. Open it and remove the token."

It startled me that he knew of the locket, let alone the token. I did as he asked and took it out.

He raised his arm and looked at his wrist. He wore a wide, silver-cuffed band, intricate in design, with a delicately carved oval-shaped feature on the top. It was in the same shape as the Orb. He waved his other hand over it, and the oval feature slid aside. A token, similar to mine, rose from inside and hovered just above the opening. He took it and held it up for us to see.

Katch looked at my token and then at his. "Oh. My. God!"

He gestured for my token. "May I?"

I handed it to him. Katch took my hand and we moved closer.

He held the two pieces so the jigsaw parts faced each other, then slowly put them together. They fit perfectly.

I heard an audible gasp from Katch as she squeezed my hand.

The seam glowed red hot, as if welding the pieces together. Then the glow died out. The seam between the two parts had disappeared, as if there never was one.

He handed the token to me, now as one piece. "Put it in your locket and keep it safe. It is our bond."

"You *are* her brother," Katch said.

"But how, Trap?" I asked. "Besides me, Mom only had one other baby, but lost it."

"Well, she did, and she didn't," he said. "I am that baby and was saved by our star family." He turned to Katch. "You know of us throughout the First Nations as the Sky People."

I couldn't wrap my head around this. "But the baby died," I said.

"No, it didn't. Or I should say, I didn't. You need to trust me on this, Melanie. When they saved me, they gave me the name Trap, after the Trapezium cluster of the Orion Nebula. Solaria felt it was an appropriate name, since the cluster is of newly born stars. You will learn more about Solaria and our star family very soon."

He took my hand and said, "Now, come."

Then he took Katch's hand. "You as well, for you are a medicine woman with special abilities. After all, you are the one who summoned me here."

I turned to see Katch in awe over this whole situation, as was I.

Trap walked us to the wall where the three stars now glowed a bright gold.

"These are the three stars of Orion's Belt, symbolic of the star system where I come from." He looked at me. "Where you belong. And, where we are going now."

"Wait a minute. We're what?" Katch asked.

He laughed. "Going there now." Then he winked at her. "What, you think you are the first of your people to make this trip?"

"So, this *is* a portal," I said.

"It is," he confirmed. "Kachina, place your hand on the bottom star. Melanie, yours on the middle one." When we did this, he placed his hand on the top star.

All three stars grew in intensity and glowed bright gold. Rays of light shot out from around our hands and between our fingers. The blue flame of fire grew in size. It encircled us. We became captured in a whirlwind of blue flame. It felt cool and welcoming.

The flame slowly dissolved, and the stones themselves separated and swirled around us. Then they also disappeared. We were now surrounded by countless pinpoints of light, floating in the vastness of the universe. Just like in my vision. Only this time, I was with Katch and Trap.

We seemed to be in some type of encapsulated craft, able to travel through dimensional time and space. Soon, the Horsehead Nebula of Orion appeared and the three stars of Orion's Belt. Not long after that, we stood on the surface of a planet not dissimilar to Earth.

A tall, Nordic-looking woman, with white hair and vibrant blue eyes, stepped forward from a group who seemed to have been waiting for us. Almost like a welcoming committee.

"Hello, Melanie. Should you have forgotten, my name is Solaria. It is good to see you again."

Trap turned to me and said, "Welcome home, Melanie."

I heard a distant sound; a loud knocking. It took me a moment to wake up and identify what it was. I sat up. Katch lay on top of the bed next to me, both of us fully clothed. We were in our room at Hotel le Tumulus.

This time a loud pounding sounded at our door.

"*Oui*. One moment, *s'il vous plaît*," I said.

I tried to remember what happened. How exactly did we get home from the dolmen last night?

Katch woke up. "What's going on? Who's pounding at the door?" She sat up, rubbed at her eyes, and ran her hands through her hair to give it some semblance of order. "What time is it?"

"I don't know, but way too early for this," I told her. "It must be urgent." I walked over and opened the door.

Eddy stood there, his fist poised, ready to pound again. He dropped it to his side and said, "Brilliant. You're already dressed. Good. Pack your things. We need to go."

I couldn't quite grasp what he meant. "What? Go where?"

"To a nearby airport. And we need to hurry. Emilee has booked a flight for you and Katch to England. I'm here to take you to the airport. We need to leave now in order to make your flight."

This was very confusing. "But why?"

"I really don't know. All she said was to tell you there was some sort of tragedy back home in America. Oh, and to be sure to let you know it has nothing to do with your boyfriends or their families."

"What kind of tragedy?"

"That, she didn't share. I am as gobsmacked as you, so don't waste your breath asking. I haven't a clue or an answer. All I know is she has packed your things at the Manor, and will meet you at Heathrow Airport when you arrive. There, you are to catch a flight back to the States. So, please, crack on with it. We need to go. Ten minutes. I'll wait downstairs." He walked away.

Katch came over and stood next to me. "Mel?"

I looked at her. "I have no idea."

Little Cracks

Portland, Oregon, 1967

Mel

I wore my black dress. The same one I wore at my mother's funeral just over a month ago. But this time, I wore it for George. It was a big funeral, with lots of police officers all decked out in their finest. A mile-long procession of police cars, their lights flashing, escorted the hearse all the way from the memorial at City Hall in Lake Oswego, to the gravesite here at River View Cemetery. Most of the town turned out for his memorial. City Hall was packed. George had been a popular police captain within the community. It was a devastating loss for everyone.

Riverview Cemetery. The same place where Mom and Dad are buried. Not far away. Just up the hill.

We stood to the back of the crowd. I didn't think it was my place to be up front. George and I had a special relationship, but other than my close-knit group, no one knew about it. I leaned against Frankie's arm and swabbed at my eyes with a handkerchief. Katch stood next to me, tucked into Beanie, doing the same. The pastor had just finished

George's eulogy. They lowered his casket into the ground. I took a deep breath, the first one in a while without a big sob attached to it.

This had all happened so fast, but it also felt like slow motion. When Katch and I landed at Heathrow Airport, Emilee met us at the gate. She told us we would spend the night in London, and then catch a flight very early in the morning for the States. We were desperate to know what had happened. Emilee refused to tell us anything until we had checked in at the hotel and eaten a decent meal first.

When we got to our room, Emilee ordered room service so we didn't have to go out anywhere. That was good, because this was tearing me apart. Why did we need to get back to Oregon so fast?

I picked at my food when it arrived. Emilee wouldn't say a word until I had eaten. It was hard to force anything down. I took little bites, just to satisfy her. But something inside gnawed at my stomach, and wouldn't let much else get down there. It took a while. I don't know if I had satisfied her, or if she had just given up. I really couldn't tell.

But finally, Emilee sat me on the bed and knelt down in front of me. She took my hands, looked me in the eyes, and then dropped the bombshell. George had died. She was trying to get us home in time for his funeral. Frankie's father had called her with the news, and to let her know the funeral arrangements. That's when Emilee jumped into action and put this all together. She knew how much I would want to be there.

I fell apart when she told me. Everything flooded back about that day in the underground area at Pike Place

Market, when George died trying to protect me. I remembered the last time I had seen him. He lay there, bleeding to death, trying to apologize to me. Like he had done something wrong, and somehow disappointed me. He didn't want me to think badly of him. And all along, that whole time, all he was trying to do was protect me.

The shock of it all must have blocked this from my mind, until Emilee told me. I fell onto the bed and curled into a ball, pulling a pillow to my face and crying into it. I could hear Katch crying as well. After a little while, Emilee helped me into bed and pulled the covers over me.

I cried myself to sleep that night. And cried again all the next day during the overseas flight. Emilee and Katch took turns comforting me. Two planes later, and too many hours and time differences to know up from down, we finally arrived in Portland. That was late yesterday.

We never had a chance to see Frankie and Beanie when we got home. The first time was a little while ago at the City Hall memorial. Our families sat together near the front, but we never got a chance to talk.

I took one last look at George's grave. People were in a little procession now, dropping white carnations into his grave. I thought of doing the same, but couldn't get myself to look down into that hole. To see where he would spend the rest of eternity. I turned to the others. "I can't be here any longer. Can we go for a walk? There's a lot to talk about."

Frankie nodded. "Good idea. Because I have something I need to give you."

I walked over to Emilee, who stood with Mrs. Fletcher and Mrs. Crowley. They all gave me hugs. Which was good, because today I needed as many hugs as I could get.

"We're going to take a walk," I said, "if that's okay? I want to see Mom and Dad. It may take a while."

Emilee gave me another hug and a reassuring smile. "That's a good idea. Take your time. I'll wait here."

"And I'll stay here as well," Mrs. Fletcher said, "to keep your grandmother company until you get back."

I thanked them and walked over to the others, who had told their parents the same thing. I took Frankie's arm and said, "Let's walk up the hill."

"Isn't that where your mom and dad are buried?" he asked.

"Yeah," I answered. "I'd like to visit them."

The four of us strolled along the winding road, past headstones, immaculate lawns, and neatly trimmed hedges. It had rained earlier, but the sun was out now. A slight breeze played with my hair, and carried the smell of wet grass and freshly laid mulch through the air.

I looked down to see the road had dried, except where little cracks wandered aimlessly across the pavement's surface. Moisture collected there and penetrated deep into those cracks, working to weaken the road.

It reminded me of a feeling I had a long time ago, when all of this first revealed itself to me; of standing on the bridge overlooking Oswego Lake, trying to figure this all out.

The clouds had opened up and big raindrops splattered the bridge's railing. There were spots where the paint had chipped away, and rust could be seen working diligently on the exposed steel underneath. I remember thinking how those few exposed spots of rust, through time, would win out, and the bridge would be gone. Just like the cracks in this road would eventually destroy it.

Back then, and here now, I wondered if the same thing could be happening to me. Little chisels tapping away at chips and cracks in my facade, trying to get through to the soft tissue underneath. Exposing it. And like the cracks in this road and the rust on that bridge, eventually breaking me.

I shook my head to get the morbid thought out of my mind.

Frankie caught it. "What's up?"

"Oh, nothing."

A seating area came into view up ahead. It was tucked into a little nook by the side of the road, with two benches facing each other. No doubt an area for visitors to reflect on life. Perfect.

I pointed to it. "Let's stop here and talk."

We walked over and sat on the benches.

I said, "There's so much we need to talk about, but I want to start with George."

"Good," Beanie said. "Because I would like to know what Captain Thornton, of the Lake Oswego Police Department, was doing up in Seattle at Pike Place Market at the exact same time you happened to be there."

I shared with them what I now remembered. How I had tried to escape with the alien debris from the men chasing me. And how George came to my rescue.

I didn't tell them he had been working with Major Burnham, since George's intentions were good. I simply told them that he followed me up there because he was worried about my safety. And ended up dying in a shootout protecting me.

One more death on my conscience.

Then I told them about getting shot, and how Trap saved me. Katch gave them a brief rundown of what happened at the dolmen, and about Trap being my brother. Frankie and Beanie were all over us about Trap. They wanted to know more about him and what happened there.

I waved them off. "I know you both have a bunch of questions, but can we talk about George a little longer? Please? I can't understand why I didn't remember him being at the market; or getting shot trying to save me." I paused. The image of him lying there flashed into my mind. "Or dying."

"You were in shock," Katch said.

"But even at the dolmen, I remembered Trap had saved me. But I didn't remember George. And he died right in my arms. I feel so guilty about it."

Frankie put his arm around me. "You shouldn't feel guilty, Mel. Like Katch said, you were in shock. Not only in seeing George die, but also in being shot yourself. It was just a way to protect yourself."

"Thanks." I kissed him on the cheek. More to make him feel better than in agreement with what he said. "But why did it take so long to find out George had died? I mean, almost three weeks?"

Frankie said, "I don't know. He was reported missing when he didn't show up for work after his vacation time was up. No one had any idea what happened to him."

I asked, "Did you know he was missing when you called me at Brightwood Manor?"

The uneasy look on his face gave me my answer. "Yes, but I didn't want to ruin your trip. I knew you would just worry about him. I tried to downplay it when you asked."

"Yeah," Beanie added, "we talked about it before we called, and decided not to tell you. It would have just freaked you out. Frankie was thinking of you, Mel."

I hugged Frankie. "I guess that was probably the right thing to do. I would have just worried about him for the rest of the trip. Besides, at the time, you didn't know he had died."

"No," Frankie said. "It took a little while for the Seattle PD, working with our police department, to confirm it was him. It was only a few days ago that the Seattle coroner brought him to a funeral home here in Lake Oswego.

"An article in the Oswego Review said he died in an altercation at Pike Place Market when some hoodlums tried to rob him. They stole his wallet, so the police didn't have a way to identify him. At least, not until they got wind through police channels that Captain Thornton was missing. That's when they looked into it, and were able to put it all together."

"Or, so they say," Beanie cut in. "I bet those government men set it all up. Since there was a big shootout, they needed to clean up the dead bodies. Including George's body. And hide the fact they had recovered the alien debris." Beanie was on one of his rolls. "I bet they took his badge and I.D., so the Seattle police wouldn't know who he was. Then pushed the robbery story on them. It was all just one huge cover-up."

Katch said, "Maybe that's why they had the whole place roped off when we walked by later that day."

"Exactly," Beanie added. "They didn't want anyone to know what really happened."

"Luckily, the Seattle police figured out who he was," Frankie said. "Or, at least, finally admitted it."

Beanie said, "I don't think they knew it was our Captain Thornton when they got his body. Maybe if it had been someone else, the body would have stayed a John Doe forever. But when they found out who he was, they had to return him. Some sort of respect thing. You know, like a police code of honor."

"I'm just glad they gave him back." I wrapped my arm around Frankie's. "I would have died to find out he was missing, and never know what happened to him."

We sat in silence for a while. Then I looked at Frankie. "Tell me about Timberline Lodge."

He shared everything, from their first visit with Mr. Zimmerman, all the way through their joyride down the side of the lodge, and then finally escaping in the back of a maintenance truck. Including who was chasing them.

"He was the same guy at your place, Mel," Frankie said. "The fake professor from the University of Washington. The guy who tried to fool you into turning over the debris."

"How do you know that? Did you recognize him?"

"No. He told us. When he showed himself at the clock. Like he was gloating that he had finally caught us, after getting captured at your place."

"Why would they still be following you?" Katch asked.

"We wondered the same thing," Beanie said, turning to me. "They got all of the alien debris at Pike Place Market."

"Maybe they think we still have more of it," I offered.

"Or, they might have found out about the Orb," Frankie added. "Why else would we still be on their radar?"

"I hope not," I said. "That would be a real problem."

"Well, it might be. If we knew where it was, but we don't," Katch pointed out.

"Did anyone follow you in England or France?" Beanie asked.

Katch and I looked at each other and immediately thought the same thing. The Martins.

"That couple from Iowa," Katch said, looking at me. "They offered us a ride to the Stones."

"It *was* quite a coincidence they had arrived at Brightwood Manor just the day before we did."

"Out of all of England?" Beanie said. "On that little island and that one place to stay?"

"Did you see them again, after you went to France?" Frankie asked.

"No. We didn't," Katch answered. "Not that we noticed, anyway."

"Then maybe it wasn't anything," I said. I leaned into Frankie and hugged him. "All the same, I'm impressed at how you escaped Roberts and his men."

Katch gave Beanie a big kiss. "No kidding. Sliding down the side of Timberline Lodge? Sometimes, you amaze me."

He looked at her in surprise and said, "Only sometimes?"

Then Frankie told us about the magnificent tree clock. I stopped him when he mentioned the designs on the tree.

"Wait. There were three symbols on it?" I asked.

"Yes," Frankie said. "Like stars, angled from top to bottom. I didn't remember at the time, but they were a lot like the ones on the locket you showed me before you left for England."

Katch leaned in, her eyes wide. "The stars of Orion's Belt."

I nodded as I thought about what it could mean. And what an intricate web this all seemed to be.

Tomorrow

Mel

Frankie took a box from his pocket. "This is what we found in the clock."

"What is it?" Katch asked.

"We don't know," Beanie said.

Frankie handed it to me. "We didn't think it was our place to open it. Your dad left it for you."

The box was about seven inches square and made of thick, white cardboard. It had white paper tape wrapped around it to seal it shut. I studied my dad's handwriting on the tape. He had written, 'Mel Belle.' I ran my fingers over the writing.

Beanie finally said, "Well, are you going to open it?"

I looked up to see Frankie and Katch with the same question in their eyes.

"Here ... now?"

"Yes, here, now!" they all pleaded.

"Okay, okay!"

Everyone leaned over the box. I took my fingernail and ran it along the seam to cut the tape on both sides, then lifted the top off. It held a small reel of movie film, like the reels we had seen at Professor Lofton's.

"Another film," Beanie said. "It must be of your dad!"

"What's underneath it?" Katch asked.

I hadn't noticed, but there was a folded piece of paper under the reel. I took the film out. Written on the paper were the words, 'For my Mel Belle.'

I looked at everyone. "It must be a letter from my dad." I took the paper out.

Katch said, "Here. Let me have the box and film."

I handed them to her.

"Can you read it to us?" Frankie asked. "If that's okay?"

"I guess for what I've put you all through, you have as much right to hear this as I do."

I unfolded the paper and read it to them:

> Mel Belle,
>
> I had no doubt that if you made it to Professor Lofton's and received the key, you would be able to locate the hidden compartment in the clock up at Timberline Lodge. I have left you this film because I knew that one day you would be in charge of the Orb. It came to me in a vision at a buried dolmen near the Carnac Stones in France.
>
> I was originally given charge of the Orb by an alien at a spaceship crash long ago in 1947. He told me our universe is interconnected, much like a spider's web. A web of energy that ties our universe together. Tap on

one end, and it vibrates all the way to the other.

He also said the universe is in a state of chaos, and has been this way for generations of time. That chaos has spread across the web. And the reason why we, here on our planet, are in such turmoil.

Long ago, after the chaos began, a prophecy foretold of a being they call the Intrepid One, who will be able to still the threads and end the chaos.

You are next in line to safeguard the Orb until the Intrepid One can receive it. You must protect it at all costs. This film will show how to work with the Orb and understand its purpose.

I know you will want to try and find it, but don't. I have hidden the Orb as it directed me to do so. When it deems you are ready, the Orb will guide you to it.

Always know I love you and your mother with all my heart.

Love,
   Dad

I stared at the letter for a moment, then folded it up. No one said anything for a while.

Then Beanie broke the ice. "It reminds me of the first letter your dad wrote. Remember?" He looked at Katch. "You weren't here then. That letter was in the backpack when Mel first found the alien debris. I thought it was a quest, but had no idea it would turn out like this."

Frankie shook his head. "Man. We were so innocent back then."

Katch handed me the box and film reel. "What are you thinking, Mel?"

"I don't know," I told her. "There is so much to think about."

"Well, we might as well forget about looking for the Orb now," Katch suggested. "Like your dad said in the letter, the Orb will direct you to it when you are ready."

"Good point." I stood. "Let's keep going. I want to see Mom and Dad. Especially now."

We walked up the hill toward their graves. Frankie held my hand.

I looked up ahead. "I think if we follow this curve around those trees, we will be there."

We came around the curve and I recognized the maple tree that sat like an umbrella above their gravestones. Then I saw a man, his back to us. It looked like he was standing at their graves.

"Who is that?" Katch asked. "Someone from the funeral?"

"I don't know," I said. "But I guess we'll find out."

We left the road and walked up the grassy slope toward the site. When we got closer, he turned toward us.

Katch said, "Mel, that's Trap."

It *was* Trap, dressed in a dark suit, white shirt, and tie.

"Hello, Melanie, Kachina," he said, then turned back to the gravestones.

We walked over and stood next to him.

"Why are you here, Trap?" I asked.

His answer came without looking up. "I've never been here. I needed to come, now that you and I are family again. To pay my respects to our mom and dad."

Frankie turned to me. "Seriously, this is your brother?"

"In the flesh," Katch confirmed.

I thought Frankie might say more, or Beanie, for that matter. But both kept quiet. Maybe they figured it wasn't their place. I had no doubt I would get peppered with tons of questions later.

Frankie stood on one side of me and Trap on the other. I locked my arms into each of theirs. "I'm glad all of us are here together. This is my family."

We stood in silence for a while.

"So, what's the big plan now, Mel?" Beanie asked.

"I don't know. Maybe try to get back to a normal life. School isn't far off."

Trap said, "Actually … there is another reason I came. You know, the whole destiny thing you've been battling with?" He turned to me and smiled. "You have no idea what is ahead of you, Melanie. There is so much to learn. And, although I have the highest respect for Grandmother and your friends, there is another family you must get to know."

"What is he talking about?" Frankie asked.

"Solaria, and the others," Katch said. "The Sky People."

I turned to Frankie. His whole body oozed with confusion.

"Boy, do we have a lot to talk about later," I told him.

He looked like he wanted to ask a million more questions, but just nodded.

"So," Trap said, taking a few steps away and turning to me. "Are you ready?"

"What do you mean?" I asked.

He looked at the others and then studied me for a moment. His form wavered, kind of mirage-like. Similar to what you might see when looking into the distance on a hot day.

"To get started," he said. "We mustn't delay. That's why we're finally together. A great danger awaits us, and we must prepare. We'll start tomorrow."

Then he disappeared.

Beanie blurted, "What the hell was that? Did he just freakin' disappear?"

"Yeah," Frankie said. "It sure looks like it." Then he turned to me. "What did he mean? Start what?"

I shrugged. "My future, I guess."

Call to Action!

If you really enjoyed *The Stones of Carnac*, please go back to the site where you purchased the novel and write a review. We authors live and die by the review. They are the air we breathe. Please help me get the word out about Melanie's amazing novel series!

Sign up for my newsletter by dropping me an email and I will send you an exclusive novella or short story currently only available to followers through my newsletter. I will then be able to keep you up to date on future releases, exclusive peeks at upcoming work, events, and appearances.

Follow me on Facebook www.**facebook.com/DJSchneiderWriter**
Visit my website www.**SchneiderWriter.com**
You can also reach out to me by email at:
 DJSchneider1947@gmail.com

Acknowledgements

First, I wish to thank my editor, Suzi Wiser, who has more resilience than a Teflon pan when it comes to making my manuscripts look good. Thank you, Suzi, for the relentless time you have spent making this novel so much better than it would have been without you—and for discovering my ineptitude in the use of question marks. Also, I need to thank the Gresham Writer's Group: Tiffany Martin, Nannette Taylor, Dave Baker, and Jennifer Helgerson for the many hours they spent editing this work, chapter by chapter. And to my new friends at the NIWA (Northwest Independent Writers Association) where I have found a haven for my novels, and a wonderful environment of friends with which to promote our work together. Visit us at www.niwa.com and support our organization by purchasing our works.

I also, and always, am indebted to the pioneer investigators who uncovered the greatest government cover-up in UFO history in the crash outside Roswell, New Mexico (Yes, I know, Corona, Mr. Friedman). Without their work, we may have never known what happened. They are: Stanton T. Friedman, Kevin Randle, Donald Schmitt, Charles Berlitz, William Moore, and Col. Philip J. Corso (Ret.). Without their great investigative work and dedication, I wouldn't have known about Roswell, and the seed for this novel series would never have been planted, sprouted, and grown into the wonderful tree it is, branches stretching toward the universe.

About the Author

DJ developed his creative writing skills at the San Francisco Art Institute, and then at the Log Cabin Literary Center in Boise, Idaho with a writing group called the Magnificent Seven. DJ also spent many years in the advertising and marketing fields writing and producing creative content for radio, print, and television. When DJ isn't out traveling the stars following Melanie Simpson around and documenting her great adventures, he is buried deep in an Oregon burrow he calls The Writing Cave, honing his craft and building his novels. It is there under the light of a gooseneck lamp he can be found diligently working on Melanie's next story, and on an upmarket novel titled *River of Dreams*.

Made in the USA
Columbia, SC
10 October 2024